Imaginarium

First Edition

By Lee McQueen

McQueen  Press

By Lee McQueen

Published by McQueen Press
info@mcqueenpress.com
http://www.mcqueenpress.com

About the Author
Lee McQueen has been both a librarian and bookstore owner. With a Master of Library & Information Science from SUNY-Buffalo, she indexes and abstracts, works with databases, and takes on research and writing assignments. She writes short stories, poems, novels, and screenplays.

Stories 1-7 registered as "Confessions of the Dreamers & Other Stories" and stories 8-14 registered as "A Day in the Life of ARES & Other Stories" by Lee McQueen.

Interior design and typesetting by Lee McQueen

Logo registered mark of McQueen Press.

© 2006 Lee McQueen
1st Edition, 1st Printing
Printed in the United States of America

McQueen, Lee
Imaginarium/Lee McQueen-1st Edition
ISBN 978-0-9798515-0-6 (pbk)

Works by Lee McQueen

Short Story Collection

The Dark Fantastic

Poetry Collection

Things I Forgot to Tell You

Novel

Kenzi

Jeannie East, then West

Screenplay

The Angel and the Lion (original)

Kindred (adapted)

Non-Fiction

Writer in the Library! (editor)

Inside the Imaginarium,

the Dreamers know when to take a chance

…and the Heroes know when to take a stand

For Mom, Dad, Sis, and Bubba

Contents

Introduction
Sudden Impact: The Short Story

Short stories condense a lifetime within one page, twenty pages, or sometimes forty pages. Then suddenly, you have a novella or perhaps even a novel. But the benefit of a short story is quick set-up, intense dialogue, and tight plot structure. All this hopefully culminates in a high-impact conclusion that ties the strings together and sums up the theme, giving the reader something profound to consider. Short stories prove impossible for this author to resist.

The Angel and the Lion began as an action/adventure screenplay. Just picture a North American woman carrying guns leading a caravan of Sudanese women and children across the desert. How could this particular event happen to this particular person?

Risk is action/suspense involving a mild-mannered, if rather dizzy, heroine distracted by her own creativity who encounters the complete opposite personality in an exacting publisher distracted by cold objectivity. After three memorable encounters in the course of one day, their views of one another and themselves change drastically.

The slice-of-life vignette in the collection, *Labyrinth of the Labor Realm*, follows an unpublished, unemployed, or under-employed writer through her sarcastically-tortured mind. While entirely fictional, many of the moments indicate that sometimes life is stranger than fiction and that the darkest hours still come before dawn.

I Would Sing Along reveals the deeper issues within a marriage during the aftermath of a couple's attendance at a Prince concert. Like marriage, a romantic comedy isn't always fun and games. But while love sometimes hurts, love also heals.

Along the love hurts line, countless women's magazines geared towards North American women often discuss the dismal marriage possibilities for women who hesitate to explore outside their own race or culture. On the other hand, *For Rent by Owner* is the worst-case scenario that occurs when one woman decides to step outside her comfort zone.

Charlatan and Masquerade provides the end-story to the absentee father phenomenon and its continuous effect on future generations... until someone decides to take a stand. Guilt, revenge, anger, and sadness struggle with hope, forgiveness, faith, and love.

This ushers in *The Confessions of the Dreamers*, dramatic suspense about a middle-class family in Somewhere, America that destroys and devours itself by an inability to let go of the past.

The short story, whether literary or speculative fiction, permits the writer the opportunity to briefly step outside the parameter of ordinary events for just a moment in time. The hardest thing for people to do is to know *when* is the right time for *what* action. How to overcome years, decades, and centuries of "this is the way things are." Often, the choice made in that one moment saves lives. But sometimes, it doesn't. Still, not making a choice *is* a choice. And no decision *is* a decision. And the only thing left to say is, "Well, that's just the way it went."

The literary collection, stories one 1-7, explains the human circumstances behind so many changes and choices and decisions.

Speculative fiction is a wonderful medium allowing both the reader and writer to ask the question, "What if?" What if something wonderful happened? What if something horrible happened? Then where would we be? And what would we do once we got there? In stories 8-14, you'll find seven such stories answering these questions.

The Reversal speculates that certain restrictive social policies cause the North American public to stage a modern version of the Boston Tea Party through the inspiration of a new type of hero. Quiet, low-key rebellion forces a nation to action.

Ever and Again sees a glass that actually is half-empty, half-full. From a series of terrible events initiated by people of questionable character, the future of mankind grows. And much like Earth-bound exploration, these scenes involving Mars exploration will likely not be included in any textbook of the future.

What if a wolf fell in love with a mermaid? And what if that mermaid existed as part of a larger, underwater population that transformed and mutated ordinary people and animals into something fantastic? The *Waterscape* fantasy answers hidden mysteries gliding below the surface.

Who knows how many mammals in the circuses, rodeos, zoos, pet shops, farms, ranches, and private homes of the world are biding their time, just waiting for that one moment, that perfect confluence of key circumstances that affords them the opportunity to wreak Mother Nature's revenge against a human population? *A Day in the Life of ARES* tells of four people caught inside just such a zoological doomsday scenario.

Children of the Golden Ra speculates a technological advance in energy with far-reaching future impact that is discovered by those considered inconsequential, almost invisible by larger society.

The Lovebirds tells a story so horrific that it almost qualifies for that genre. Instead, it is a speculative history with an almost mythic quality that explores one unspoken aspect of slavery. Perhaps unspoken because such things never happened. Or perhaps unspoken because such things did.

Finally, in *Welcome to Aztlan!*, the long-dreaded race war bubbles to the surface due to advances in robotics. One woman trying to save her family from persecution flees with them to the Texas-Mexico border where she is forced to make hard choices.

The speculative stories reveal the possibilities of what could happen, what would happen, and sometimes, what should happen... in an ideal world.

Originally, the literary and speculative stories were to be published as two separate collections under two separate titles. However, they seemed to belong together as one collection under one title. Hence, Imaginarium.

The short story, whether literary or speculative fiction, permits the writer the opportunity to briefly step outside the parameter of ordinary events for just a moment in time. Sometimes, one moment is all that is necessary to change the fate of the world. And sometimes, the least of us have the greatest ability to influence the future of us all.

Lee McQueen
1 October 2006

The most powerful
player in the game…

Story 1

The Angel and the Lion

Davey came to in a dimly lit, moving space that rattled over the sound of a loud motor. Lifting her aching head gingerly, she saw that she wasn't alone. She was with the other women – fourteen all together. All of them were black.

She was American with shoulder-length braids. They were southern Sudanese with scarves and head wraps. The red surge of pain inside her skull receded to a dull throb which allowed her small intervals to remember the betrayal.

Congressman Bradley, warned her three weeks ago.

"Davey, don't go. I know you feel that you owe Minister Thompson for helping you when you were incarcerated, but negotiating large sums of money with individuals who have already shown a degree of immorality by buying and selling humans, is too high a price to pay. You don't owe him or the United Church of Peace Mission your life."

"Congressman, you are the father I never had and I love you for that. But I want to make peace with the world. I've done a lot of taking and a lot of hurting. At least I can say that I tried. It's just for three weeks."

"Davina Lewis…"

"Minister Thompson has faith in me, Congressman. I wish that you did."

They compromised. Davey accepted a text messenger and promised to send Congressman Bradley daily updates from Sudan.

She'd come a long way from the streets of South Dallas and the gangster life she'd led most of her younger years on the liquor and convenience store circuit. During her two-year prison sentence, she met Minister Thompson who helped her to study for her G.E.D. Once paroled, she worked for his organization, The United Church of Peace Mission.

One day, Congressman Bradley strode into the mission and laughingly asked her to cease sending all those letters to his office about the Sudan slave trade – Minister Thompson's crusade. After she completed her parole, Congressman Bradley invited her to work in his office because, "Despite all those trees you killed, the letters were well-done."

And now, despite Congressman Bradley's warning, despite preparation and Christian goodwill, Davey, twenty-five and rehabilitated, hung from a chain attached to shackles on her wrists that twisted around a bar in the back of the truck. She watched miles of Sudan desert and the occasional tamarisk tree rush away in clouds of sand and dust through the back opening with growing despair.

The United Church of Peace Mission's effort to redeem slaves in Sudan was not only a dismal failure. It was a slaughter.

They arrived to Khartoum that morning and met their guide, Salim, on the tarmac.

"You are exactly on time. Welcome to Sudan. Did you have a good flight?"

Minister Thompson briskly took charge.

"Great flight! We're ready to go to work. Are we all set to meet them?"

"It has been arranged."

And now they all knew what it was that had been arranged. After a pleasant tour of Khartoum, Salim drove them a few miles north where the slavers held thirteen captives. The mission participants, college students and middle-class retirees, looked at the slaves they came to redeem in the back of the truck. While the others went to negotiate up front, Davey lingered.

"How long have you been here?"

The slaves stared back at her silently. The entire scenario seemed so unbelievably obscene… and wrong. Congressman Bradley told them Western dollars only fueled the trade by driving up the price. He'd told them.

Davey swallowed.

"We're doing what we can to free you."

Still no response.

Davey peeked around the truck and watched money exchange hands. She pulled out the text messenger:

YES 13 SLVS

Chaos erupted loudly in front of the truck. A quick glance revealed screams of fear, streaks of blood, and twitching bodies in blazing afternoon heat. Quickly, she sent another message:

ATTK SOS

No place to hide. Under the truck? In the back of the truck? Run for the desert? It happened too quickly. The slavers grabbed her. She struggled. They hit her. And now, like her own ancestors, she was a slave.

"Where are we going? Where are they taking us?"

No answer. She could speak neither Dinka nor Arabic. Davey had never felt so alone. Not even during her week in solitary for beating another inmate near to death. She lost the text messenger. No one knew where she was or where she was going. She didn't even know. Davey rocked back and forth as the truck rattled over endless desert terrain.

A few hours later, the slavers opened the truck and pulled them all roughly to the ground.

"Atbarah," she heard one of the slaves whisper to another.

When the slavers traded them again and led them to another truck, Davey noticed the headlights of a car in the darkness. After another half hour of rough terrain, they led the captives into a warehouse with a main room and a few smaller rooms.

The men threw food on the hard floor and poured water into a bucket. Davey drank water from her hands.

She heard a voice shouting Arabic roughly and turned to see one of the slavers waving his gun. The women around her sat and faced the wall. Davey quickly did the same. From behind, she heard the sounds of a struggle.

"Davey, are you okay? We're going to get out of here."

Minister Thompson must have been held in the car.

"Davey, don't fight them. Do as they say!"

Davey heard angry, rapidly-spoken Arabic reprimanding him. She half-turned and then quickly faced the wall again. Sure enough, she heard the meaty sound of a gun butt striking her mentor in the gut as he was led away.

One by one, they dragged the women into a smaller room. The screaming started and stopped as the women returned. Even if Congressman Bradley received her text message, he would not be in time. Davey heard the by now familiar Arabic command followed by a smack of the gun butt directed at the young Dinka girl beside her.

She looked about ten-years-old.

Davey thought of those days long ago on the streets of Dallas. Talking loud but saying nothing really as the cop snapped the cuffs on her and told her she needed to do something with her life. There was more to the world than the streets she and her friends thought they controlled. There was also more to friendship than mutual self-destruction. She received not a single visit or letter from her crew during her two years inside.

The little girl cried.

Davey looked down in shame at her own powerlessness. She felt prickles of fear.

She was next in line.

She told Minister Thompson on his first visit that she only agreed to see him to break up the boredom of her day. He told her about Shadrach, Meshach, and Abedneggo.

"I Been a Negro, too," was her sarcastic response.

Minister Thompson laughed and told her that was funny. She had to laugh with him. She could never rattle him and eventually, she stopped trying. He'd persuaded her to read the story of Daniel in the lion's den aloud.

With a quick prayer to God to deliver her from the lions too, Davey stood up slowly, still facing the wall. The inevitable angry shouts and curses rained down upon her. She felt the gun butt strike her in her back but spoke calmly.

"Take me instead."

The girl gasped. Outrage ensued. The slaver dug the gun barrel crunchily against her spine.

"English? Or American?"

Davey winced.

"American."

With that, they grabbed her braids and dragged her into another of the smaller rooms. Minister Thompson sat opposite the desk of the leader in some sort of macabre interview.

The slaver holding her hair spoke rapid Arabic. She heard the word "American" tossed out indignantly as he shook her. The man behind the desk smiled with polite mockery as he spoke in British-accented English.

"I am Asaad el Haak. The Lion of Truth. Welcome. Please remain standing as there are only two chairs and we are still in deep discussion."

El Haak turned back to Minister Thompson in thoughtful contemplation.

"The Great America. The new land for the children of the old lands. Were you born an American, Minister Thompson?"

"Yes."

"Where in America were you born?"

"El Paso."

"How about you, Miss…"

"Dallas."

He didn't need to know her name.

"Two Texans!" El Haak was delighted. "The cowboy and his cowgirl from the Wild West. JR Ewing. The land of oil and greed." He paused. "Texas was a slave state prior to America's own Civil War. With great fields of cotton picked by, I believe it was… slaves. Am I right, Minister Thompson."

"That's true, for a brief period."

"Would it not be a most intriguing irony to learn that your ancestor's once owned Miss Dallas' ancestors? And now you are here to make amends by teaching Miss Dallas how to set slaves free."

Minister Thompson remained silent. The baiting continued.

"You must feel very at home in the Middle East, Minister Thompson. It is not so different. Do you like it here? You are here. Therefore, you must surely like it here."

Davey's head ached from the fist in her hair and the sound of El Haak's hateful, mocking voice.

"You have already experienced so much of the joy and pain there is to find here in the desert -your unfortunate pain, my everlasting joy. There is not much else to know."

El Haak waited. She and Minister Thompson waited.

The interview disappointed El Haak. She could tell, though he smiled, that their passivity puzzled and irritated him. She felt El Haak's hard, black gaze travel up and down her body and then shift back to Minister Thompson as if making up his mind.

That type of cruelty, she'd seen once before. In a tiny apartment in a South Dallas slum, her father questioned her mother… and then strangled her as Davey watched from underneath a table.

El Haak's gaze focused on Minister Thompson with finality. Davey's eyes filled with tears as she looked at El Haak pleadingly.

Davey heard Minister Thompson's voice from far away.

"Don't cry, Davey."

El Haak glanced back at Davey and smiled, finally satisfied. From behind the desk, he withdrew a sword with a metallic hiss.

What good did crying ever do anyone?

Asaad El Haak lifted his sword and cut off Minister Thompson's head amid Davey's screams of protest. Davey's knees weakened as his skull thumped to the floor.

The fist in her braids snapped her back upright to meet El Haak's smiling contemplation as her tears mingled with Minister Thompson's blood.

"Minister Thompson will always be part of Sudan," he informed her conversationally.

He held the sword against her neck… and waited.

Davey closed her eyes and tried to still her shaking body as the blade scraped up and down slowly, softly. Her breath choked in and out.

"I think you will too, Miss *Davey* of Dallas. My assistants appear extremely eager to introduce you to our special ways."

The slaver holding her led her to where she sat before. She heard El Haak shout something and two slavers guarding the other women went into his office and carried out both parts of Minister Thompson's body.

Davey shivered violently. The women who had been to the small room and the women yet to go had all been completely cowed by the sound of Davey screaming.

Davey looked down to avoid the hard gaze of the remaining slaver as he approached her. Something acrid bubbled in the back of her throat. He hit her with the gun butt.

If Davey understood Arabic, she would have heard, "Get up filthy black American slut! *We* are your god now!" She understood enough to stand. She followed him in a trance.

The slaver watched her undress slowly. If she cooperated, maybe she wouldn't be hurt. She was down to her underwear. She unhooked her bra.

But was she willing to die?

He put down his gun. He reached down and pulled himself out of his pants.

Yes.

Davey kicked him hard and cut off his scream with a hard blow to the throat. She forgave her father as she strangled the slaver. He had no further need of his gun, knife, or radio. She took them. Dressed quickly. Peeking out of the room, she saw that the other women remained unguarded. *Mother, I was too young and too small to help you.* Davey swallowed.

"Ssss."

They all turned to her. She passed all except the gun to the first woman who had been raped.

The other two slavers, finished with Minister Thompson, were on their way back inside – probably to take their turn with her judging by the laughter.

Davey positioned herself and brained the first slaver who entered. Three of the women dragged down the other slaver before he could raise his gun. While Davey snatched their guns and radios away, the women quietly, viciously took their revenge with the knives.

Now, three of them had guns.

Davey felt a glimmer of hope. They might have a chance.

"Who speaks English?" she whispered. The women shook their heads. "English!" she demanded desperately.

The little girl who sat next to her earlier spoke up.

"I speak English."

"You!" Davey was exasperated, "Then why..."

The girl was contrite. "I was afraid."

Understandable.

Davey decided rapidly. "Tell them we're gonna take a truck!"

The girl translated for the women and they all nodded, agreed. The slavers, mutilated and bloodied, said nothing.

El Haak raised the alarm from his office doorway. Davey aimed and fired. Missed.

No turning back.

She could hear other slavers responding to El Haak's shouts. They outnumbered the women.

Davey screamed, "Fight for your lives! Fight them!" She shot down two henchmen as they ran into the room.

"Get the guns!"

The odds turned. Caught unaware because they didn't expect the women to fight back, five more henchmen fell screaming and cursing, twitching.

Nine women gunned with her.

"Stay with me!" she told the girl.

They ran into the night for the same truck in which they'd arrived, shouting and shooting at everything and everyone who moved to stop them.

Davey took weapons detail in the passenger seat. The universe brought her full circle to her first after-school job.

The woman behind the wheel announced to Davey, via the girl, "We head for Gondor through Kassala!" The other women continued shooting out of the back of the truck as they fishtailed wildly away from the warehouse.

Good-bye, Minister Thompson.

"I'll contact Congressman Bradley from Ethiopia. He'll help us." Davey replied.

If the Lion of Truth followed, she would pray to God to give her the strength to close his mouth and destroy him.

Perhaps a sandstorm would hide them.

For now, at least, they were safe.

Story 2

Labyrinth of the Labor Realm

My name is Taylor McElroy. My life, my labor, and my love are all dead-end streets littered and polluted with my failures and broken dreams. I watch passively as the rain falls and makes an oily, gritty, gray-black porridge of my past mistakes.

On this cold, dreary Monday in January, I await judgment.

"$45.00, that's it. That's the best I can do." The pawnbroker waits with an expression that is supposed to be objective – like a doctor. However, he has no bedside manner to speak of and I see the condescension seep into his face.

"Take it or leave it."

I am insulted. But I am also broke and desperate to raise rent money. Next Monday, the sentence of my eviction at high noon will be carried out. The system, my landlord assures me, works.

"Sign here."

I sign there. I take the money.

The postal worker is nice. I like him. We shoot the breeze now and then.

"Another manuscript, huh? $5.88, including the envelope." I slip a five and a one off my damp wad of pawnshop money carefully. It is pathetic how much I anticipate the twelve cents in return.

"Good luck to ya, this time, Ms McElroy."

This time. Unlike the last time. Unlike all the other last times. Good luck to me. The postal worker allows me the dignity of delusion. We never speak of the many collection letters that arrive in plain brown envelopes to my post office box. He's cool like that.

I have a job interview. I am hopeful. But it is an employer's market. Therefore, my plan is to dance to the employer's fiddle while the employer calls out the number. The ad in the paper says, "Telephone Operator needed for answering service." I can do this. I know that I can.

The man who interviews me resembles David Bowie, complete with strange, rather sinister charisma. He speaks slowly. He looks slowly, as well. I mean, he takes pauses between words and stares at me. If I were a serial killer or a vampire, I would put his face in my newspaper ad to solicit fresh prey.

I am afraid to look evil in the eyes. But I need this job. I really, really need this job. I glance around his office instead. He notices me not looking at him.

"The swords are souvenirs from my travels."

Travel where? To the fiery pits of Hell where these phallic metallic blades of penetrating destroying destruction were surely forged? Ice-cold, pale blue eyes rest again on my face. He heard my thoughts. Or he read my mind. I may not make it out of this office alive.

"Give me... a second... to... look through your... application."

He pauses again as if to give me a generous head start in a mad dash from the room. I really need this job. I smile vaguely and stare vacantly over his right shoulder. My life and sanity tick-tock away.

"Are you... married?"

Ice blue laser stare. I swallow and shake my head.

"Do you have... any children?"

I am single and childless. However, the common sense answer to this question and the previous is a loud, proud "Yes." Yes! YES! I have a huge, hairy, ugly, jealous husband that I will meet at the domestic violence counselor's office right after this interview and five messy children to pick up from elementary school who need to be immunized from the Red Death at the free clinic.

I shake my head again even as my brain screams out, "Lie! Lie!" Sometimes, I am not so bright.

"You have a... wonderful... speaking voice. So clear and articulate. Very... warm and soft... feminine."

I need this job. I need this job. I need this job.

"You're... very pretty."

Embarrassed cough. Smile. Glance to the door to measure the distance. Of course he sees me looking at the door. Those eyes can see the wind blow.

"You see that door? That door leads... to my private residence. If you ever... need anything... you can just... knock. As a matter of fact," He pauses.

Here it comes. Don't say it, weird freak. Please don't say it.

"I'd like... for you to knock."

Damn. He said it.

On the way home I ask myself why this happens to me. Do I know where I'm going to? I'm either hysterical or I have the flu. Do I know?

The serial killer in him brings out the serial killer in me. I want to set his David Bowie face and his office on fire then make him explain the reason why to my landlord. A jail cell can't be that much worse than a homeless shelter. Three hots, a cot, and free shower shoes.

I eat crackers and peanut butter. My dessert is hot tea with sugar, cinnamon, and black pepper. My entertainment is the battered copy of a writing magazine that lies crumpled at the bottom of my satchel.

I read the call for submissions again.

"Writing Contest - Poetry, short story, script, play, full length novel submissions." I hug the contest rules to my chest. I curl around the smeared, wrinkled, food and oil-stained magazine clipping in the fetal position and allow my dreams to take over and accomplish all that I could not while awake.

Tuesday, I pound my way along the pavement. This ain't a stroll. The employment, or rather, *unemployment* office (depends upon one's level of optimism, I suppose), has alerted me of to job opening at a large hotel. I am optimistic. I can do this job. I know that I can.

I fill out an application and write, "Front Desk Clerk," in the blank that asks, "Position applied for?" I hand the clipboard back to a polished woman with coiffed, frosted hair and many white teeth.

The lower half of her face unhinges and the brilliant white of her smile blinds me. "The clerk position has been filled, but we can always use happy smiling faces to serve in the kitchen."

Happy like yours? The top half of her face is inert. I don't mean calm. I mean, inert. The surface of the skin around her cheeks, nose, eyes and forehead doesn't move.

I try to match her grin. I want to be a team player. Now my face hurts.

I am back at the unemployment office speaking with a woman at the front desk.

"I don't know why they told you that. The clerk job is still open."

The woman and I exchange that look that only she and I could understand. Further words need not be spoken. She and I, her mother and sister, my mother and my sister, her friends and my friends are new neither to the art of bait and switch, nor to the look of disbelief and shock when our mainstream telephone voices and resumes are matched with our non-mainstream faces. I should go back and picket the hotel. I really should. And I would, but I'm light-headed.

Hunger strike!

No. Sticking my neck out is what got me here in the first place. I go home to rest. The phone rings. I answer.

Click.

It's called star 69, you idiot.

Now his turn to answer.

"Who is this?"

I generously attribute the disconnection to a probable mistake by the telephone company. I practice being a team player on everyone now.

"Is this Taylor?"

Who is trying to get their crank call on? My number is unlisted.

"Taylor McElroy?"

I am silent.

"You applied for a clerk position?"

Okay, yes.

"What... Where are you from? What have you done?"

This is the interview?

"This is the owner. Come in for an interview."

Never underestimate the power of unspoken implication.

I don't pound the pavement. This time, I step lightly because I'm really not sure what to expect.

The owner wears Good Ole Boy aura like the smoke of smuggled Cuban cigars. I bet he hasn't eaten peanut butter in years.

"So you're sure you wanted to apply for the clerk position instead of the server position?"

The owner turns to his left-hand man.

"Remember that thing I had to do? I'm gonna step out."

Excuse me?

Left-Hand-Man emanates Redneck through his pores like a second skin.

"You know, you should try for the auditor's position. It's the hardest so if you prove that you can do night auditing, then you can do anything. Including front desk clerk. I do see that you don't have much accounting experience though. No certification or anything. We'll just have to see how you measure up against all the other applicants."

Baited and switched. *Again.*

After making my rounds at the grocery store, picking up samples from the deli, the bakery, the produce section, and the frozen food aisle, I return home to wash it all down with peppermint mouthwash on the rocks. The tingle from the mouthwash doesn't get me high, but it sure helps me to think. There is money here somewhere.

Wednesday, I am at the monstrous entertainment juggernaut - conglomerate, if you will. I know that I certainly will if no one else does.

"You've got eclectic taste. Real sexy. I can't believe you're letting some of these go."

Hurt me.

"I mean, jeez. Double and triple cd greatest hits. Some rare and foreign too."

This is the day the music died.

My ears ache and starve in mourning.

"These DVDs are classic cinema you don't ever see much. Real cult status."

After an average of thirty viewings each, I should be happy to be freed from the cult of cinema. But the indoctrination is so deeply ingrained that I yearn to chant the dialogue I've memorized.

"I can give you $120 for the lot."

And so, I say goodbye to yesterday.

It is important to me to equalize the negotiation so I pick up a free weekly magazine on the way out. After all, I don't come *that* cheap and easy.

I stop at the grocery store. No samples out today. I wonder if my repeated tour yesterday had anything to do with that.

"That's $1.22, ma'am."

I open my change purse with a wince, a small smile, and a hushed apology that the shoppers behind me in line cannot hear. I don't want to break the twenties I just received. That's an extra special delight I reserve for my landlord's eyes only.

"No problem at all, ma'am. Pennies spend as well as any other money."

This I know, having searched late at night under many a closed drive-through window for the pennies that spend so well.

I read each page of the weekly sitting on a free bench in a free park breathing free air, eating cookies from the "hurt food" basket. For fifty cents, I don't mind that someone aided my digestion by crushing the cookies for me. For sixty cents, I don't mind that my three cans of juice are dented. That makes the juice easier to pour and that's certainly all right with me. The back page of the weekly says, "Poets and song writers sought."

So much despair.

I can do this. I know that I can.

So little paper.

Late fees and interest mean one step back for two steps forward. Life is like a game of "Mother, May I?" Forward, then back. Forward then... oops! I forget to ask, "Mother, may I?" Back I go.

I speak with the pawnbroker once again. Other customers mill about. I can't believe what I am about to do. Two steps forward. One step back.

"Computers lose value faster than cars. Faster than any other merchandise we handle. $50.00, take it or leave it."

The regulars look to me for a reaction. I look back at them blank-faced. I have no idea. They don't either. Neither does the floor. Neither does the ceiling. Neither does the counter.

"Look, lady, make up your mind. People are waiting."

Was there ever really any question? Wasn't all this hesitation just a show for myself? I mean, really. In my heart I know I would have accepted $25 for a computer that cost me $1000 four years ago. Good thing the pawnbroker didn't know that.

I am still a writer. Have pencil, have crayon, have charred stick, have safety pin and blood in the tip of my finger, will write. There is a letter in my mailbox.

"...disconnect your service in seven (7) days..."

Seven more days of heat and light. Would spring come in time? I should not chance it. I reluctantly break seventy dollars off from my stash. Two steps forward. One step back. Somewhere, the landlord's skin turns cold as if from a bad daydream.

Back to the unemployment office that same afternoon.

"You have so much experience. And a master's degree. Why would you apply to work at a fried chicken fast food restaurant?"

The pity in his eyes mingles with the shame in my own. Only because the unemployment office allows me to make free copies do I not flee sobbing. Someday, I will hold my head up. But that day is not today.

I spend a little more of the landlord's money.

"Sardines, crackers, and peanut butter. Congratulations."

I cock my head to the side because I can't imagine why the cashier considers this a winning combination.

"You're expecting, right?"

I remember the pitying look from the employment counselor. Once today was enough. I nod the affirmative and feel tiny prickles under my arms.

"Well, congratulations, ma'am."

Fake smile and then out the door.

The postal worker kills me softly.

$3.65 altogether, ma'am."

Fake smile and then out that door too.

At the library, I see what's new on the Internet. Lots of screenplay contests. I can do this. I know that I can. Entrance fees, "$40, $25, $45, etc." I can, but then again, I can't. At least not right now.

At a popular discount chain store, an irritated woman tells me, "Not hiring," and points to the sign on her door I missed in my puppy-like eagerness to show initiative. I stupidly repeat the phrase back to her as a question.

"No, ma'am. We just laid some people off. I don't even know if I'm gonna have a job."

Oh. I shuffle away feeling great concern for her and myself.

The light blinks on my answering machine. It is a job! I won the lottery! One of my many submissions hit the jackpot!

The landlord is fed up.

"Rent is due on the 1st, Ms. McElroy. Not the 9th, not the 14th, and not the 25th. That is your signature at the bottom of your lease, isn't it? I'm not kidding around with you. You have until Monday. Read the lease!"

My eyes seek desperately and I find. Here I go back out the door.

"You must have been collecting for like years. Yeah, but we can only offer $112 because some of the spines are creased and the paper is kinda yellow."

He is young.

"Well, yeah, they probably are rare, but the thing is they're just so old.

Let me explain.

"They're like, not what's hot right now. And besides, once I give a quote, I kinda have to stick with it."

He has a job because he follows the rules. I have no job.

"It's like our policy or something."

I should learn from his example.

At the post office, the postal worker lets me know, "There's going to be a postage rate increase next month."

If this day got any better, I wouldn't be able to stand it.

The sun goes down. On the way back to the library, a stocky, pasty-faced weirdo drives along beside me. I quicken my pace.

"How ya doin' gal? Wanna party?"

I change direction and cut down an alley. He circles to find me again a block away.

"Heh, heh, heh."

I walk through someone's back yard, reverse, cut through another back yard, then across a store parking lot. A dog barks at me indignantly from inside an SUV.

"Heh, heh, heh."

Time for the double-reverse around the block and back again switchback? No. I'm tired. It's been a long day. I walk towards his car. Stop in the name of mace! He guns his motor and roars off.

This day just had to get better, didn't it?

A male and female police officer chit chat in the evening dusk.

"You need some help, ma'am?"

I describe my problem.

"A lot of women solicit in this neighborhood. Where do you live? Why are you walking this direction?"

The police woman makes no effort to mask her up and down perusal of my clothing. If she were not a cop, if she were not standing next to her beefy partner, if she did not wear a gun, if she did not have the entire weight of police training riding on her ability to profile, I would smack her stupid hat off.

"So you say you're going to the library, huh? You a college student? No?"

Her partner, at least, has the courtesy to get into his vehicle and drive around for a look-see. She blathers on while her partner reports back on the radio that the man who fits my description zooms away when spotted.

On the library's computer screen, I stare at the words I write. "Little paper cuts and spitted poison today." I'm not sure. I mean, I'm no expert, but I think I may be losing my mind.

The librarian has a job and does the job she has well.

"You'll have to log off now. Someone else needs the computer."

I want to just log off the entire day and allow someone else to breathe my oxygen for me. No. Not that. Not quite that. I just need some sleep.

Thursday is here now. Monday is not far behind. I should pack. When the sheriff comes and tosses out my belongings, I'd rather they be in boxes than scattered about. Because I have class.

The fast food restaurant manager doesn't like me. Petulance oozes through my telephone speaker.

"Look, if we need someone, we'll call you. You don't have to call in to check. We'll-call-*you*."

Okay. Cross out "For here or to go" and proceed to the next item on the list which is, "Re-read rejection letter." The publisher treats me with professional respect and gives careful consideration to my submission. The paper is expensive and thick. I wonder if they're hiring?

"...develop your major character more in-depth so the reader can easily identify the emotional motivation..."

Two steps forward.

With that, I catapult myself to lay siege to the Mexican food restaurant. The manager is pretty friendly. No irritation. No creep vibes.

"You speak Spanish fluently?"

¡Claro que sí!

"It's good you have customer service experience. We need a hostess and a cashier."

Yes, I'm that somebody.

"Why don't you come in for a second interview this afternoon with the owner?"

Yes! I need a win. I really, really need a win right now. This may be it. I groom again, carefully. Rehearse. Practice my smile. Think of some witty repartee. I arrive half an hour early.

I window shop at a nearby candy store to kill a little extra time. If I could run fast, if I had a car, if I were handy with tools, if I had a sense of direction, if I had bus fare, if I had a bike with a basket, I could rob this store. I sigh instead. I'm so damn hungry.

Five minutes into the interview, the restaurant owner sings a song very different from that of his manager.

"I've made a business decision to not extend an offer of employment to you Ms. McElroy."

I am too stunned to react. Does he know I'm hungry? Eventually, I settle on confusion. Yes, definitely confusion.

"I made a business decision to not extend an offer of employment."

Where did I go wrong?

"It's just a business decision."

Did I mention I do windows?

"Just a business decision."

He stands up to indicate the interview is over and that I should leave the premises.

"Just business."

I hold out my hand. The least he can do is shake it.

"Nice to meet you, Ms McElroy."

He shakes my hand. I do not leave empty-handed. I carry his sweat away with me on my palm.

Why? Why? Why?

That afternoon, I sit at the computer screen of a computer kiosk inside a big, box store that has everything – including jobs – I could ever think to ask for.

The computer quizzes my psychological state of mind. Yeah right. *You can't handle the truth.*

"Have you ever received counseling for depression, addictions, or any other work-related issue?"

"Have you ever removed office supplies from your place of employment without asking?"

"Do you feel marijuana is equal to the drinking of alcohol?"

"Have you ever filed a worker's compensation claim?"

"Have you ever been absent from work?"

"Have you ever been late to work?"

"Do you feel some people are hired based on 'who they know' rather than merit?"

"Do you feel a non-conformist has a place in a corporate atmosphere?"

I want to confess to the computer my deepest thoughts and fears and philosophies on life. But I also want to tell the computer whatever the hell it needs to hear in order to recommend me to other humans as a good bet to push grocery carts towards customers entering the store. This is my dilemma.

I can do this. I know that I can.

At the library, I check out writing books to replace the books I sold. I use the bathroom. I drink from the fountain. I use the Internet. I build up immunity against every germ circulating through the ventilation system and coating every nook and cranny of the computer keyboard.

"…while a worthy and fascinating read, does not fit the subject parameters and profile…" another publisher tells me in an email.

"We just hired someone," the librarian tells me at the front desk. It is my theme song. I know every word. I sing it aloud as I walk to the day labor office.

"Sorry. Nothing's available today."

I make a few phone calls.

"You need to talk to my friend over at the development office. Tell him Charlie sent you. He'll fix you right up."

I call the development office.

"We're not hiring, Taylor. Charlie knows that even though he keeps sending people this way."

A lawyer needs a secretary like a starving, soon-to-be homeless woman needs a check.

"You're not from around here are you? I can tell by your voice. Where are you from and how'd you end up here applying for this job?"

A clothing store needs a cashier like a desperate, near-sighted woman needs insurance coverage for her eyes.

"Why would we hold your graduate degree against you, Ms. McElroy? It's not that at all. We just feel you aren't a good fit for what we're looking for here. Good day, ma'am."

A newspaper needs a receptionist like a broke, newly-thin woman needs to buy a belt to hold up clothing that still remembers more prosperous times.

"How long have you been sitting there? Someone should have told me you were here. I've just been yapping away on the phone."

Indeed.

"Okay, we'll let you know."

Promise? You promise to call me?

Speaking of clothing that remembers more prosperous times, I pull out a suit that is now two or three sizes too large. The consignment shop less than a mile away tells me, "We can give you $10.00"

Deal!

Back on the street, I feel encouraged. One more application.

"We'll get in touch if something comes up."

I don't move.

"We'll let you know."

I search for my significance in her eyes. On the other side of that counter, do I really matter?

"We'll-call-you."

I look at the floor. I will not cry.

"Bye-bye now."

I recover and hurry from the store just before the manager's hand reaches the panic button.

I'm too tired to eat that evening.

Friday morning, I have a classic hunger headache. For one sick moment, I enjoy the high, the tingling, numb sensation in my face and finger-tips. It is all I have to let me know that I am awake until I eat half a pot of rice flavored with salt, pepper, basil, and oregano. I run out of tea so I mix cinnamon with pepper and sugar and pour hot water over it.

I wrap my coat around me and pull the belt tight. My waist is smaller. Actually, I look kind of nice.

"We have a job in hotel housekeeping." The woman at the day labor office checks her files. "That's all we have for the next several weeks. Everything else is industrial, heavy lifting."

I rush out with the work ticket before she changes her mind.

Back at the same hotel where I was not hired as a front desk clerk by the owner, the owner doesn't recognize me now wearing an apron as I push a cart laden with cleaning supplies and toiletries past him, across the lobby, towards the elevator.

The hotel guest in the fourth room is glad to see me standing in the hallway. He stands in the doorway of his room wearing a towel. Beyond him, I see the wastebasket filled with ice and beer.

"Come on in, sweetheart. You're just in time to clean me up. I'm real dirty."

The towel slips down a little.

I am not dumb. But I am smart enough to play dumb when circumstances call for that state of mind. I slowly unpack towels, soap, and shampoo from the cart. His towel comes off completely when I extend my hand and the toiletries drop to the floor at his feet. I frantically push the cart to the next room and ignore his laughter. It doesn't matter. He complains. I am fired.

I collect my earnings, all twenty dollars, from the day labor office.

"Don't spend it all in one place."

I'll be sure to pass that on to the landlord after I stock up at the grocery store.

"You must really love beans and rice."

I am just so very tired.

"Are you a vegetarian? How well does that work with your pregnancy?"

It does wonders for my pregnancy.

Someone dropped today's paper on a bench at the bus stop. Heigh, ho. Straight to the classified ads I go.

"One year in Iraq, tax-free. Free flight to and from. Lucrative contract reestablishing communications infrastructure in post-conflict environment. Security provided. Safety not guaranteed. Visit www.arenco.com."

They need an information specialist. God, help me. I may not make it back alive, but I know that I can do this.

An older gentleman drives by. He is not a bus driver. He is not a cab driver. And... he's actually no gentleman.

"Psst. You wanna ride?"

I shake my head.

"I bet you ride real good."

Unfortunately, my mace sits on my kitchen counter today.

"You sure now, honey?" He changes tactics. Street smart guy, he is. In milliseconds, he assesses me and realizes that manipulative chivalry rather than gross lechery will break me down quicker. To illustrate this, my empty stomach claws at me and curses me for my ignorant ingratitude.

"You look like you could use a little help."

My stomach tries to escape from my abdomen to jump into the car with a potential sugar daddy. My brain, my analytical, logical, writer/researcher brain betrays me and joins in with my stomach's disgust and frustration. The headache pounding against my skull jars me to focus once more on the situation at hand.

My heart weeps for me to hold on to the person I used to be before the fateful day I blow the whistle and discover why the chasm between right and wrong yawns so wide. Virtue without a financial safety net is like church with no heavenly reward. Sounds good, but what's the use?

I escape into the nearest store. It is some sort of punk, skater-boy hang-out. Generation Y and X wait for the Age of Aquarius to take off and relive his by-gone days of youth elsewhere.

Late that Friday afternoon, the day labor office remains my last hope.

"Well, okay." The dispatcher is not convinced. "You sure now? You have to be at the barn at five tomorrow morning."

I'm sure that I will fake it till I make it.

But the sanitation worker is not convinced. He looks around at the trees and into passing cars for a hidden camera and microphone as we hold on to the back of the truck. Oh, if only.

"I can't believe they sent you out here."

I can't believe it either.

"You go to school?"

Fake it. I shake my head.

"Me neither. We have about ten more blocks and then we're finished."

Till I make it. Or not. He has to work harder to make up for my feeble attempts to keep pace. I see the driver of the truck's lips move as he stares sourly at me in the rear view mirror. He wants to back the truck over me. It's not like I could run away. My arms, back, and shoulders feel as though they are encased in concrete.

"Sorry it didn't work out, miss. You did better than some for the first day. Make sure you soak in a hot bath. You're gonna be real sore tomorrow."

I'm sore right now.

I am a failure at everything I try.

Opportunities to whore, steal, and cheat passed me by. My invitation to flip burgers got lost in the mail. I fail to take out the city's garbage. I don't even deserve to take out my own garbage for someone else to pick up. Let it sit there in my kitchen and reek all night.

Because the sanitation worker is kind enough to not report me, I am paid for a full day's work. I don't deserve that either. But I take it.

I whimper pitifully as I retrieve my mail. I'm not gonna read it. I'm just gonna enjoy this hot water while it lasts. I will remember every moment in this tub when l soap myself down in my neighbor's sprinklers next week. I will give thanks for the psycho who waters his lawn even when it's too cold for grass to grow. I will give thanks for this heating pad inside my sleeping bag (I sold my furniture to pay the previous month's rent).

Tomorrow is Sunday and I will give thanks for air and sunlight.

The morning is crisp, dry, and clear. It is cool and warm at the same time. Cold wind. Hot sun. February will begin soon. I creep to the coffee shop still a little stiff. Just a little treat for me. One last feast before I join my people, the transitory guests of the tax-paying public. I should use the rest of today to get to know them better. Find my place among them. The bright side is that since so much of my stuff is already sold, I don't have that much to pack. I give thanks for this too.

I sidle in, avoiding the front counter. I bring my own cup from home. I know where the hot water for refills sits. Hot water, sugar, cinnamon, and lemon make a good tea. I call it that. I sit and spread my paperwork out. I need to get organized and caught up on my life. Handle my business. Make some decisions. Plead my case with those who will listen to reason. Prepare for the worst from those who have tired of my excuses. Rank them all in order. But first, a note to myself:

Painted

Awaken

Awaken and see an empty room

The sun, the sky, the tree, the air, the Earth, the moon

Locked inside

Locked inside sexy silver glass

Cannot hide

Cannot hide just break me don't ask

The Hated

Make it

Make it all ready to face that way

Little paper cuts and spitted poison today

Perfect diction

Phony fiction of regular reality

Shake the hand

Smile so wide then devour all of me

The Hated

Jaded

Jaded 'cause you said it with no proof

Do you ever see what I see ever, do you?

The other side

The other side you hide away from me

Diamond filter

Killer glitter distorted reality

You painted

Naked

Fake it no money shield for you

The lock, the bar, the gate, the wall, the gun real soon

And you lied

You lied just like you lied in the past

So much pride

So much pride grasping and crass

The Hated

Crap.

No wonder I haven't published. Now my tea is cold. Tears come to my eyes. I should have stayed at home and taken another bath.

The voice nudges me. "Now I guess I know what my face looked like when you got on the back of the truck with me."

The depressed stupor makes it hard for me to understand what he's saying. He tries again.

"What's your poison? It smells like cinnamon."

The sanitation worker from yesterday holds a steaming pot of water. He works here. Interestingly enough, he doesn't appear as if he's been beaten with rubber hoses the way I do after a day of garbage tossing.

"I didn't see you come in."

Busted. My life as a transient begins in T minus...

"That kind of day, huh?"

I smile, embarrassed. I wonder if there is a panic button behind the coffee shop's counter. Will I meet the police woman who wonders how I get any business wearing scuffed tennis shoes instead of gold stilettos once more? I should have been friendlier. Hindsight is always twenty-twenty vision.

"Tell you what," he sets down a paper cup and pours hot water into it. "Try chamomile and mint. You'll like it." He stands over me. He will not leave unless I try the tea.

My face is hot as I pull my empty wallet out of my bag.

"Don't."

He turns and walks away.

The tea is delicious the way I remember real tea being so long ago. Before I open my big mouth and mind someone else's business.

Done with the poem, I shuffle and play with invoices a while longer. No matter how I stack them, I come up deeply in debt. Well, on to yesterday's mail. More news is bad news.

He's back.

"Didn't mean to startle you earlier. I feel bad about that. I spotted you over here and I wanted you to know I wasn't just a garbage man. I shouldn't have stepped to you like that. Chip on my shoulder and all. So... let me make it up to you. I really think you should take this caramel apple butter cake for a test drive."

I draw back.

"What? You on a diet?"

Not intentionally. I cough and clear my throat.

"Allergic?"

What is with this guy? I sigh, mumble something, and shake my head.

"You know it's on me, right?"

Right.

Payment for services not rendered? I already owe him for carrying me on the sanitation route yesterday. Now the tea. Now the cake. I'm not going down this road. If I go, I'll never return to who I used to be.

"Well, the water's free anyway. So's the honey and lemon."

He waits for me to speak. I wait for him to walk away. We wait together. And wait. It's a push.

"Look, you mind if I sit with you a few minutes? I'm on break."

Who am I to say whether... He sits down even before I finish the thought.

"So what's your story?"

My story lays between us, spread across the table, in glaring, large, capitalized words of chastisement from various creditors. My face is red. I am embarrassed. He is good-looking, kind, and generous. I am a big mouth, a tattletale, unemployed, and maybe a deadbeat. He points to the envelope in my hand.

"What's that?"

I shrug. Could be a million dollars. Could be another bill. Could be January. Could be June. I am indifferent to just about everything these days. I open it, then change my mind. I don't care anymore. What does a homeless person need with mail?

"You're not gonna read it?

I shrug and stir the chamomile, mint, and honey in my cup. The water goes round and round.

He picks up the envelope and opens it. Shameless. A guy like that's gonna go places, I just know it. He reads aloud in amusement as I wait to find out to whom else I owe money.

" 'Dear Ms. Taylor McElroy.'" He looks up at me. "Taylor? Nice name. I'm Rick."

I nod and continue stirring. Could be Rick. Could be James.

He speaks quietly. "You got heart, Taylor. Much heart."

I finally stop stirring and stare at him.

"'After careful review of your submission, the editor of Gemini-Wilder Press has decided to publish your short story collection with the requested revisions sent under separate cover... advance per contract details will follow upon condition...' "

Time stands still. I see his mouth moving, but I don't hear anything else. There is a rushing sound in my ears, a swimming sensation in my head, and a choking sound from my throat. I can't help it. I begin to cry. This is not a gentle weeping. Oh no. Not this. Various liquids explode from my eyes, nose, and mouth. I don't even notice the other customers in the shop looking towards me to see if I've been assaulted by the large man smiling proudly at me across the table.

"Well, since you already have desert in front of you, how about lunch on me to celebrate? I finish here in two hours."

I cover my face. Does the hunk have a hankie?

"Unless you already have plans?"

Cancel the flight to Iraq.

I'm eating cake.

Story 3

Risk

Ten o'clock Tuesday morning, honey-brown eyes stared with a puzzling combination of anguish and hope across Dallas Joliet's desk. Siobhan Frederick anxiously made her pitch to two brilliant blue lights that glittered with lighter flecks of crystal and gray beneath raven's wing black hair and black brows.

"It is the story of three lonely children of a single mother in a northern urban ghetto who are starved for affection the mother is too busy and too tired to provide. They find love and warmth when they visit their grandmother's rural property in the South." Earnest with excitement, Siobhan finished proudly, "I also have illustrations."

Joliet Publishing, a small, quirky family-owned press on Esplanade Avenue, had been her last chance. October was *her* month. The 31st was *the* day. She'd spent hours working on her manuscripts and her illustrations. Not only that, she'd defied humidity by pulling back fifteen inches of wild, orangey-brown afro into a tight French braid that rested between her shoulders. Off came a funky skirt and denim jacket. On came her faithful, no-nonsense, navy blue suit and navy pumps. Her business-sized side bag was plain, black leather that went with every outfit in her closet. Her business cards were crisp and her breath was fresh. She'd rehearsed, she'd practiced, she'd groomed.

The pale marble statue across from her viewed her blankly for a moment, then replied with somewhat robotic indifference, "I'm sorry, Ms. Frederick. Your work is significant and has merit. But, unfortunately, it doesn't quite fit Joliet's goals."

Siobhan's heart sank as he continued killing her softly. "In addition, it would require more editorial work than what could be provided with the size of our staff."

Including welcome, introduction, handshake, chit chat about the misty weather, and the pitch itself, the entire interview took about fifteen minutes.

She'd spotted the framed picture of Mr. Joliet and a small boy with the same shockingly bright eyes son on the desk when she walked in. *One last chance.*

"Mr. Joliet, I see that you're a father…"

The publisher held up his right hand in a "stop" gesture. "You just ended the interview, Ms. Frederick," he clipped out firmly.

He stood and smoothly turned the same hand to the side for a well-practiced, dismissive handshake. There was nothing left for her to do in the face of a silvery-blue reflection of her own disgust but leave.

"Looney-tune reflections of a looney-tune mind." he decided. He needed her to be on the other side of the threshold before the weeping began. As editor and publisher, he'd learned from his father, the founder of Joliet Publishing, to remember it was "Always Business, Never Personal." He'd told the woman nothing but the truth. Once she mentioned his son, however, she'd gotten exactly what she deserved. Shown the door.

Dallas felt uncomfortable with the hurt look in the woman's eyes. The intensity and melodrama she wore like cologne, despite the business attire, might require police profiling, or medication, but definitely not publication, he told himself. He pressed the intercom button.

"Janet, if Lily calls, put her through to my cell." *Like she'd really call.*

"Yes sir."

"And try to get all the arrangements completed before 11:30 so we can lock up early."

"Yes sir!"

Janet knew that Mikey's birthday was an excuse for everyone to enjoy a half day to themselves.

Ignoring the parade of mimes, street musicians, and costumed tourists, Siobhan slowly climbed the stairs to her third-floor room in the elegant, decaying mansion she shared with graduate and doctoral students as well as a few artists. She took off the navy blue suit and released her wild mane of hair from its tight braid opting for a loose scrunchie.

Wild, but contained. That was how she liked it. Because straight-laced and repressed had gotten her nothing but shown to the door. Well, that and an awful attempt to pander to what she thought was his human side. She grimaced with embarrassment at the morning's disastrous meeting.

At the very least, she could stop for some California rolls and a caramel cappuccino to enjoy in the small park area by the river. Yes, she was near broke, but, "I deserve a little treat," she said to the mirror. The sun would take away the chill from Dallas Joliet's icy indifference still crawling around her neck and she could watch the costumes walk by. Once she recovered equilibrium, she would cash her check from Wind Publishers, the company that contracted her for encyclopedia entries. Plans in place, she left the house at a brisk pace. Still, the tears came back.

The community telephone inside the entryway rang. She heard her name. She waved one of her tousle-headed housemates away as she hurried blindly down the street.

"Ricky, take a message!" she called over her shoulder.

The woman waiting in line in front of him fumbled through a large, black purse muttering to herself. Gigantic, red-brown hair swung left and right. A floor-length gauzy concoction floated and rustled around her. That and Mikey's constant stream of excited chatter dizzied him. Thank goodness, this day came but once per year.

"At Carnival Pizza, they wear hats on your birthday. And you get a cake." Mikey shook his hand urgently. "Daddy! You get a cake!"

Dallas barely listened. He really wasn't used to being the full focus of Mikey's attention. That was why God invented a babysitter, a maid, and a daycare. And that's also why God invented a mother... if only she weren't such a selfish, self-serving, cold-hearted, gold digging b...

"Next in line, please," the teller sang.

The morning's drama with the weird woman, picking up Mikey, this new detail of dropping off last night's deposit, and forthcoming over-priced fun with the clowns at the local pizzeria exhausted him. It was only two in the afternoon and he could hardly wait to have a drink, lie down, and sleep it all off.

Dallas waited a beat and then walked around the wild-looking chocolate-cinnamon pastry (or whatever it's costume was supposed to be) in front of him. He heard a voice say, "I'm next. I'm just looking for my..." The rustling continued. "It should be here."

He clipped over his shoulder, "We're kind of in a rush, ma'am."

She lifted her head then and he got a good look at her. Mutual recognition and dislike greeted him.

Siobhan sighed, "Go ahead."

Guess he wins this round too.

She smiled at the little boy who stared back at her with open-mouthed, wide-eyed fascination. Moonlike orbs glowed at her in a perky little face. Now perched on the side of an enormous indoor garden of tall plants, she felt more insistently through the contents of her bag. Out of the corner of her eye, she watched Dallas Joliet step smartly up to teller's window.

"Hi Marlena, this is last night's deposit."

Siobhan screwed up her face and mocked him behind his back.

Hi Marlena, this is last night's deposit.

His son, still staring at her with bright eyes, laughed. She smiled back at him and sighed, a little ashamed. Her wallet was not here. Wonderful. Now she'd have to walk back home and get it. Was it at home? Let's see. Her room. Then the Japanese restaurant. Coffee shop... She'd used the twenty in her pocket. Park. Did she drop it at the park? Did someone bump into her...

She clearly remembered holding the wallet in her hand this morning. Slightly flustered, she'd taken out her business card with fingers trembling pathetically with hope. In the background chatter of the bank she could hear Dallas Joliet's light banter with the bank teller as he told some lame joke while the teller threw her head back and laughed as if her life depended on it. Now... back to... then she set her wallet on Dallas Joliet's desk.

She sighed and shook her head in disgust. *Why did I do that?*

But then why did he just stand there watching her search, knowing the entire time he had her wallet? And then he just cut in front of her. He knew he had her wallet! Cold-blooded, unfeeling, frozen, popsicle, ice cream cone-looking... Oh, as soon as he stepped away from the counter she would tell him exactly what she thought of him.

Whoosh!, the bank's lobby door swung open. Three men dressed in head-to-toe loose-fitting black jackets and jeans walked in. They were either brothers or good friends, moving in unison. *Like a pack*, her imagination said. Their hair hung long and limp. Greasy. There was a hardness about them – something hostile, something desperate. There was a grayish, sickly unnatural tinge to their faces. Something prickled the back of her neck and under her arms. *Not costumes*. Now was probably a good time to leave to find her wallet. But she saw with growing uneasiness that the three of them remained in front of the door.

Bad, bad, bad she heard in her head.

Siobhan crooked her finger at the child watching her and gestured him towards her. He approached closer with a mischievous smile. The three men inclined their heads to each other as if in a discreet business consultation. She edged the child further behind the plants towards a dim hallway missing a light bulb. Just as they started to turn the corner, Dallas Joliet looked up and frowned with alarm.

"Hey! Wait a minute!"

Chaos erupted.

Curses roared amid screams and shots fired into the ceiling and walls. Siobhan fled down dark hallway and tried various doors.

"Call the police!" she told the bank manager who ran out of his office.

She chose an unmarked door that was unlocked. A quick flash showed her a large trashcan and shelves. Janitor's closet. She shut the door behind her and the child who was crying. She heard more gunshots.

"Everybody out! Get the fuck out!"

Doors opened and slammed shut in the hallway. Women screamed.

She climbed inside the empty large-sized trash can on rollers and heaved the little boy over the side into her lap. The trash can creaked and rolled. Footsteps pounded past the door.

"Sssh! Ssh! Sssh! Don't let them find us!" She tried to quiet the boy who whimpered in fright.

The trash can stopped against a shelf. Metal aerosol containers and bottles of cleaning supplies rattled just as the janitor's door was yanked open.

"Who's in here? I'll kill you!" The rough voice filled the small space. *She didn't think to lock the door.* Siobhan clutched boy in her arms tight. *Please.* The criminal in the doorway laughed and turned around to shout at his colleague.

"Did you get him?" An undistinguishable curse was the reply. "Well then get the fucking code! What the fuck are you standing around looking at me for? Get the code!"

The door to the janitor's closet shut with a bang. More cursing from outside the door faded as the criminals walked away. The vibration from the door's slam caused items to fall off the shelf onto Siobhan and the boy with soft thuds.

In her arms, the boy flinched with fright. Some of them hit her too, but her hair shielded her and the boy for the most part. The noise outside the door was probably loud enough to cover the noise inside the closet, but still she whispered, "Ssh. Ssh. Don't let them hear you. We don't want them to find us. If they find us, they might hurt us. So ssh."

"I want my dad."

"I know. It won't be long. We just have to wait for the bad people to go away."

"I want my dad."

"He'll come. Someone will help us."

They heard the approaching wail sirens. The bank manager must have had just enough time to either dial 9-1-1, or to hit a panic button.

"Do you hear that? That's the police, sweetheart. Police are good. They'll help make the bad people go away so you can see your dad. We just have to wait and be very quiet."

She waited a beat to see what the boy would do. He was absolutely silent. Thank God. She lucked out on a kid that followed directions.

"What's your name?" she whispered.

"Mikey," he whispered back.

"Like the cereal commercial."

"What cereal?"

"Nevermind. Where's your mom? Is she at home?"

"I don't have a mom."

"Oh."

Change subject.

"Um… so do you go a lot of places with your dad?"

"Today. It's my birthday."

"Happy Birthday, Mikey. How old are you?"

"Five. We're going to Carnival Pizza for my party."

Not today, you won't. She decided it would be best to play along to keep him calm.

"Carnival Pizza? Wow. That sounds like fun."

"My dad's gonna wear a hat and a big nose."

"Wow. A hat and a big nose? That'll be funny. Make sure you get a picture." The thought of that stuck-up snob in a clown outfit was absolutely delicious.

"My dad has a camera."

Some poor writer or photographer probably left the camera on Dallas's desk and he took it for himself, Siobhan thought nastily.

Aloud, she asked, "Are your grandparents or some other kids coming to the party?"

"No. Just me and my dad."

In the lobby, they all lay flat on the ground. He wanted to lift his head to check for Mikey. But the last person who turned around to ask a question got kicked in the ribs.

Lily was long gone. Divorced from him and Mikey. Living the high life with a low life in Paris. And it didn't matter to Lily where the money came from. All that mattered was where it went – into claws that grasped with acrylic tips. That should have been his first clue about her true nature. Joliet Publishing barely made it through the burden of her alimony payments. The Parisian married her just in time and now Joliet was in tentative recovery. After two years, of no contact, Mikey didn't remember his mother. Dallas wished *he* didn't.

Isolated, shy, and lonely, Mikey was another Dallas Joliet waiting to grow up while Dallas watched passively on the sidelines. Black boots stalked back and forth among them, maintaining order. Dallas stared into space. Mikey was fed and clothed. His teeth were cleaned on schedule. His immunizations were up-to-date. What else could he have done?

Dallas closed his eyes in despair.

He could have called up some parents of the children from the daycare, maybe some of his neighbor's kids to attend the party with Mikey. How much trouble would it have been, really? Mikey was the only thing worth a damn in his life anymore and he didn't even make the effort to show him how important he was. Mikey was cared for by other people even though he maintained prideful custody.

Mikey! Mikey, my son, if we make it out of this alive, I'm gonna be better for you.

"What's your name?"

"Siobhan."

"Siobhan?"

"Yep."

"Your hair looks like cotton candy."

"Oh really." She laughed. "Like cotton candy, huh?"

"Like chocolate cotton candy."

"Oh my God!" She hugged him. "Mikey, you're the best little boy ever!"

Mikey lay back against her for comfort.

"Don't you break my heart," she whispered.

Boyfriends came. Boyfriends went. Career goals crashed and burned. One day you turn around and you're thirty-five, working freelance, with no real prospects in sight. Years ago, she'd promised herself to have her first book published by thirty. Ha! She was supposed to be married with one child and another on the way in a rambling country home that needed repairs only once in a while. Double ha! T.V. dinners, pizza, movie rentals, walks in the park around, through, beside, in front, and in back of families picnicking and playing games was as close as she got and maybe would get.

Where did I go wrong?

Sudden loud shouts and gun shots from the bank lobby caused her to flinch. Mikey woke from his light doze with a start.

"Siobhan!"

"Ssh… ssh… I'm here. We have to be quiet, Mikey. We can't let them find us."

"I'm scared!"

"Me too. But as long as they can't find us, we're safe."

"My daddy…"

"I know."

"I wanna go home."

"What do you do at home?"

"Watch t.v. Play games."

"What games?"

"Cards."

"What kind of cards."

"Pig knuckle."

"Pig knucke?"

She felt his head nod.

"What? Is that a… wait… are you talking about… pinochle?"

"Yeah. Pig knuckle."

Siobhan swallowed down laughter. He was so cute. But still. *How does a five-year-old learn pinochle?*

"So, who do you play, uh, pig knuckle with?"

"I play by myself."

"By yourself?" Siobhan frowned remembering the birthday party arrangements. The kid didn't have a lot of friends. "So, how does the game go?"

"You get some cards. You get a whole deck of cards. Then you throw them down one on top of another. Then you have a big pile."

Mikey stopped talking at this point, apparently satisfied with the explanation.

"I see." She really didn't. "Sooo…" Siobhan paused trying to understand. "Okaaay." Mikey still remained silent. "You throw the cards down…" Still nothing. "I give up. Do I have to tickle you? Then what happens?"

The tickle threat got him talking. "Then you try to get a card without moving the other cards 'til you get 'em all. Then you win."

"Wow," she said for lack of anything else. "That sounds like, um…" *Fun?* She wasn't going to lie to him. "Sounds like, pig knuckle."

"If we had cards, we could play pig knuckle till the bad guys leave."

Siobhan smiled in the dark.

More shooting and shouting came from the lobby. Two hours passed in darkness with little whispers back and forth.

"I'm hungry, Siobhan."

"Me too. If only we had some real chocolate cotton candy."

Mikey giggled.

"I like cotton candy."

"We should send a letter to the cotton candy company and tell them to send us a big bag of chocolate-flavored cotton candy."

"Yeppy."

"Then I'd put a big piece on your head so you looked like me."

"But I wanna eat it!"

"I wanna eat it too!" Siobhan laughed mischievously. "I'd eat it while it was still on your head before you could!"

Mikey's giggles were cut off by the police who yelled through a bull horn. The thugs yelled back angrily. A phone rang, was picked up, then slammed down with curses. *Ring. Slam. Ring. Slam. Ring. Ring. Ring. Ring. Yank!*

Something hard crashed against a wall then clattered to the floor.

"I have to use the bathroom."

"Mikey, you have to wait."

"I can't. I have to go."

"Mikey."

Mikey was in agony. "Please!"

"Okay. Ssh. Stay calm, okay Mikey? I think there's a bathroom in the hallway. But you have to be very, very, very, very quiet. Okay?"

"Okay."

"You can't make a single sound and you can't talk. Okay?"

"Okay."

"Very quiet."

"Okay!"

"I'm sorry, Mikey."

She didn't blame him. Her own hissy had been so rudely interrupted earlier. This day really sucked all around. She lifted Mikey out of the trash can. She told him to hold the trash can for her so it wouldn't move this time. Still, as she struggled over the side, it jostled the shelf with the cleaning supplies. She managed to catch a can of air freshener that tipped over as Mikey watched with both hands over his mouth.

The hallway was still dim. The bathroom was darker. She dared not turn on the light. From the open doorway she saw three stalls. The stall furthest away was outfitted for special access with handrails. She chose that one and closed the door quietly behind them.

"You have to use it in the dark and you can't flush or wash your hands, okay?"

"Daddy said I always have to wash my hands."

"If you turn the water on they'll hear you."

"Daddy said..."

"You can wash your hands when you get home, Mikey. After the bad people go away."

This was an acceptable compromise.

"Don't look!"

"I'm not.

He used the toilet and then she took a turn.

"You don't look either."

"Okay."

They'd been whispering in the dark while she zipped up. When she heard the first kick at the door to the bathroom, she broke off talking and breathing.

"Fuck!" A rough voice swore.

She clutched Mikey reflexively.

The bathroom's door was heavy. She remembered because she'd shut it slowly and carefully behind them. Otherwise, it would swing back hard to close in the face of the unsuspecting. The extra two seconds allowed her to haul Mikey into her lap again as she sat on the handicap bar and put her feet on the toilet seat for balance. The second kick was harder, angrier.

Whack! The door bounced against the tile wall.

The prickles crawled from under her arms, towards her neck, and across her scalp.

"Can't see shit!" The lights flicked on.

Just in time, she bent her head to the right to hide her huge hair below the wall of the stall. Where the air hit her skin, now covered in a fine sheen of sweat, she felt cold. She fought her body's natural instinct to shiver. She fought the urge to scream in fright. She fought the urge to sob and cry. The little boy was quiet but she could feel his poor little heart racing. They both sat terrified.

In the stall right next to them, the thug went a noisy number one that splashed on the floor and the wall. Then he went an agonizingly difficult number two, with a foul-smelling discharge of gas to finish it all off.

She was terrified the boy would make a noise of disgust, or worse, giggle. She couldn't stop trembling. Her shaking shook Mikey. Finally, he finished. She heard the scrape of metal as he picked up his gun from the floor. He didn't bother to flush or use toilet paper. Nor did he wash his hands.

This monster doesn't deserve to shoot me.

What little decency that existed within him inspired him to conserve electricity. He flipped the light switch on his way out, leaving her and Mikey in the dark once more.

"Ssh," she breathed shallowly.

"It smells," Mikey whispered.

"I know, but ssh. He might come back. Or someone else."

Ten minutes later, he brought a woman to the bathroom. Siobhan recognized his voice when he shouted, "Leave the door open, bitch!" He cursed the woman out the entire time she used the first stall of the bathroom. At the very least he didn't make her sit in the mess he left in the middle stall.

"Bitch! Don't ask me for shit else! Wipe your ass off and get the fuck back!"

The woman screamed when he hit her. This time he left the light on. Siobhan and Mikey sat quietly in the third stall next to the wall. Three years of therapy for Mikey. At least six months of therapy for her. The woman's sobs faded as she was shoved (or maybe kicked) back to the lobby. This wasn't a good hiding place. They needed to get back to the janitor's closet.

"Stay here," she ordered.

Siobhan peeked her head out and looked down the dim hallway. Voices and shadows emerged around the corner from the lobby. She raced back to the last stall, snatched Mikey in her arms, and tilted her head to the right just as the bathroom door opened.

"Any of you assholes try anything and I'll blow your fucking nuts off. Take a shit and be your asses done with it!"

He brought men this time then. Two. Siobhan held her breath.

One person went into the first stall, unzipped, and started.

The second person paused by the middle stall, saw the mess, and hesitated. A gravelly voice laughed.

"Too dirty for ya, pretty boy?"

Pretty boy?

The door to the stall with her and Mikey opened. Her heart dropped to her stomach.

His son sat in the lap of a terrified gypsy cringing against the side of the stall. How does a day even turn out like this? The gypsy, he remembered now her name was Siobhan, gently but firmly restrained Mikey as Mikey silently struggled to get free. Dallas quickly put a finger for silence over his mouth and sternly shook his head as he cleared his throat loudly.

"Hurry the fuck up! You got your head knocked in once already, pretty boy. If I have to come in there…"

Dallas Joliet eyed Siobhan Frederick questioningly. Her head was in an awkward angle. He looked at his son with frustrated indecision. He should try something. A flush came from the first stall.

She shook her head, terrified.

Whatever you're thinking of, please don't.

Dallas coughed to buy himself time. The response was metallic banging against the stall door.

"What the fuck!"

"Uh, give me a second." Dallas unzipped his pants. "I'm just a little nervous."

Siobhan sat in disbelieving embarrassment. Dallas's face glowed scarlet around the angry red bruise on the left side of his face. But what else could he do? Neither of them wanted to involve the little boy in a shoot-out.

"I ain't giving you shit! Hurry the fuck up, asshole! What the fuck you doin' in there, pretty boy? This ain't your time to get off!" Another bang against the door emphasized his point.

As annoyed with Dallas as she had been earlier, Siobhan couldn't contribute to this strange humiliation. But she dared not move her head. So she simply closed her eyes as Dallas Joliet, the coldly proud ice sculpture who'd dismissed her from his presence twice that day, urinated into the toilet bowl under her feet while his son watched the frightfully bizarre charade with his anxious wide eyes. Ten years of therapy for Mikey and at least three for her. Maybe one for Dallas.

Dallas flushed the toilet. Under the noise of the churning water he hugged his son quickly. It was safe to open her eyes. Before he left the stall, Dallas gave her an imploring look and mouthed the words, "Emergency exit." His last shaky smile was for Mikey.

Verbal and physical abuse accompanied both men all the way back to the lobby. From far away she and Mikey heard more gunshots and screams. Their trash can haven and their survival in the bathroom was a miracle. But how far would good fortune carry them?

"Stay here," she told Mikey again.

The faint, outline of the door at the end of the hall wasn't another office or another closet.

"Caution, alarm will sound," the sign said.

It was the emergency exit. If the alarm sounded, could they get away in time?

Siobhan swallowed. The dilemma. The known fear and the unknown terror. The rock, the hard place, the devil, and the deep blue sea. Choose door number one or door number two? Stay? Or go.

She had permission for the risk. Mikey's father told her, begged her with his brilliant eyes softened to a quiet, gray clarity. Siobhan covered her face with her hands. She was afraid. Nothing in her under-achieving life had prepared her for this. She'd never been a girl scout. She wasn't athletic and had never played a sport in school. Mikey, waiting in the stall, was obediently silent.

Dallas kept his head and his eyes down. The mood was grimmer than a graveyard, which was what the lobby had become. The security guard and a customer who'd reached for the security guard's gun lay dead. Vicious kicks, pistol-whipping, and shouts kept everyone else intimidated. They didn't have to look at the pools of blood congealing underneath the dead bodies to know to stay in line.

Siobhan and Mikey sat together on the handrail again. Siobhan took a deep breath and exhaled it in a sigh over Mikey's head.

Pretty soon, others would come to the bathroom. Inevitably, someone would give them away. To stay, was to die. She had to do it. The unpublished writer who couldn't keep track of her own belongings was supposed to save the day. She held back a hysterical whimper. She was scared. She was tired. But so was Mikey. He was so trusting. He put his hand in hers and waited patiently for her to take care of it. The poor little boy leaned against her tiredly. He no longer asked for his father. She'd warned Mikey not to break her heart. Too late now. Siobhan sighed and rubbed her forehead, undecided.

She'd done one thing right, at least. That first tingle of warning she felt when the thugs walked in was the only reason she and Mikey got away. What was it? Tired thoughts drifted disconnectedly through her exhausted mind. Tears coursed silently down her face as she continued deadly procrastination. That look in their eyes... the stone-like expressions... the stalking walk of the predator...

They weren't wearing masks.

No masks, even on this day. And no phone negotiation.

Siobhan! bounced inside her skull.

It wasn't robbery.

Siobhan! echoed urgently.

That was what she'd seen – dead men walking. Living bodies that had already given up the soul and would take everyone else's with them. The police were to finish what was already started. Nothing left to lose. No one left to live. No one to leave alive. One final spree to usher in never-ending dark. Dallas - cold, proud, haughty Dallas – must have known.

The indecision, the mission. What's it gonna be, Siobhan?

"Mikey. Listen." She gulped. "We're gonna go in the hallway. I'm gonna push open the emergency exit. And then we're gonna run outside very fast." *Say it like you mean it, Siobhan.* "As fast as we can! Okay?"

"Okay."

"Can you run fast?"

"I think so."

"Even if you see me fall, you keep running. Don't stop. No matter what, run as fast as you can."

Mikey nodded.

"Okay?" She had to hear him say it.

"Okay."

"Now listen, if I can open that door, if the door opens, run outside. Run FAST!"

"Run fast!" he repeated solemnly.

"If I can't get the door open, then run back into the bathroom - right here - and stand on the toilet so they can't see your feet."

"Stand here?"

"Yes. You know why?"

"Yes."

"Why?"

"I don't know." She smiled briefly against his head.

"When I push the door, it'll make the alarm go off and the bad guys will come. They'll know we're here. But if they don't see you, they'll just think it's me while you hide. It'll be a trick. Okay?"

Mikey nodded again vigorously.

"Okay."

"If I can't open the door, HIDE! But if I do open the door, then RUN! Got it?"

"Okay."

"Okay?" She gave him playful squeeze.

"Okay!" She had to laugh. Mikey would be all right. She kissed him and then took his hand.

She took his hand. "Here we go, Mikey!"

Properly-rehearsed, she and Mikey snuck to the emergency exit. She lifted a trembling hand to the bar...

A shuffling step in the hallway behind them preceded the curse of outrage.

She and the gravel-voiced thug on another bathroom run stared at each other in shock. She felt a small tug at her arm in the same moment the thug lifted his gun. She and Mikey threw their weight against the door. The alarm sounded. The door caught on something – rust from the sound the hinges made.

"Oh my God!" she sobbed.

A bullet whizzed by her ear. She screamed. Mikey screamed. The furious shooter shouted. She vaguely heard other voices and sounds of struggle. The alarm assaulted her eardrums. She and Mikey, as a coordinated unit, threw themselves against the door again.

Outside, all was brilliantly white except for the sky. The sky was dark but light shone everywhere else. She couldn't see anything.

Click. Click. Click.

"Wait!" she screamed. "Don't shoot us!"

From the emergency exit door, she heard a shout and then a sharp report.

She shoved Mikey forward, then changed her mind and picked him up.

She zigzagged with Mikey across the parking lot to avoid getting hit. Another shot rang out. Somewhat disoriented, she ran towards the lights. She still couldn't see but help was behind the lights, she knew. She heard a bullhorn. She heard shouts from every direction.

"Here! Run here!"

Run where?

Which way?

As she pivoted, her left leg folded in on itself. She fell sideways before she realized she'd even been hit.

"Oh God! Aaaaah! Shit!"

And now for the pain.

She barely remembered to release her hold on him.

Good fortune ends here.

"Mikey, run!" She screamed as she pushed him. "Run!"

Dallas, closed his eyes when the alarm sounded. Two more people had been shot at the hallway entrance. If she was successful, Mikey would live. And as long as Mikey lived, then what happened next wouldn't matter.

Mikey cried. She heard his tiny child's voice screaming at her.

"Siobhan! Come on!" He tugged at her arm. "Siobhan!"

She shoved him away again.

"Go! Mikey, go! I told you! Go!"

A volley of bullets whistled overhead. She couldn't tell from which direction.

"Mikey, stop it! Don't!"

"Who went out the back door?" The thug guarding the bank lobby screamed at them. "Who was it?" He stalked his black boots among them again. "One of you knows!" He handed out kicks and slaps yelling in vain for his two partners to come back to the lobby. Dallas received another metal-against-bone crunching slap of the gun barrel himself. "Somebody better say something!" the thug roared. "Hunh, pretty boy?" As his head ricocheted from the blow, Dallas kept his face carefully devoid of expression.

This is my gift to you, my son.

Blue and red swirled over the gaping crowd. White light flashed and strobed. *Is it Christmas? I thought it was Halloween.* Shouts, shots, and running feet swirled into a dark mist. No pain anymore. She smiled in gratitude. A curtain of liquid silk finally splashed down and somehow, it was okay. *No pain.* All of it was really okay.

"Sir, are you okay?"

"Yes," Dallas rushed out. "I have a son... my son, Mikey... is he okay?"

"He's right over here, sir." The cop guided him towards the ambulance. What little color remained in his face washed away completely.

"Oh, my God. Mikey, Mikey..." Anguish pierced his voice.

"He's not hurt, sir. Absolutely fine. Nothing wrong with him. Just scared."

"Daddy!" Upon hearing his father's voice, Mikey jumped out of the back of the truck.

Mikey burst into tears as Dallas ran to pick him up, openly crying now. The ambulance drivers took that opportunity to slam the back doors shut and rush away with a scream of sirens

Later that night, for the first time in his life, Dallas Joliet was a father to his son. He carefully cut off bread crusts as the guilty self-recriminations continued.

Why couldn't I have fixed my own child some damn food before now? It only took ten minutes to do this.

He had a lot of ten-minute missed opportunities out of five years to make up for.

He carried peanut butter and honey sandwiches, sliced pears, milk for Mikey, and a long-awaited glass of wine for himself into Mikey's room. Earlier, while Mikey splashed in the tub, he'd called the babysitter, the maid, Mikey's daycare, and Joliet Publishing and left messages to explain his and Mikey's much-needed week off from the world.

Side by side on Mikey's bed, they silently ate their dinner. And yet, Dallas still felt like a failure. *Why can't I think of anything to say to him?* He'd allowed his son to be nearly killed. Someone else had to save him. *What kind of parent am I?* His hands trembled with frustrated defeat. But just as he stood up to clear away the dishes, Mikey quickly called out, "Daddy, can you read me a story?"

The kid still wanted him. Dallas cast his eyes about Mikey's room desperately. He had better make this good. And there it sat in silent accusation - the black leather satchel the cop handed him that matched the messy wallet on his desk. Just like that wallet, he'd messed up all day long today.

Television news anchors triumphantly broadcast the story:

"…hostages wrestled with gunman… heroic escape… out the emergency exit… police with necessary information before she… logistics inside the bank…"

In her wallet had been a rubber-banded wad of business cards from other publishers. The corresponding rejection letters were in her satchel. Within her manuscripts were the same hopes, dreams, fears, anguish, love, and loss he'd seen in her eyes each time he met her.

Dallas felt himself pitch forward into the warm pool of liquid, golden-brown honey spread across the hospital bed. She was subdued, but watchful which was an interesting switch from the anxious, scatter-brained routine from yesterday morning. Also gone today was the terror from late yesterday afternoon. He thought he knew all about her but the cinnamon gypsy still surprised him.

Dallas cleared his throat. "My new reviewer and I both believe *Magic Grandma's* a great way to announce Joliet Publishing's forthcoming Children's Division," he told her. He turned away to stop the swimming sensation in his head. "Right Mikey?"

"Right!" Mikey jumped up and down clapping his hands.

"Of course, uh, Siobhan," Dallas coughed discreetly as he deliberately spoke her first name aloud, "I made some editorial notes for clarity and structure, but…"

Siobhan took a deep breath.

"It's definitely doable," Dallas finished.

Siobhan exhaled. "Wow."

"And, uh, Mikey has something he wants to ask you."

She sat up with a wide white flash of a warm smile for his son. Dallas felt a brief, unexpected pang of envy. Where did that come from? Did he wish the smile were for him instead of Mikey? Or that he were able to show that same type of affection so easily to his son.

"Yes, sweetie?"

"Siobhan, will you come to my birthday party?"

Siobhan's eyes opened wide with pleasure. "Of course, honey. Carnival Pizza!"

"Ah, perhaps something a little quieter at our home," Dallas recommended with alarm.

Siobhan smiled at Dallas with a teasing, knowing expression before she turned back to Mikey.

"We can play pig knuckle!"

Dallas felt warmth seep back through him as his son giggled. Whatever pig knuckle was, if Mikey liked it, then he loved it.

"Mikey," Siobhan took a serious tone. "I might need your help with my next children's book, Chocolate Cotton Candy. Okay?"

"Okay." Mikey nodded.

"Okay?" Siobhan grinned.

"Okay." Mikey danced.

"Okaaay?" Siobhan laughed.

"Okay!" Mikey screamed out.

Siobhan and Mikey collapsed into giggles at their inside joke.

Over Mikey's head, Siobhan saw the frozen look creep back into Dallas's face. She hated that remote expression. But she understood it and herself a little better now. People deserved a chance to make things right. She squeezed Dallas's hand. And a thrill traveled up her arm and circulated when Dallas squeezed her hand back.

Hard.

Story 4

I Would Sing Along

Jesse and Anna argued in loud whispers in the hallway. Their friends inside playing a board game heard them before they knocked.

"You guys get in here and quit disturbing the peace!" Freddy called through the closed door. Freddy and his wife, Sheila's, place served as the informal gathering spot for the thirty-somethings in their circle. Children weren't allowed on Friday nights which was Couple's Night, so the crowd varied by who could arrange babysitters.

"What's going on with you guys? Who started it? Jesse!" Sheila laughed as Jesse and Anna entered.

Anna was embarrassed. "Sorry you guys. You know how it is when you have a difference of opinion."

"The difference of opinion in this house does kitchen duty," Sheila smiled slyly at Freddy.

"Hey! Hey now!" Freddy smacked Sheila's bottom. "That's personal business."

Sheila sat on Freddy's lap and put her arms around his neck and hugged him. She turned back to Jesse and Anna.

"Come on in! You know where the food is. Take your coats off."

Anna and Jesse followed instructions tossing their coats on Sheila and Freddy's bed. They fixed plates of hot wings, chips, veggies, and cake in the kitchen.

"Drinks are out here you guys!" Sheila called.

Anna and Jesse silently came back into the living area where Freddie waited expectantly.

"So how was it?"

"You don't want to know," was Jesse's sullen reply.

Anna rolled her eyes.

Sheila widened her eyes curiously. "What happened? Both of you look like you sucked a lemon and forgot the ice tea and sugar."

Jesse sighed and shook his head.

"How was what?" Rhonda sat with her husband, Paul, shaking dice. "Somebody talk."

Jesse couldn't stand it. "We had an *episode* at the Prince concert tonight."

Rhonda was excited. "No, you did *not* see Prince! Those tickets were expensive!"

"Tell me about it," Jesse declared gloomily.

"Tell *us* about it. So we can pretend we had enough ends to go too." Freddy punched Jesse in the arm.

Jesse looked at Anna who stared straight ahead in patient endurance at the difficulty of being his wife.

"Fine!" Jesse settled back. "First, you pay through the nose for the good seats then he tries to make you feel better about it by making your woman think..." Jesse shook his head in disbelief.

Anna spoke up at last. "He didn't make me think anything, Jesse. He did it."

Sheila, a Prince fan herself, was instantly alert. "Did what? What did Prince do?"

Anna and Jesse exchanged a long look. This was obviously the source of their argument. Jesse gestured with a sarcastic if gentlemanly flourish.

"Gone tell 'em. Brag all about it."

"Brag about WHAT!" Sheila and Rhonda screeched.

Freddy's shoulders shook from laughter. "Oh man! We may not even want to know now. But tell us anyway. Ain't nothin' goin' on around here except me winnin' and sendin' folks to jail."

"Yeah right," always low-key Paul finally announced his presence. "Who got all the money?" Paul spread his huge handful and waved it at Freddy, laughing.

"You better go downtown and put some of that money on Rhonda's books 'cause she ain't leavin' jail anytime soon. Not till she pays me my rent!"

Paul joined Freddy's teasing. "Maybe after I leave the toilet seat up a few nights she ain't home."

Rhonda punched Paul then Freddy. "Ya'll stop! And that toilet seat better be down when I get out of jail!"

Sheila shushed them. "Quit changing the subject!" She looked eagerly at Anna. "What did Prince do, Anna?"

Anna laughed. "Jesse can tell you. He's the one who brought it up."

"But you're the one who talked about it all the way home."

"No, *you're* the one who argued about it and wouldn't let it go."

"No, *you* wouldn't let it go."

Sheila finally lost patience. "Dammit! Put them hot wings down. Don't nobody get to eat nothin' till I hear what Prince did. Freddy, you better tell them fools not to mess with me!" Sheila laughed with her husband who handed her a drink.

"Baby, you need to just calm down and relax."

Jesse eyed the hot wings hungrily. "All right. This is it. Anna swears all around the world and back again that Prince pointed her out in the audience and sang to her." Jesse laughed and snatched a hot wing with his teeth savagely.

Anna stared at him coldly. "Well he did! There's no need for you to be jealous about it." To the others she added with wonder, "He sang to *me* ya'll! I can't believe it!"

Squeals rose immediately from Sheila and Rhonda.

Jesse waved his hand dismissively. "I bet he can't believe it either. But think what you want." Anna opened her mouth to speak, but Jesse continued on. "Tell them the rest of it, Anna."

Anna silently chewed her chips.

Now Rhonda lost her cool. "Jesse, your ass about to get fired from storytelling!"

"Fine. Fine." Jesse got up to pour himself and Anna a drink who accepted hers with mumbled thanks. "Imma tell it before you all hear about it from someone else."

Anna made an exasperated noise. "I got a little bit excited."

Jesse snorted. "Anna, jumping up and down and screaming 'Prince I love you. I love you. I wanna have your baby!' in a high-pitched shriek is not a little excited. That's a crackhead needing a fix."

The room erupted into laughter as Anna threw Jesse an evil glare. "It didn't really happen like that, Jesse!"

"So you didn't carry on like the fat lady at our church? Can't even hear the music over Holy Ghost Crazy, knocking folks over." Jesse's wounded expression sent the room to a fever pitch. "That's how it was at the concert tonight."

"I didn't knock anyone over!"

"I saw a security guard eyeing you. I thought I was gonna have to fight our way out of there."

"Jesse, you know you're exaggerating." Anna looked around the room for support. "He's exaggerating ya'll!"

"My wife, standing next to me at a concert that cost damn near a month's rent…"

"You wanted to go too!"

"Screaming about having another man's baby. Did Prince buy your ticket? Did he send a limousine? Who drove you?"

Anna tried to cut in again but Jesse was on a roll.

"People looking at me like I'm supposed to blow a tranquilizer dart at her through a straw."

Freddy rolled from side to side on the couch giggling like a school girl.

Anna was angry. "Okay what would you all have done? This is PRINCE! Keep it real now. Freddy, you and Paul keep it real too!"

Sheila, at least, understood. "Which song was it?"

Jesse was derisive. "What the…"

"Pink. Cashmere." Anna enunciated carefully.

Sheila's expression was tortured. "Oh my God. What part? Was it that part where he sings real high…"

Jesse saw support swing Anna's direction.

"Sheila. Are you kidding?"

"Honey, if Prince sang to me I…" Sheila caught Freddy's interested gaze, "…would sing along." She took a long sip of her drink. Freddy smoothly took her glass away.

"You've obviously had enough." He grunted. "It ain't like Prince is gonna…" Freddy saw Sheila's eyes narrow in warning. "I mean he's married anyway. Like we all are. Happily married. Right?" Freddy patted Sheila's knee.

Rhonda persisted. "But how was the concert overall?"

Jesse and Anna's mumbles blended together vaguely. "Okay. Yeah it was fine, I guess."

Jesse changed the subject.

"Whoever brought the hot wings, now these… these are goin' on! I'm gonna get some more because I know ya'll already had a head start."

Paul, a natural peacemaker to his wife's outspoken nature, was game to get the conversation going another direction.

"Me and Rhonda brought them. Just bring the whole pan in here so we can finish it."

Rhonda gave a quick wink to Anna and played along. "...so that one part where Samuel L. Jackson walked into the room and told the other guy..."

Eventually, Rhonda and Paul took their leave while Anna and Jesse helped to straighten up their host's living area.

Sheila fetched their coats while Freddy enthused about his new entertainment center. "We'll have movie night when the big screen arrives."

Sheila chuckled as she handed the coats over. "I can't put Freddy out on the couch anymore 'cause it won't be a real punishment."

Anna giggled. "Well, you can always confiscate the remote."

"Like I won't have a back up remote behind a glass panel." Freddy triumphantly made a chopping gesture. "Break in case of emergencies."

Jesse laughed as they shared the black male handshake.

"He will too, ya'll," Sheila declared as she hugged Jesse. "I wanna thank you and Anna for the most entertaining couple's night ever!" Sheila chuckled slyly. "You know that story's gonna get around, right? Especially since Rhonda was here."

"But at least you know our side of it," Jesse replied.

"You know my side," Anna added.

"Well, there's your side, my side, Prince's side, and the side of what actually happened." He held up his hand to stop Anna's indignant response. "Okay, you guys, we're going. We wanna get invited back sometime."

"Now you know you're always welcome here," Sheila tapped Jesse playfully as she and Freddy exchanged hugs with Anna.

"Get your black asses out!" Freddy grumbled loudly. "At least till I get that big screen. They're gonna deliver it tomorrow morning."

Jesse paused in the doorway. "You need help setting it up?"

"Yeah, I might. I'll call you, man."

"Okay, we're taking our black asses home," Jesse laughed.

As they crossed the hallway to their own apartment, Anna and Jesse listened to the loud eruption of laughter behind Freddy and Sheila's closed door. Inside, their own apartment, Anna and Jesse laughed a full five minutes at themselves.

"Oh, Jesse," Anna looked up at him lovingly, "Thank you so much for taking me to see Prince. I'm sorry I embarrassed you, babe. But I was excited. Actually," she smiled, "I'm still a little excited."

Jesse remembered her passion at the concert as she gyrated, her passion in the car as she argued and her very passionate declaration of gratitude as she pressed her leg between his. He pulled her tighter into his arms.

"You know what? Let's put in a Prince CD. See what happens. Who knows who'll be the most thankful tonight?"

Anna laughed throatily as she led Jesse to their bedroom.

It might have ended there if not for Freddy's big screen television.

Late Saturday morning, Freddy entreated, "We don't want to fall asleep or cry any man tears. So please, no I-Shot-My-Husband-And-Now-I'm-Gonna-Make-It-On-My-Own-Cause-I-Know-Karate, movies."

"You wanna come with us?" Sheila asked him.

"Naw. Just get something you know I'll like."

"We are not watching Girl's Locker Room Chainsaw Madness. Forget it."

"I already watched that last week anyway."

Anna laughed. "We can get Denzel's latest spy thriller and that one science fiction where some black people actually make it to the end. I forget the name but I'll know it if I see it."

"That sounds good, sweetheart." Jesse smiled at Anna approvingly.

"*Whatever!*" Sheila made Freddy talk to her hand on the way out the door.

Sheila and Anna walked to Anna's car parked in the street.

"Sweetheart, hunh? Looks like you guys made up last night."

"It's all good, girl. Jesse isn't mad at Prince anymore. He's thanking him."

Sheila grinned and laughed. "Okay? That's what I'm *sayin'* girl. Hello? If these men only knew!"

Back at the apartment, Freddy punched Jesse.

"Sweetheart? I guess you got some last night."

"Please man! I get some every night."

"The way you guys left out of here, I thought I was gonna have to call a domestic hotline for one or the other of you."

"Naw, naw. It's all good. The house is in order."

They tried to hook up the big screen without reading the directions. Then they tried with the directions. Then they tried with the directions written in English.

In the video store's parking lot, Anna parked near a street vendor with a table full of bootleg CDs, DVDs, and video games. "They kill me just being right in front of the video store."

"What gets me is they usually have what you can't even find at the video store. They'll have it pressed, packaged, and priced two minutes after a release. Of course you'll see someone's head blocking the screen and maybe some static. Don't ask me how I know about that."

"Someone told you, right?" Anna laughed.

"I had heard it from Boogie and them." Sheila laughed with her as they entered the store.

Thirty minutes later, they found their selections.

"All that drama about these movies. He better have that big screen ready to go by the time we get back." Sheila's tone was a mock threat on their way out.

"They better remember the pizza, I'm starved," Anna replied.

The street vendor still hustled amidst an even larger crowd. Anna and Sheila drew closer. And there it was waiting for them.

"That can't be the concert from last night!" Sheila's eyes were wide.

"It is! You can tell by the cover! That's the outfit he wore last night."

The guy was running out. There were six copies left.

Anna stood indecisively. "Should I?"

Three left. The street vendor waved them like a fan in his hand.

"Prince, live in concert! Okay, my man. Thanks for the business." He waved one in each hand. "Two left!" He looked at Anna. "You look familiar. I seen you before?"

Anna felt her face redden. "No. Unless you saw me go in the store earlier."

Hustle Man shook his head. "Somewhere else."

"Well, look. I didn't get to see the concert." Sheila felt for Anna, but oh well! This was PRINCE! She snatched the last DVD out of the vendor's hand just as someone else reached for it.

As she drove home, Anna mused aloud. "I don't know if I want to relive the experience. I actually am a little embarrassed."

"We can skip over Pink Cashmere," Sheila assured.

"You should probably watch it without me."

"What about the guys?"

"The guys?"

"Keep it on the low?"

"For the love of God... yes!"

Crystal clear, detailed picture and phenomenal sound. Movie and Pizza Afternoon would be the new institution amongst their friends, Freddie decided. Even better, the women fell asleep on the third movie.

"Sheila loves to talk movies," he muttered to Jesse.

"Yeah, I noticed," Jesse chuckled.

Freddy felt for the next DVD in the room darkened by early dusk.

"What's that one?" Jesse asked him.

Freddy hesitated. Whatever they saw on this DVD while the girls slept would prove embarrassing to at least one, maybe two people in the room. Still, he was damn curious after all the hoopla last night. Besides, he was an admitted jerk. So what?

"Check it, man!"

Jesse groaned at the familiar image of Mr. Purple Wonderful. These bootleg guys were something else.

"Sheez! Turn it down and skip ahead towards the end." Jesse glanced at the sofa where Anna dozed oblivious to guitar riffs.

Freddy never did read the directions.

The volume increased to a level that would have awakened the dead.

Four people looked at each other with variations of shock, accusation, violation, irritation, anger, guilt, and *oops!*

Freddy fumbled again for the controls. "I... uh... we saw... we don't have to..."

Anna stopped him. "No Freddy. Obviously, my husband was interested in seeing this DVD, so let's all watch it."

Jesse looked pleadingly at Anna. "Anna, sweetheart, why don't we..."

Anna's voice was sickeningly sweet syrup poured over gritty concrete littered with broken glass. "Yes, *sweetheart*. I agree. Why don't we watch this again and see if we'll all learn something new about life in general and ourselves in particular?"

Movie and Pizza Afternoon became a hostage-taking. It was their apartment. It was their television. It was their DVD. But neither Freddie nor Sheila dared to speak aloud.

The soft, opening melody of Pink Cashmere emitted in high-definition from the surround sound speakers.

Jesse stood up in front of the screen. "Anna…"

Anna said only one word. "Move."

Sheila and Freddy looked at Jesse apprehensively. Their last chance for rescue shrugged helplessly and sat back down.

Prince pointed into the crowd. They heard Anna's voice. "…love you… baby…" Everyone sat up straighter. Anna held her head up stoically, biting her bottom lip.

Their eyes searched the screen. "…Prince… love you…" The camera operator tried to find Anna in the crowd and zoomed in dizzyingly on false targets then zoomed back out to try again. "Oooo!" Hands waved as the crowd sang with Prince. "Oooo!"

The camera operator gave up on the crowd and focused back on Prince, now deep into the chorus of Pink Cashmere.

Anna, Jesse, Sheila, and Freddy took a collective breath and sat back in their seats. No one said anything. Freddy stared at the remote in his hand. He would be on the couch tonight. He passed the remote to Sheila quietly. Anna and Jesse both appeared to be at a loss. Sheila caught Jesse's eye and prompted him with a significant glance that said, "Say something!"

Freddy looked up at the ceiling and prayed that Jesse would do the right thing. He liked Jesse and Anna. And he loved his wife who, as always, held his happiness in the palm of her hands.

They came together at the end of the day, went to sleep together at night and woke together in the morning. Right now, Anna's expression was unreadable. But Jesse knew her. She needed him to be on her side. And if it took a little illusion and delusion to smooth out the rough spots, then that was still a marriage.

"Anna. I owe you an apology," Jesse spoke quietly. "Clearly Prince sang to you. You were the most beautiful woman in the room."

He cuddled her close as she smiled the smile she wore last night while they…

Jesse glanced at his hosts. Sheila beamed back at him in approval. Freddy gave him a surreptitious thumbs-up sign.

Prince finished singing and the instrumental part of the song continued. As for the heavy-set crew member adjusting the elevated speaker behind Jesse and

Anna at the concert, he said nothing all. For he was the man who wasn't there for the split-second he was there.

Jesse stood pulling Anna up with him. "Well, it looks like Movie Afternoon is definitely gonna be a hit, Freddy. But, my friends, we'll have to cut tonight short. Right Anna?

"Jesse, I wanna have your baby."

Anna and Jesse waved a cheery goodnight to Sheila and Freddy.

Story 5

For Rent by Owner

"Jenny Vireo, a single mother from The City's south side, remains a person of interest in connection with the death of a terrorist operative she married. Any person with knowledge of Jenny Vireo's whereabouts should contact the anonymous police tip line. In other news, three members of a white supremacist group operating in The City were shot…"

Perry, the Information Officer at Griffin Research clicked off the television. He had a nose for news and an ear always to the ground. He turned to Jay, his newest hire, other than the janitor who mopped small wet circles around the room.

"You wanted your chance to move up. Well, this is it, kid. She used to work for a woman named Naomi who ran a temp agency before being busted as a marriage broker. Street name, Jacana. The police feel she hasn't told everything she knows."

Jay met Jacana at her office. Showed her his credentials.

"Jenny told me a little about herself. A fool for love, that girl. She held drugs for her boyfriend, Hawkins."

"Boyfriend? I thought…"

"You gonna listen, or what??

"Okay. Sorry."

"Seven years ago, they picked him up on attempted murder. No witnesses. They tried to turn her on him for the drug charge. She refused. He got ten for attempted murder. She got five years for possession and conspiracy to attempted murder."

"But she wasn't in on the murder attempt?"

"Naw. But they wanted to punish her. She had a baby for Hawkins in prison. They placed the child in foster care with this bourghie couple."

"That's too bad."

"Yeah, too bad." Jacana took a long pull on the cigarette. "But that's not all." She looked down at the burning end as she exhaled a long stream of smoke. "I didn't tell this to the cops." She eyed Jay.

"But Jenny told me," she hesitated, "that inside, they sold her among the guards for the next four years. They gambled for her. Played her like the lottery. Wrecked her by the time she came to me."

"After she served her time?"

"After they freed her, I was the only job she could get. She did day labor for my agency."

"What sort of work?"

"Janitorial. Cleaning offices, hotel rooms. Things like that."

"How did it come about that you knew so much of her background? You two clicked or something?"

"Naw. We didn't like each other at first. She had a pulse and she did the work. I paid her. That was it for a long time. Then, something changed. I'm not sure exactly how it happened."

"Here." In her bare walled, thin carpeted, non-descript storefront office, Jacana handed Jenny her check for the day's work at the hotel. "Be here tomorrow morning at 4:30."

"Yes, ma'am." Jenny didn't move.

Jacana looked up and frowned. "What? You gotta problem with your pay?"

"No ma'am. I was just wonderin' if you had other work."

"Oh," Jacana crossed her arms and leaned back slowly. "So cleaning shit out of toilets don't cut it anymore?"

"No ma'am. I mean. Yes."

Jacana threw Jenny a hard glance. "Don't you know?"

"What I meant..."

"Seems to me," Jacana idly shuffled through papers on her desk, "that an *ex-felon*," she glanced up at Jenny, then stacked the papers, "would be glad for an opportunity to rejoin society. Get off other people's taxes. Take care of your own business. Unless, you have an interview lined up with the mayor's office." Jacana snorted then laughed aloud. "Yeah, they'll be real glad to see you down there."

Jenny remained standing, check in hand, waiting for Jacana to get bored with the sound of her own laughter. Jenny didn't laugh at anything anymore.

"I would like to do more work in addition to the hotel and office cleaning," she stated quietly.

Jacana, looked away a moment. Shook her head and pursed her lips. "Damn." She sighed. "Look, sorry about all that. I misunderstood."

Jenny nodded.

"I know your background. I make it my business to know about these things. I keep it real. You need more money, don't you?"

Jenny nodded.

Jacana thought a moment. "You know what? We're all for rent in this world. That hooker on the corner? She's for rent. That prissy northside woman? She's for rent. Wifey in the suburbs? She's for rent. We're all for rent."

Jacana watched Jenny's expression carefully. Jenny wondered where the conversation would go.

"It's all a game, girl. Give 'em what they want, get paid for your time and labor. That's what you're doing here. And that's what you did before you got here."

Jenny flinched.

"Oh, I know, Jenny. I know what they do to you inside. Especially a pretty girl. That's why many of them try to get that gig in the women's prison. The fringe benefits everyone knows about but no one admits to."

Jacana indicated the chair in front of the desk. Jenny sat down.

"You see, twenty years ago, I got sent up. They liked me, oh yes, they did. I had two babies for them. They took 'em away. I don't know where they are now. They made me abort the third."

Jacana shook a cigarette out of box. Lit it. Took a drag.

"I got a job for you. Long cash."

Jenny waited and watched Jacana blow clouds of smoke to the ceiling. Jacana didn't speak though.

Jenny shifted and looked at her hands. "I have a son. He's four now. I don't know where he is. But… I want to," she swallowed, "I want to buy a home for us for when I do find him."

This time, Jacana nodded.

"I don't know if it's possible, but I'm trying to save."

"And?"

"And if you have anything I extra I can do, I'll do it."

"Uhm hmm. Well, Jenny, if you handle yourself like a business woman, you can make things happen."

"I can do that."

"That's all I needed to hear."

"That's when I told her about the other business I ran."

"As a marriage broker."

"Whatever you want to call it."

"Better than…"

"Prostitution?" Jacana laughed. "Sometimes."

"And so you arranged…"

"*Fuck…* you can come out and say it. I got immunity. Yeah, I *arranged* it. But it took a while. Jenny had to overcome the moral factor. Had to work it out for herself."

"I see."

"Yeah, you see. She saw too. But she had the nerve to get a little self-righteous on me. After she dealt with her son's foster parents, though, she came around."

"How did she find out who they were?"

"I told her."

"You knew?"

"I found out. I told you, I like to know things. Plus, I wanted to give Jenny a little incentive," Jacana smiled.

"She met them?" Jacana nodded slyly.

"Did they allow her to see her son?"

"Nope, but she managed to track down his school on her own. She saw this little boy who looked just like Hawkins and she knew him right away."

Jacana ground her cigarette in the ashtray on her desk.

"Jenny was smarter than anyone, including me, took her for. Long-range planner, that girl."

"Where did she live before?"

"Some dump."

"Yeah, she still owes me back rent. Skipped out, two years ago, the little whore. I heard about her. The police came and wrecked this place." Jenny's former landlord indicated dry wall still full of jagged holes, electrical sockets covered in fine white powder, dangling light fixtures. "Who's gonna pay for that? I'm gonna have to fix it myself. Do a story on that."

"How would you describe Jenny Vireo's personality?"

"She was a looker, and she knew it. She used to parade in and out of here givin' me the eye. Then she got mad when I tried to help her out. She was a tease."

"She teased... you?" Jay eyed the balding, heavyset man whose skin reeked of alcohol at noon. Either he recovered from the previous night's binge or he prepared for tonight's binge.

The landlord scowled at him a moment, then searched for a way to save face.

"You see. I saw her strugglin'. She had a son somewhere. She was workin' for that day labor agency. But she didn't make much. The cops watched her so she couldn't contact her boyfriend or his people. But rent don't stop for drama. However, I'm generally a compassionate man. So I offered her a discount."

"A discount."

"Yeah," he grinned and rubbed his belly.

Jay felt queasy.

"The little bitch cursed me and pulled a knife. Then, one night, I come up here to throw her out and she's gone. Never heard from her again. I told the cops that when they came here and tore the place up. Whatever you're looking for here, Mister, you ain't gonna find it."

Jay nodded, "You're probably right," and walked away.

Jay ate lunch and consulted the profile on Valerian. Eastern European, male Caucasian, approximately thirty-eight-years of age wanted in connection with countless bank robberies, hijackings, and bombings. He wondered whether Jenny knew the whole story before she agreed to marry him.

Jay finished and headed for his next appointment.

"We cared for her son like our own child. We even tried to adopt him," the upper-middle housewife sat next to her financial manager husband.

"She agreed to serve as a surrogate..." the manager began.

"No, that was later."

"Well, we met with her and offered her a contract to serve as our surrogate. My wife…"

"I couldn't have children."

"We wanted a sister or brother for Mark."

"Mark?"

"That was his name," the wife began to weep.

"It's still his name," the manager reassured her, holding her in his arms.

"She refused the contract, at first and kept asking us to let her see Martin. She kept calling him Martin, the name *she* gave him. *Martin, Martin, Martin.* She obviously didn't accept that we were Mark's parents. I should have known right then that she was up to something."

"When did you see her the second time?"

The manager looked at his wife. She nodded slightly then turned to look out the window.

"About six months later, she contacted us. She'd changed her mind."

"About being a surrogate?"

"Yes." The manager stopped talking and looked down at his hands.

"So," Jay prompted. "How did you arrange… well, wait… Did she ever say what changed her mind?"

The wife turned to look at them. "The money, obviously. She used the money we paid her to steal our son away and flee the country. Our son and the two little ones."

"The twin girls."

"They were to be our children too." The wife covered her mouth with a hand as if to keep from screaming the words.

"So, how did you arrange for her to be a surrogate? Did you use a fertility clinic or…"

"No."

"A private medical facility?"

"No."

The middle class couple tensed, bracing themselves for his next question. Jay turned to the manager.

"Did you and she," he cleared his throat, "you and Jenny?"

The manager nodded and sagged back against the couch, not looking at his wife who continued to occupy herself with the window.

"We investigated her. We already knew she was an ex-felon. But when I discovered that she'd married a man of questionable background and criminality, that's when I knew we had a clear chance to give the children the type of life they deserved."

"So… you blackmailed her to…"

"She cooperated! No one forced her to do anything. She accepted our money. Then she stole our children! We want them back. If you find out anything…"

Jay rose abruptly and shook the manager's hand.

"I'll keep in touch." He squeezed the manager's hand perhaps a little too hard. "Protective Services thanks you for your help."

Jay visited Hawkins in prison.

"I got two-and-a-half years left. I keep myself to myself." The large, solidly-built man shifted in his chair.

"There's been mention of early parole."

"Yeah right. I don't believe nothin' nobody says till I see it."

"She's smarter than people realized."

"That's right," he snorted. "Don't ever under-estimate her."

"No," Jay said slowly. "I wouldn't."

Hawkins smiled with approval, then abruptly laughed aloud.

"Nobody knows where she is. She fooled everybody."

"Including you."

"Especially me."

"What about that guy she married?" Jay searched Hawkins' eyes carefully. "What about him?"

All humor left Hawkins' face. "I hear he's dead."

"Shot execution style."

"You live hard, you die harder."

"Did Jenny tell you about him?"

Hawkins eyed Jay suspiciously. Thought a moment. Made up his mind.

"That guy was a straight up psycho. He probably shot himself."

Jay raised his eyebrows.

"You think?"

"Don't get me wrong. I mean, I know. Who is an *alleged* drug dealer to judge anyone, right? But see, that kind of crime has money as a motivation. Somebody doesn't have money, they take yours. Sometimes they give you a happy feeling in return for your money. Sometimes they don't give you anything at all. But economics motivates that. Now terrorism?" Hawkins whistled. "Something else entirely. Crazy."

"When Jenny visited here, did you speak about her... marriage proposal?"

"She told me. I didn't like it."

"Did she tell you about another offer she received?"

Hawkins frowned. "Oh. Yeah. The rich bitch who wanted Jenny to fuck her husband."

Jay widened his eyes. Hawkins snorted.

"Yeah. Jenny told me. We took care of that."

"You took ..."

"Me and Jenny had a conjugal visit."

"I see."

"Do you?"

Jay coughed. "No idea where she is?"

"None."

"Not even the children? Your children?"

"Nope."

"Thank you, Hawkins."

The two men shook hands.

In the parking lot, Jay spoke softly into his tape recorder adding the pieces of Jenny's story together. Then he called Perry.

"Birds of Prey, rookie. They supposedly disbanded when the streets got too hot. But rumor is that they just went further underground. Became shadows. Some went legit and served as fronts for the more dangerous members."

"So Hawkins still has connections on the street?"

"In the street, in the boardroom, in the banks, wherever they are, he is."

"So, for instance, if Hawkins had an issue with his girlfriend's husband, he could take care of it from the inside then arrange for her to vanish."

"That could happen."

"Thanks, Perry."

On a hunch, Jay went back into the prison and found a guard willing to talk.

"He had two visits with her."

"He only told me about one of them."

"Did you actually ask about another?"

"No."

"Well," The guard shrugged already bored.

"Do you remember anything about the visit?"

The guard stared at him as if Jay had just said, "Squeak blah beep beep toot." Jay passed him a twenty. This time, the guard looked at the twenty as though Jay had just defecated in his hand. Jay sighed, cleared his throat, and laid another twenty in the guard's hand. Suddenly, they were on the same page.

"She brought him a book."

"Why is that strange?"

"Hawkins can't read."

The house where Jenny lived for six months as Valerian's wife was a definite step up from the apartment slum she'd been living before. The neighbor on the left side of the house slammed the door in his face. The neighbor on the right side, an elderly woman, invited him in, impressed by the quick flash inside his wallet.

"Something about that guy sent chills down my back. I never looked him directly in the eye. Not that he looked at anyone anyway. So cold and unfriendly. I felt sorry for her."

"Because he was unfriendly?"

The old woman shook her head. "He hit her. I used to hear them. I like fresh air, you know," she explained carefully, "so I keep the windows open."

Sure enough, a breeze blew through her house.

"I overheard him smacking her around, throwing things, knocking things over. She screamed a couple of times. It was just awful. You want to help someone in that situation, but she didn't seem to want anyone to talk to her. She kept to herself too. But not in a cold way. More, in a scared way."

The old lady refilled her teacup and offered more to Jay who shook his head, "no."

"And then one day, I overhead him threaten her."

"In what way?"

"He said, 'I'll kill him! I'll kill him and his son!' I didn't know quite what he was talking about. She didn't have a son, not yet. She was pregnant with his child, I thought. But one doesn't always quite know these things, does one? And maybe that was why he was angry. He didn't quite know, I think. But then," she drew herself up scornfully, "he was crazy, after all."

She smiled generously at Jay. "You can use that quote for your show, if you like."

Jay thanked her profusely and left.

Jay received a call.

"Meet you for what?"

"Hurry up."

The phone disconnected.

In the shadows, a slight form sidled up to Jay, beckoned him nearer. Jay stiffened.

"Harrier."

"Yeah." The slight man thrust a book forward under Jay's nose causing him to flinch back reflexively.

"What's that?" he demanded.

"Just take it."

Jay took it, looked it over. Read aloud, "*Sea Ducks and Black Scoters of Canada.* I met you for this? What's this supposed to mean?"

Jay eyed the slight man sharply who sidled away. "Keep looking. You'll find it."

Jay flipped the pages impatiently. "Find what?" he called after the man who melted into the darkness.

That night, he flipped back and forth, forth and back through the book. On the news, he heard another mention of Jenny's disappearance followed by an update on the White Raptors, the white supremacist group. Jay's mind heaved with the effort to put the pieces together.

"...unknown witness say a man of small stature, approximately five feet, four inches executed all three..."

Jay started and looked at the book in his hands. He'd ripped off the hardback cover by the spine, flipped through the pages, checked for handwritten notes. Nothing. But this had to be the same book Jenny had given Hawkins. Otherwise, what was the point?

> "…similar style to the execution of terrorist, Valerian, by person or persons unknown whose wife remains at large…"

Jay flinched. Somehow, he'd become a player in this, whatever it was. Not just an investigation. Not just research. Somehow, he was being used in part of the action. He had a role in the drama. The book was his cue to enter stage right. Jay sat back in his chair. Sat a long time. The ring of his phone woke him again.

"Yeah?"

"Perry. You watching television?" Perry hung up.

> "…suspect that a prison guard assisted in the escape although there is no clear proof at this time. The guard had undefined connections with a white supremacist group and had a reputation for making hostile statements about minority groups so it is not clear what would motivate this person to assist in the escape of Hawkins."

Jay looked at the torn-up book in disgust. The cover lay askew on the floor where he'd thrown it. *Sea Ducks and Black Scoters of Canada.* Canada…

If someone needed to move large sums of money, kidnap a child, forge papers, and cross borders… a relationship with an alleged drug dealer and marriage to a terrorist would be quite educational. The school of hard knocks taught such lessons very well.

Jay got a road atlas of North America from his shelf.

"Where are you, Jenny Vireo?"

Keep looking. You'll find it.

Jay decided to read the entire book if he had to. He carefully turned the title page after examining it for hidden marks. He looked carefully at the copyright page with its dense legal statements and disclaimers. He saw the call number for library shelving. He looked lower. And then, he saw it – the isbn number used on all books. Whenever he purchased a book from the bookstore, the cashier always scanned the barcode with the isbn number on the back. This isbn on the copyright page had been carefully, almost invisibly erased. Someone typed in another number over it. It didn't match the number on the back cover. Bank account number?

And phone number. *In the street, in the boardroom, in the banks…*

From one of The City's scarce public pay phones, he made the call.

A breathless voice answered, "Yes?"

Jay hesitated a moment. The silence stretched.

"This is Jay, Ms. Vireo. I work for Perry."

Silence.

"I have the book."

"Ask Jacana to give you my last payroll check."

Jenny Vireo hung up the phone.

"So it was for you all this time, hunh?"

"Apparently." Jay shrugged.

"They told me that I owed her. I happen to operate on the buyer beware principle, you know. I had no idea the world of hurt Valerian would put her through."

"Yeah." Jay waited.

"But whatever. Here." She handed him a sealed envelope. "It's the same way she gave it to me. I don't know nothin' 'bout nothin' and I don't wanna know."

"Thanks, Naomi."

Naomi started. "Thank you… for calling me by my real name," she replied.

Jay smiled. "We all play the hand life deals us. Looks like Jenny played to win, doesn't it?"

"She'll be all right?"

"She'll… be fine. I'll see to it."

Jacana stared at him a moment and nodded.

At home, Jay counted the thick stack of bills inside the envelope that also contained her confession. *Don't ever under-estimate her.* He sat a long time considering his own future. *Do the good thing, the bad thing, or the right thing?* With a sigh, Jay deleted his recordings and burned the book.

"Dead end," he told Perry back at the office.

Perry grunted. "That's your story and you're sticking to it, eh?"

"Some stories don't need to be told."

"Oh really?" Perry narrowed his eyes and lasered Jay with a sharp gaze. Jay responded with unyielding silence. Perry glanced at the janitor who'd come in to quietly empty the wastepaper basket. The janitor, staring down at the trash bag in his hand nodded imperceptibly. Then he left.

Perry was quietly triumphant.

"We knew from the moment Jenny Vireo received the wire that we had our man." Jay stiffened as Perry walked around the desk with its *Philip Peregrine* nameplate.

Perry shook Jay's hand.

"Filling in the empty spaces takes independent thought, Jay. And much discretion. I had a feeling about you. A very good feeling. Congratulations."

He clapped Jay on the back. "How does it feel?"

Jay smiled thoughtfully.

"Feels like flying, Perry."

Tomorrow, Jenny would send her fee to Griffin Research. Jacana would receive the janitor's official resignation and go on with the rest of her life, forgiven. Griffin Research would test another recruit.

Thankfully, they could allow *this* recruit to live.

Story 6

Charlatan and Masquerade

Mr. Kensington knew from experience that a banker often discovers the very uncomfortable truth about his customers during times of crisis. A natural disaster, a divorce, a funeral...

The young woman in black entered First Bank at a brisk clip. She paused, turned sharply on a high heel and headed his way with a *click-clack* keeping a steady rhythm.

He invited her into his office.

"Mr. Kensington, my lawyer said to give you these forms." She handed a familiar set of papers across the desk.

"I'm very sorry that we meet under these circumstances." He spoke the standard line in the standard concerned tone as an older man in a wheel chair wheezed his way slowly into the room and parked next to the young woman's chair.

The woman didn't look his way, merely shook her head dismissively and made an annoyed gesture of impatience at Mr. Kensington as if to say, *Get on with this.*

Mr. Kensington led her to the safety deposit box with the older man - father, uncle, lover, lawyer, friend – following slowly behind. He discreetly withdrew and left her to it. Twenty minutes passed. The woman rushed into his office red-faced to return the key. She was crying. In the hallway, Mr. Kensington saw the wheelchair creak slowly to a stop. She walked jerkily out the door and this time, gripped the wheelchair handle, bent towards the old man and whispered to him reassuringly. She then straightened, set her shoulders back, and *click-clacked* the wheelchair out the First Bank double doors.

Mr. Kensington shrugged and returned to his office. On the floor lay a small booklet that he knew she must have dropped in her rush. The uncomfortable truth, it could only be.

Well, why not?

He picked up the booklet and began to read:

On this Saturday in July, I sit here writing this, almost not believing the things I said and did. Even though I won't read this ever again, maybe someday, Robbie, you'll learn things about me you might have suspected, but mercifully overlooked. But will you *understand?* That's what I don't know. I do know that you must remember.

"His insurance doesn't cover it," the nurse told me. Which meant that I would, she seemed to imply. Long ago, my father, Lennox, told me that what money he spent raising me served as an investment in his future. *His* future. Not mine.

And as I spoke with the nurse about his condition and the need for major surgery to correct it, I decided what the return on Lennox's investment, for I did not call him "father" anymore, would be. Oh yes, indeed, I did.

Robbie, you played with your dolly a little ways down the hall. As I looked at you so happy, I decided that your future was the important thing. No matter what.

"Thank you, Sharon," I told her. "I will see what can be done." *Nothing*, I'd already decided by then.

I called to you, "Robbie!" And we left.

I just dropped you off to your piano class. I feel so proud of you, Robbie. I want you to be wonderful. More wonderful than you ever dreamed you could be.

I thought about what you asked me, "Is Grandpa gonna die?" You looked so sad. So young. So innocent. So free.

And I told you, "Hospital care is expensive, sweetheart. Especially if his insurance and my insurance don't cover special procedures. My job covers us only just so much. Any extra, well," I cleared my throat and looked at passing traffic, "Well, hospital care is expensive sweetheart."

And then you went inside to Miss Ross, the best piano teacher my money could buy. And I sit here now. I'm drinking coffee. I'm reflecting on the past.

Well, you just assured me you had a good day with Miss Ross. But when I paid her, she told me you didn't seem to focus. I really didn't feel up to talking to you about it. Besides, we only had time for a quick snack before ballet.

"Destiny has a puppy."

"Well, Destiny's parents must not mind a carpet cleaning bill."

"She said they toilet-trained him."

I just smiled at the windshield while I drove you to the studio.

"Alex has a bird. It's a parakeet. It sings all the time. He said they're easy to take care of."

"I don't know, sweetie. You're so busy with all these classes. When would you find the time?"

You didn't answer. I'm sorry, Robbie, but rules are rules and I fully intend to be there for you as the parent I never had.

I told you, "I'll be back, soon." You still didn't answer. Why didn't you answer me, Robbie?

But I didn't dwell on it too long. My cell phone rang. Sharon told me, "Your father is asking for you, Ms. York."

"Okay, Sharon. I'm on my way."

I knew you'd be an hour at class, so I drove back to the nursing home. I guess I had to clear all this up.

And he, who used to be so big, lay there now, so small.

"Caroline, I..."

"Lennox. I cannot afford the surgery. I have a child to care for, you know. She comes first."

Lennox stared at the ceiling as he listened. Too proud to beg or cry, I decided. Fine.

"I'm saving for Robin's college education. I don't want her to take out loans, or work herself into a walking coma, or have to call home to beg for grocery money. I wouldn't do that to her. I actually don't know what kind of parent would."

He didn't respond. But then, I expected that. I walked across the room, leaned against a table and looked at him.

"I also have a car and a mortgage to pay off. Because unlike a certain person we both know, I won't leave my daughter with no resources for her future. Unlike a certain person who allowed his second wife and her adult children to accumulate his wealth, everything that I'm worth, all of that goes to Robin. Because that's the type of person I am."

I looked at the mass-produced pastel painting on the wall by the door.

"I also have student loans to pay off because you refused to help me pay off tuition even though you promised the State and my mother that you would. I sold my future to the federal government. There's nothing left for you. Don't you remember?"

I paced back and forth. I wasn't in a hurry. Not with my captive audience. I'd practiced this speech for years and I wanted to get it right. Lennox needed to know exactly what he meant to me.

"I work for a living, Lennox. I have no one and nothing to fall back on but myself. I made the mistake of marrying a man who treated me and Robin the same way you treated Mom and me."

I stopped pacing at the table and sat in the chair. "And Robin deserves so much better from Jason. She's a great kid. The best, as a matter of fact."

Lennox looked at me briefly.

"Oh yes, she is, Lennox. And you would know that if you'd bothered to take time away from your other family to get to know her."

I drummed my fingers against the table.

"I thought about moving you into my house. But that would have required retro-fitting the stairs and doorways. Installing all this equipment," I waved away the hardware hooked to his bed. "Just too expensive and not a lot of room."

I looked at Lennox to check his reaction. Still nothing. He stared upward at the ceiling. No apology. No excuses. No regrets. Nothing at all.

I smiled coldly. Lennox's own special smile that I learned to replicate. But his coldness no longer hurt me as much as it did when I was young and frantically desperate to prove myself worthy. Instead, I mocked it.

"By the way, I brought you something."

He didn't look.

So I held up the newspaper classified ad section with various jobs circled so he could see them as he lay there. "Work from Home, Read Books for Money, Stuff Envelopes and Become a Millionaire!!!" I read them aloud to Lennox in my best television infomercial voice.

"Remember when I called you senior year terrified that I wouldn't be able to pay my final tuition bill in time to graduate? You sent me these same advertisements. My professors gave me the emotional support that you withheld. And I did day labor to scrounge up just enough. It was me and the ex-convicts out there picking up trash out of the gutter for three weeks."

And that's when Lennox's expression changed. I saw his eyes fill. But I didn't care.

"How many nights do you think I cried alone in the dark because they disconnected my lights and phone? If the restaurant didn't allow me a meal per shift I don't know what I would have done. I carried twenty-one hours that last semester. I worked those gutter jobs and kept up with class work while you sneered from a distance. All those snide remarks I took from your wife's family and you said not one word in my defense. Why didn't you, Lennox? Is it because you agreed?

I let the news clipping slip from my fingers onto his blanket.

"Do you remember what you said to me when I told you I was pregnant with Robin?"

Lennox turned his head to wall. I still felt that bitterness in my heart towards him.

"You do remember."

I moved away from his bed and paced again.

"But I want to know, how does it feel, Lennox? Tell me how does it feel to suffer while someone berates and looks down on you and ridicules you? I've felt it for a full thirty-two years. But how does it feel to you?"

I snorted and shook my head.

"You think I didn't know this day would come? I've always known. I waited for it. And now here we both are."

Her father still faced the wall.

"The worst? The very worst is that Mom worked herself into a heart attack just to help me pay off the rest of my tuition bill. She literally drove herself into the ground. For me."

I took gasps of air as the words rushed out.

"You do remember your first wife, don't you? The woman you left with a mortgage and a car to pay off? A daughter to feed and clothe? One day, we had everything. The next, we squeezed into the darkest, tiniest, bug-filled apartment in the city just to try to make it. And then I had the nerve to attend college so no one could ever do to me what you did to her."

I laughed with a bitterness so strong I nearly choked on it.

"Every time I asked you why, why, why, you always said, 'They need a father figure in their lives.' Guess what, Lennox? I needed you! I needed the father figure! Holidays and birthdays, where were you? There. With them. Always way over there with them. You gave the best years of your life to *her* children because their own father didn't! Oh, the irony of it all. They didn't even give a damn whether you lived or died as long as you paid for their house and their food and their light bills and their phone bills and their cars and their bail and food and shelter for their friends and cousins and boyfriends and girlfriends. And now that they've screwed you over, the back of your head is still all you have to offer me, your own daughter. Isn't that right?"

I don't even know if Lennox went to sleep at that point. But I didn't care anymore. I spoke fiercely to the back of his head, the only part he ever allowed me to see after he left me and Mom. The triumph of moral superiority washed over me in dizzying waves as I brought it all home.

"This is who I am, Lennox! This is what you created! That return on your investment… it's payback. That's it! That's all you get! Do you really feel that you deserve what you're asking from me, Lennox? Do you honestly feel that you've earned the right to even ask?"

He didn't answer.

"How. Dare. You?"

I finally took a deep breath to calm my pounding heart. The wife who divorced him and took his assets for her own children did this to him. Not me. I finished quietly.

"I have to pick up Robin. I have a child to care for. She will never lack for love. She will never go hungry. She will never feel unworthy. I will never put another person's child over her. I take care of my child. She is the most wonderful person you never even showed the slightest interest in knowing. But I love her. Everyone who has a heart loves her."

And with that, I left.

I picked you up just as all the other students streamed outside the studio. You chattered on and on about that puppy. This time, I was the one who didn't answer.

Finally, I asked you, "Robbie, do you actually like piano and ballet class?"

You looked at me as if afraid to say what we both already knew. You're my daughter, Robbie. I knew you before you took your first breath. I'm the one who raised you.

"It's okay, honey. Be honest."

"No," you whispered so quietly, afraid to tell me, your own mother, not meeting my eyes.

"What do you like to do, then?"

"I like animals. I like the zoo. I like playing on the play ground and riding my bike."

I gripped the steering wheel tightly because I couldn't see so well. The tears in my eyes blurred me for a second so I slowed the car down slightly.

I cleared my throat.

"Well, I'll see if the zoo has children's workshops. Or, we might find a pet store that needs volunteers. How about that?"

"Mommy! Do you mean it?"

You overwhelmed me with such eager gratitude that I felt... almost sick inside. What had I done?

"Does that mean I don't have to go to piano and ballet?" you asked me.

I trembled a little. Did you see it? "If you really don't like it and don't want to do it anymore, you don't have to."

"Maybe you can use the piano and ballet money to help Grandpa."

At that, I almost lost control of the car. I felt a knife in my heart. How could you? How did you know, Robbie? How did you know who your mother was so deep inside? How did you know?

So I fixed your dinner in silence while you went on and on about all the different animals at the zoo. I put you to bed and you dropped off easily as always. But I lay awake for hours. I cried in my bathroom. I knew that I would never sleep again if I didn't do something. So I woke you.

"Robbie, we're going to see your grandfather again."

"But it's dark."

"I know, but we really have to see him. It's important."

I persuaded the night shift to allow us inside. And you sat right there next to me at his bedside when I told him, "Your granddaughter decided to use the money for her piano and ballet classes to pay for the surgery."

You didn't see me scowl, watching him, daring him to treat you as if you didn't deserve to live. The way he'd treated me. Lennox looked from me to you. I stared lasers into his eyes. And then, I saw it. I saw the human I'd searched for so long within my father at last. You did that, Robbie. You.

"Robbie is a wonderful child, you know." I smoothed your hair and pulled your pajama-clad body onto my lap and hugged you. While you talked to your grandfather, caught up on the missing years, I hid behind you so that I could cry again.

Before we left, I authorized the procedure. One day, I told myself on the ride home, you would understand that sometimes things work out differently than we plan. Sometimes, you do what's right at the right time for whatever reason with no regrets and no second-guessing.

And if you're reading this, Robbie, then I've passed on to the next life. Maybe your grandfather has as well. Even though I couldn't leave you the legacy I intended, I know that you'll make it. You're a wonderful girl. And you should always know that when I needed you most of all you saved me. Robbie, you saved *us*. All of us. I just wanted you to know that.

We've seen the road behind. We know what's back there. There's nothing back there for us anymore. It's time to look at what's ahead and to expect the very best, no matter what. You'll get there one day. I know you will. I promise you.

Do you understand now, Robbie? Wherever and whatever you are now, you are everything that I intended you to be and I'm so very proud.

I love you always, my wonderful girl.

Mama.

Mr. Kensington sighed. Money launderers, drug dealers, organized crime moguls, embezzlers, jewel thieves, gold diggers… a banker sees all. But this, this was something to make a grown man cry and shut the office door so that none of his colleagues could see or hear.

That older gentleman… had to be either the father or grandfather. But maybe that didn't even matter.

He walked back to the safety deposit box and almost placed the book inside. He stood and thought a moment, then locked the empty box. Back in his office, he put the booklet in an envelope, sealed it, and locked it into his desk. If she returned, he'd simply hand the envelope over remaining bland and unknowing of the uncomfortable truth. So many things were better left unsaid.

And some lessons last a lifetime. He really didn't think he would ever see her again.

Story 7

The Confessions of the Dreamers

Early Sunday morning, Roy paused in the doorway to his daughter's room in his condo on the suburban outskirts of the city and marveled at Mother Nature's ability to replicate his dark brown hair and hazel eyes in female form. John, his veterinarian buddy, often joked that it looked as though he had given birth to Marietta all by himself. She was so much like him – studious, quiet, serious, given to daydreaming. Pretty low maintenance, for a teenager. Roy sighed. Like him, Marietta would soon have to adjust to the soul-killing realities of life.

"Marietta, we're going to have to cut the weekend short. Your Aunt Stephanie died this morning."

Marietta looked up from her poetry homework. "Aunt Stephanie?"

Her mother's identical twin existed only in sinister whispers on the fringes of the family circle. Her name rarely came up in conversation. On the rare occasion someone said, "Stephanie," out loud, eyes looked left, right, and then downward. An awkward pause would settle like gray gloom.

Then another someone would break the spell. "Think it might rain?" with a puzzled glance at the crystal clear sky. "Who won the game?" as the scoreboard blinked rapidly on television. "How did Susan get the potato salad so creamy?" Susan would stare at the lumpy potato salad without reply. Then more voices hurried to fill the silence.

Following protocol, Marietta looked left, right, and finally, down at her poem. "How did she die?" Even to a sixteen-year-old, thirty-six was still young.

"Susan's already on her way to pick you up. It's probably better that you hear it from her."

Her father hesitated.

"Marietta, she… Well, the funny thing is Stephanie sent you something care of me. It arrived this morning. I opened the box to make sure it was okay. But this," her father handed her a thick book, "is still in the wrapper, so it should be fine."

"A Bible?" Marietta hefted the book up and down. "That's weird. I mean, I didn't think she was religious." None of them were, really. When Grandma died months before, she took all the religion with her. No one else bothered to pretend.

Roy shrugged. "Well, there's a lot about Stephanie that no one ever knew. And now maybe never will." He hugged her. "Go ahead and get packed, sweetheart."

Low murmuring drifted up the stairs. Roy's voice held a familiar pleading tone.

"Susan, I'm... I'm sorry."

A long silence then, "Really." One quiet word swirled with layers of meaning.

"It... doesn't have to be like this." Marietta remembered that same whimper used to crawl around their house just before Roy left for the suburbs.

"But it *is* like this. You made sure of that." Cold. Final. Unforgettable, Susan. Marietta slung her duffel bag over her shoulder and hurried down the stairs. She loved her father. She did not want to see a grown man cry. Not again.

Wide, open spaces on the road compacted as traffic increased on the drive back into the city.

"Mom, what happened to Aunt Stephanie?"

Susan checked over her shoulder as she raced other vehicles to their exit. "She was shot to death by police." Bam! Flat out. Just like that.

"What?"

Her mother sighed patiently and smoothed a pale hand over her raven hair pulled back into a tight French twist. "Marietta, you remember that I told you Stephanie was unstable?"

"Yes."

"Sometimes, when you walk a tightrope, you make it to the other side. Other times, you fall off." Her dark eyes flashed as she shot Marietta a glance. "Stephanie made it across many times. As a matter of fact, she got good at it. But, she crossed one time too many."

Marietta looked at Susan's creamy hands as she turned the steering wheel. "Why did they shoot her?"

"They didn't have a choice." Susan's fingers tightened to a bloodless white color as if to choke the car to death. "Marietta, it's probably going to be on the evening news. That's why I came early to get you, so you'd know ahead of time."

Marietta hid in her room upstairs. Their answering machine was full of messages and her mother fielded more calls as the phone rang through the rest of the night. She went back downstairs once to heat a plate of leftovers in the microwave. Between the monotonous Midwestern-accented announcement of Aunt Stephanie's death on television and the hum of the microwave, she overheard Susan talking to someone on the telephone.

"The deceased, Stephanie Madison purchased her weapon…"

"…threatened me just last week."

"… serial number matched… was not loaded… at this time…"

"…Something just told me it…"

"… family members that she had a history… no further…"

"… the last time I would see her alive."

Marietta poured a glass of juice, and tried not to hear Susan.

"…her wallet… a business card from an abortion doctor… I don't know… Stephanie…"

Susan sighed loudly.

"I was afraid for Marietta…"

Marietta raced back upstairs and quietly closed her bedroom door.

Six days later, afternoon stretched into evening. The minister had to stop talking. The congregation had to cease waving programs and handkerchiefs in the air. The fat lady, Sister Margarita, had to sing. The show was finally over. Everyone left.

Home once more, Marietta finished putting away containers filled with amazing casserole and salad mixtures. Dear, sweet Sister Gracie. Just because sweet potatoes, carrots, and cheddar cheese were all orange, that didn't mean they were supposed to be combined.

Susan systematically straightened the living room and tied down loose ends of fabric the same way she systematically straightened and clamped down the disobedient edges of her hair with metal clips. Life would go on. Marietta knew her mother disturbed a groove only in extreme emergencies. Routines were not accidents waiting to happen. They were *routines*. And Roy needed to understand that.

"You should have asked me first, Roy."

"I probably should have, but I wanted Marietta to have a chance to see him."

Marietta cringed at the quiet verbal war waged in her honor. Susan said something in the low voice specifically-tuned to cut Roy down to size. Surprisingly, it didn't work this time. Her father didn't back down and the discussion continued.

Exasperated, her mother called, "Marietta!"

The fluffy, golden dog yipped and barked eagerly. It smelled the bacon-cabbage stir fry on Marietta's hands. She couldn't help laughing at his silliness.

"Oh, he's beautiful. He's so friendly."

Her mother made an impatient sound that her father quickly covered with, "He's yours, Marietta. You get to name him."

"How about Jesse?"

"Jesse Brazil." Roy repeated the name, pleased. Roy's hazel eyes met Susan's dark brown eyes squarely as he answered Marietta with triumph. "Sounds good to me."

This was a new dynamic to her father and mother's relationship that Marietta knew her mother didn't appreciate. "Marietta, this dog is your responsibility. You're going to feed him and walk him." Susan frowned a crease into her smooth cream-colored skin. "And he sleeps outside."

"Mom."

"Marietta."

"Can't he sleep in my room?" Marietta looked at her father who looked away. *Don't push it, kid.*

"Marietta you don't know what he might be carrying."

"He has a clean bill of health from John," Roy announced loudly.

"Alright." Susan still looked dubious.

"Susan, you're running out of reasons. He's fine."

"I said alright!" *Shut up, Roy*, her mother seemed to want to say. Instead, she turned to Marietta. "But Marietta, remember the rules."

Jesse raced from Marietta to Roy to Susan and back to Marietta excitedly. "Okay, Mom."

All day Sunday, Marietta set up Jesse's backyard home. She hauled food and supplies from the store in the ancient family station wagon - her first car. Jesse rode along with her pointing his nose insistently into the wind.

She'd missed school all week and had gotten her assignments from sympathetic teachers by phone and email. It was while she put the finishing touches on her poetry assignments due Monday morning that she discovered Stephanie's secret.

Marietta had removed the plastic from the Bible, noting that it wasn't the plastic retailers used. It was ordinary plastic wrap that hugged the book as if someone had gone over it with a blow-dryer. But whatever. She carried the Bible to the funeral for appearance sake, but hadn't bothered to open it. Neither had she gone up to view Aunt Stephanie's body. She could see Stephanie's resemblance to her own mother well enough from where she sat. It felt creepy.

Now Jesse nosed around her room all restless, whining curiosity. He knocked the Bible off her nightstand. For the first time, under Jesse's paws, the Bible Stephanie sent her lay open. On the left page were verses. On the right page was a neatly typewritten sheet of white paper, cut exactly to tuck into the spine without sticking out.

> "She's doing it again. How does she do it? I remember playing with fire in a vacant lot a long time ago. I pretended that I was a cave woman in prehistoric times. When I got home, Mama beat me like a slave. Like Kunta Kinte. Like my name was Toby. The only way Mama could have known was her. How did she do it?"

Marietta slammed the Bible shut in fear. What kind of creepy message did Aunt Stephanie want to send her? In the holy book of all things. Curiosity got the best of her, so Marietta allowed the book to flop open to a random page. Another sheet of paper held a poem.

Yellow Rain

Everything has reason
I always knew
Get a clue
No longer pleasin'
Introduce you to truth
Get your due

Trust in you
Things you say
Games you play
Only a fool
Tries to stay
Not walk away

Used to hear
No yellow rain
Pissed in my face
Lies my dear
Bring the pain
Hell for my brain

Stories cannot last
When you smile at me
And let the lie free
While I laugh
Get a clue
No trust in you

Stephanie was nuts. Just like everyone said.

The dreams began that night. In a mist of water and smoke, she heard splashing and gurgling. Someone called to her. She couldn't see anything. The mist closed in then rose upward. A voice screamed, "Marietta!"

Marietta jerked awake, sweating, terrified. She was in her room. It was silent. Outside her window, the moon was full. Clouds gave it a cottony appearance. In the backyard, Jesse barked angrily. Marietta hurried downstairs to shut him up before her mother or a neighbor complained.

"Eeeeeeyowrrrr!"

That scream. A cat?

By the time she reached the backyard, Jesse's enemy invader had left. She shushed him from the patio door and went back to bed.

Monday morning, Susan shoved Jesse's nose away from her while she finished clipping dead leaves off her rose hedges. Their neighbor, Mr. Johnson, was of the classic nosy variety which is why Susan insisted that Roy plant the hedges in the backyard instead of the front yard. No matter. Mr. Johnson, who liked Susan's beautiful face as well as her rose hedges, soon found a small opening through the hedge and spoke through it now.

"Poor kitty. I found it when I turned off my sprinklers and buried it so it wouldn't draw rodents."

"Disgusting. People are so irresponsible with their animals." Susan hacked more viciously than necessary at the hedge, hoping Mr. Johnson would get the hint.

Mr. Johnson nodded agreement and peered with interest at Jesse chasing butterflies, barking gaily. Susan abruptly turned away rewarding Mr. Johnson a view of her backside marching stiffly away.

Marietta spread honey on toast as Susan shut the patio door in Jesse's eager face.

"Mom, I was just thinking about Aunt Stephanie again."

Washing her hands, Susan spoke automatically "You know you can always talk to me, Marietta. That's what I'm here for."

"When do you think they'll stop showing the video of her... you know?"

The slow-motion ballet of Stephanie's last stand made for breathless public affairs commentary. Wild, black hair swirled around a face that looked more gray than beige. Her mouth screamed a black hole and to Marietta's eyes, Stephanie appeared to age ten years before she hit the hood of her car and dropped the gun. The unloaded gun. Marietta's classmates stopped asking her questions about it once they realized she wouldn't provide details.

"The next big fire or three-mile pile up will do it. Everyone's got a video camera these days, you know. And whenever the police are around, that's when they pull them out and turn them on. Blood money."

"People seem so angry."

Susan sighed and sat down. "They're agitating for... action against the police department. But I let them and the police know that the family wasn't interested in scandal. It's over. Besides, Stephanie... wanted to die."

So cold.

"Do you miss her?"

"Yes. Yes, I do. Despite all the negative episodes, she was my sister."

"When was the last time you saw her before she died?"

Susan fiddled with the salt and pepper shakers. "Months ago." *...threatened me last week...* "She'd fallen into a bad crowd. So-called revolutionaries. Drinking. Probably drugs. Different men." She shook her head, sorrowfully. "I didn't want any of that around my house or my daughter." Susan stood up. "She threatened to hurt you, you know. That's when I cut her off completely."

Marietta's eyes widened in surprise. She remembered with a mixture of shame and uneasiness a homeless bag lady standing motionless across the street from her junior high school. "Look at that," one of her friends laughed and pointed. Marietta looked and walked away quickly in fear that Aunt Stephanie would call to her and embarrass her in front of the entire school yard. She never told anyone and decided not to mention anything now. Not like it mattered anymore anyway.

Susan spoke over her shoulder as she went upstairs. "Remember to feed and walk Jesse before you go to school."

Absently, Marietta dumped half a bag of dog food in a mixing bowl and filled the plastic sink tub with water. Then she shoved it all out the patio door with her foot.

That night, she met Roy for dinner at their favorite seafood restaurant. It was to make up for missing their past weekend because of the funeral and cutting the previous weekend short because of Aunt Stephanie's....

"Dad, did Aunt Stephanie hate me?"

Roy's hands stilled from cutting his steak. "Stephanie had a hard time in life. She... often acted out her pain and anger because she didn't know a better way to deal with it. I wouldn't say she hated you, though." He shook his head. "No."

"Is she happy now?"

"I don't know. I'd like to think so."

"Did anyone love her?"

Roy put down his knife and fork. "Of course, honey. She was loved." He picked up his glass of lemonade.

"Did you love her?" This time, Roy paused so long Marietta didn't think he would answer. He finally remembered to take a drink and set down the glass.

Her father was uneasy, Marietta knew. It was something kind of strange, the stick with which he'd been beaten.

"She was part of the family."

The house was dark.

"You'll be okay?"

"Dad, I'm sixteen, not six. Mom's just out with friends. She'll probably be back by ten."

Roy laughed. "Okay, I'm sorry. See you soon, sweetheart."

Marietta waved him away as she closed the door behind her. An empty house meant opportunity. Opportunity meant exploration. Exploration meant answers. Maybe. In the medicine cabinet sat a half-empty bottle of Susan's "nerve" pills. On the back of a mirror hung on the door of Susan's closet, hung a restraining order dated a week previous to Stephanie's death. Inside a barely visible slot built underneath the night stand, lay a gun.

Headlights beamed into the room and Marietta heard a familiar engine cut off. From the driveway, Susan watched expressionless as her bedroom light switched off.

In the still of that night, Marietta worked up courage to open the journal again. None of the pages were dated. She had no way of knowing really when Stephanie recorded her thoughts. Marietta closed her eyes and let the book fall open randomly.

> "Papa, to me, was a superhero. Large and tall. Always helping people and fixing things. Sometimes he told us about the war. Two wars he'd been in. Three, if you count the war at home for Civil Rights. He was like Captain America and Superman and Shaft and Luke Cage all wrapped into one. I tell myself that. I like to think so. But not really. Back then, he was the Invisible Man eclipsed by Mama's so-called godly goodness."

Behind Marietta's closed eyes, images floated in and out of her body. The smoke drifted, floated, cleared. She saw her mother. It looked like her mother? No. Not Susan. The wild hair and near fanatic glitter in her eyes gave Stephanie away everytime.

"Marietta! Where's my baby? Marietta! Where's my baby? Marietta!"

The voice intruded, clanged. It didn't fit. It jarred her awake and for once, she was grateful to hear Susan yell up the stairs.

"Marietta! Wake up! You're going to be late to school!"

She groaned and looked at the clock. Great. She overslept. She'd have to make up time after school and miss Wednesday evening poetry club.

"Marietta!"

"I'm awake!"

"Marietta, you're supposed to feed and walk Jesse."

Marietta dragged herself to the shower, scrubbed a toothbrush through her mouth, and snapped a rubber band on her tangled hair without combing it. Unbelievably, Susan was still going on about Jesse when she emerged from the bathroom. "He's jumping around all over the kitchen. You need to…"

Take the yellow pill, Mom. Jeez.

"Mom, I'm coming!"

Marietta rushed downstairs slinging her backpack over her shoulders. Sure enough, Susan's bathrobe bore Jesse's paw prints and she looked unusually disheveled this morning. Jesse urgently licked Susan's face and hands until she knocked him away. Then Jesse growled at Susan.

Marietta looked at the clock. "Mom, I have to go. I'm late for class." She grabbed fruit off the dining room table and made for the front door while Susan tried to shove Jesse out the patio door.

"Jesse, outside! Marietta…"

Jesse barked a protest.

"Marietta!" Susan's voice brought her up short. "I told you about this!" *Lady, who are you anymore anyway?* Jesse growled louder at Susan's angry tone. "Jesse, go!"

"Mom, just for today. Please?"

"Go!" Susan's shout might have been for her or Jesse. *Whatever.* Marietta shrugged and ran to her car.

Marietta pulled out of the driveway. She knew about Baby Alicia. The family synchronized their stories. Everyone presented an unshakable, united front no outsider could penetrate.

Forgiven, but never forgotten.

Even before her final breakdown, Aunt Stephanie had been urban legend. The whispers, the averted eyes, the insinuations, the tight clutching of newborns whenever she was in the vicinity… It had all been too much.

Once upon a time, way back before her memory began recording, Marietta knew she and Alicia played together. Their birthdays were only three months apart.

Marietta sighed and turned the corner. Alicia would have understood her like no other. With Alicia as her best friend, things would have turned out much differently. Marietta could have been cool.

Marietta would call Alicia on her cell. "What movie do you wanna see, girl?"

Alicia would pop gum. "I don't know. Are you and Darius still talking?"

"No. He's too immature. All he wants to do is play basketball. You know what? Reggie stepped to me the other day trying to see what was up."

Alicia would gasp from outrage. "Reggie already got a girl!"

"He sure didn't act like it!" Marietta would giggle.

Or, Alicia would hang out in Marietta's room. They would style each other's hair the same way and wear matching clothes.

"Girl, let's go to the mall." Alicia would always be down.

"Cool with me. I need some shoes. Dad already said I could go to senior prom. And if Darius doesn't get his game straight, I might go with Reggie and be like..."

Girlish laughter.

Marietta parked in the school's parking lot and hurried to the attendance office finishing her muttered conversation along the way.

There was no Alicia. Neither was there a Reggie or Darius or a senior prom. There was only her weird self, her weird thoughts, and her love of poetry... The woulds, and coulds, and shoulds and what ifs didn't exist. Because they never happened.

The phone rang about one in the afternoon as Susan cleaned and dressed herself, clamped down her hair, then disinfected the kitchen. Jesse's paw prints were all over the floor.

"Oh. It's you."

"Yeah. Exciting, isn't it?" When all else failed with Susan, sarcasm was Roy's last line of defense. "Susan, I'm worried about Marietta."

"Aren't we all? She's not taking care of that dog like she promised, Roy."

"No. I mean she asked me about Stephanie yesterday."

Roy heard Susan's indrawn breath.

"What about?"

"That got you, didn't it?"

"Roy, don't start..."

"Whether Stephanie was happy and did anyone love her."

"Well, I guess *you* would know the answer to that." Susan could be a stone-cold bitch when she really put her back into it.

"I'm moving on, Susan. This is not about you."

Silence.

"I think the Bible might have caused Marietta to think about it a little more." "What Bible?"

"She didn't tell you?"

"Tell me *what*, Roy?"

"Stephanie sent Marietta a Bible to my condo."

"Roy! We discussed this before. *Didn't we?* We weren't going to allow…"

"It was just a Bible, Susan. It was still in the wrapper."

"But still…"

"Susan, calm down! It was in the wrapper. I…"

Susan's voice sliced his ear through the phone line.

"Why didn't *you* tell me?"

"I didn't think it was that big a deal."

"Kind of like the damn dog wasn't a big deal, right? You wanted Marietta to have a chance to see it first. *Right?*"

"Susan, listen…"

"*Right?* Wait a second." Susan dropped the phone, shouted something, and then picked it up again. "Let me call you back. He's barking again."

Half an hour later, Jesse quieted down and like any other married couple, Roy and Susan picked up their argument at precisely the same point and continued back and forth at a steady pace for another hour and half.

Marietta, lost in thought at school, read Aunt Stephanie's hidden journal during lunch and dull moments in class:

> "Mother, on the other hand, was a different sort. A mad scientist who built Frankenstein's monster in her secret laboratory. I used to pretend that. But when she canned fruit and vegetables with the kitchen blazing hot, she did look a little crazy. I have to be honest. Once, she slapped me at church. I told her it seemed like a nightclub with the lead soprano as lounge singer and the offering basket collecting the cover charge. All the women dancing for the men. So, apparently, I'm a blasphemer as well as a liar and thief."

"What!" Marietta shrieked into her cell phone as she drove home after making up missed time after school.

"Marietta, I'm your father. I know you've been through a lot. First Grandma, then Aunt Stephanie... Now you're going through puberty."

"Dad. Are you kidding?"

"Well, you're at that time in life when everything changes."

"Oh my God. Dad, please don't put either of us through this. I'm begging you."

"I'm just saying that you can talk to me. Marietta, I'm not trying to be mean or anything. I'm just concerned about your health."

"Who told you I was on drugs? I mean, where is this even coming from?"

Marietta missed her turn and pulled over to the side of the road.

"Your mother and I talked it over and she..."

"Mom? Mom told you I was taking drugs?"

"Marietta..."

"Dad, it's not true! I would never do that, I promise!"

"Marietta, I know the separation must be hard on you. Hard to understand."

"But Dad..."

"I promise you, Marietta, I'm not going anywhere. We'll get it figured out real soon. It's going to be okay, sweetheart."

After her father hung up, Marietta sat shaking in the station wagon on the side of the road where she'd pulled over. Something like a shower curtain separated her from the natural world. It wasn't the windshield. It was a clear bubble covered in gray film that only she could see. Something she would have to claw through to escape. "What would you do?" She looked at Aunt Stephanie's Bible as if waiting for it to speak. She closed her eyes and let the pages fall open.

> "Arby used to look at me as if wondering the same thing. 'Did she...' I always looked away. I hate that doubt in him and me. But there's nothing I can do. Sometimes I hate my sister and the things she says and does. We can't choose our family. We just love our family. Or, at least, we tell everyone we do."

Ever since she started reading Aunt Stephanie's journal, Marietta's head was a funhouse. She saw things that weren't there, heard things that weren't said, spoke to people who disappeared into white haze. She dreamed things she was afraid to think while awake. Life was slightly off-kilter. She was off-kilter. But she certainly wasn't on drugs. This one thing she knew for sure. Someone was confused. But not her. Determined, Marietta drove home.

"Oh Marietta, Marietta. Your father is really not himself lately. I'm sure you've seen it. I think… Stephanie's death affected him more than he lets on."

Susan's dark eyes searched Marietta's hazel eyes carefully.

"I've always had my suspicions. I heard the rumors, you know. The two of them." A pause as Susan tested the atmosphere of the room. "Stephanie was… obsessed with us. Me, Roy, you."

"Me?"

Susan reluctantly nodded her head. "You represent the daughter she always wanted but wasn't woman-enough to raise. You know what happened to Baby Alicia, don't you?"

Marietta looked at her hands, nodding.

"Stephanie has always been… unwell, even when we were children. No one in the family trusted her. Even Roy. But I think maybe, he still had feelings. I know that *she* did."

Marietta felt tiny prickles at the back of her neck. The thoughts in her head, the things she'd learned the past few days shifted, clanged, and scraped against her mother's words.

"Mom, I think if Aunt Stephanie had gotten the help she needed, she wouldn't have gone over the edge. I don't think she would have hurt me."

Jesse was barking again. Susan stood up and looked out the window, irritated. "You're a child, Marietta." Susan waved away Marietta's protest dismissively.

"Yes, you are. You don't understand. Stephanie couldn't function in normal society. She was hostile and paranoid. Couldn't hold a job. Couldn't hold a man. Or a baby. Dear God, she couldn't even handle a simple thing like reality either. She thought she was some sort of freedom fighter." Susan let out a derisive laugh and looked at Marietta.

"She was a message-bearer and drug mule! And then she just…" Susan turned away from the window and looked into Marietta's mirror, speaking to her own reflection. "*That's* why she died." Marietta thought her mother never looked more like a mannequin than she did at that moment.

Susan works in mysterious ways. Someone said it long ago. Marietta cleared her throat nervously.

"Look, I mean… just as long as you know I'm not getting high, Mom."

Susan smiled, smoothed her tight bun of raven hair, and turned away from the mirror, and sat back on Marietta's bed. "Of course not, Marietta. No one who knows you and loves you would believe something like that." She paused as if a thought just occurred to her.

"Oh yes. Your father did mention one other thing – some sort of gift you received from Stephanie." So that was why she'd found her mother in her room. "He was concerned that you felt the need to be so secretive about it."

Marietta felt thin, invisible, silky filaments stroking her, feeling her, testing her, crawling across her scalp.

"I wasn't being secretive. I just didn't think it was important."

"Oh, then can I see it?"

The filaments moved downward, found a vulnerable spot on the back of her neck, and pressed lightly. "I'm... I'm still looking through it."

"That's funny. I don't remember you showing such enthusiasm for the Good Book before." The filaments gathered around Marietta's throat and tightened slightly. "As a matter of fact, I seem to remember you telling me the kids at church were phony and fake."

The soft tightening made Marietta's voice sound high and unnatural to her own ears. "Well, they are." She fiddled with objects on her nightstand.

"Marietta, Marietta, Marietta. You'll never make any friends with that uppity attitude, miss." Susan laughed lightly. "Remember your twelfth birthday? Remember that boyfriend you *nearly* had? And now look at you."

Marietta's eyes widened. "Why are you bringing that up? It was a long time ago and I don't care anymore. No one does."

"Own up to your mistakes, Marietta," Susan advised calmly.

"I'm more than the mistakes I made, Mom."

"No. You *are* the mistakes you made, Marietta. We all are." The cobweb was sticky and gross. It smothered. "Your father is going crazy trying to figure out how to please you despite it all. I'm doing all that I can. And you can't even keep your promises to us. Now you're hiding secrets and God only knows what else. When I think of all you could have been and chose not to be, I lie down and cry sometimes. Remember that summer program?"

Marietta's voice wobbled despite her effort to control it. "Mom, you're not even allowing me a chance, are you?" Her begging sounded just like her father's and she hated the sound of it.

Susan smiled then sighed sorrowfully with long-suffering impatience. "Just determined to create a nervous break-down out of thin air, aren't you?"

"I am not having a nervous breakdown! I'm just..."

"Calm down the hysterics, Marietta."

"I'm not hysterical!"

"Aren't you?" Susan *tut-tutted*. "I think I'll talk to a doctor about your anti-social behavior. I should have a long time ago. But we'll see."

"Mom, being shy is not anti-social."

"And denial is not just a river in Egypt."

"I'm not in denial! I just..."

"Sooo defensive, Marietta." Susan smiled slyly. "As I've told you before, more listening, less talking."

"Stop it!" Marietta backed away two horrified steps and held back a sob. "Just stop!"

"Marietta!" Susan reproved sharply. "I think you'd better calm down before you end up like Stephanie."

"Shut up!" Marietta ran down the stairs. "Shut up! Shut up!" Marietta yelled it over her shoulder as she slammed out the front door.

Outside, Jesse's barking anger was a distant reflection of her own frustration as she started her car and screeched away on an aimless path. She sat in a park for an hour. She watched airplanes take off and land, bright lights streaking upward and downward in the growing darkness. She ate a fast food combo meal and cried. At last, she admitted her fear.

Is she right about me?

Marietta opened Stephanie's Bible randomly and read by the car's interior light. The hopeless words of a crazy, dead woman advised her from the grave.

"Mama used to look at me so sadly as if wondering how such a crazy child came to live in her house and what should she do about it. Nothing I said ever got through to her. Or, if it did, she took the easy road. She always thought the worst of me and expected the worse from me. Pretended she didn't see. I AM NOT CRAZY!!!"

Marietta slammed the book shut, heart pounding. Stephanie… Stephanie… that's why you sent the Bible to me!

I'm moving out.

Marietta spoke aloud to the dark, "I'm gonna go home, pack up, and move out. Take Jesse with me. Live with Dad." Her mother was right on one point, at least. She hadn't looked after Jesse like she should. Poor boy.

"She's a liar! All that stuff about Dad. How could she? Just fourteen months and I can leave this place and never look back. Just make it to eighteen, Marietta. That's all you have to do. Lay low, lay in the cut, and suck it up. Finish high school and LEAVE! Go far away!"

I am not a drug addict. I am not an alcoholic. I am not anti-social. I am not uppity. I am not irresponsible. I am not in denial. I am not crazy. And I am not Aunt Stephanie! Marietta allowed herself one last sob, realizing that if she didn't act soon, she *would* be Aunt Stephanie.

"That's how she gets you." She turned the key in the ignition. "She whips you with your own emotions. That's how she got Stephanie. That's how she got Dad. Don't let her get you."

She's not gonna get me.

"Play it cool for fourteen more months. Just stay calm."

Marietta muttered the words as a mantra to herself all the way home. "Don't go out like that." Distracted in the dark, she misjudged the distance of the driveway.

"Maintain your composure."

She also didn't see Susan dumping something into the trashcan on the curb until the headlights marked her as a target. Marietta gasped and slammed the brake.

Except it was the accelerator.

Susan screamed. Marietta screamed and swerved. Then, scraped and gouged by the brick corner of the garage at sixty miles per hour, the station wagon screamed. Marietta lay across the car horn. Susan lay across the driveway.

Pain. No. Not quite pain. White mists, drifting smoke, cloudy light. Fog. Indoors or outdoors? Marietta lay for a few minutes trying to figure it out. She was breathing. Air went in. Air went out. But someone else breathed too.

"Where am I?"

She heard a voice. "Marietta, you're in the hospital. It's Friday morning."

She focused her eyes in the same direction as the voice. Roy looked back at her grief-stricken.

"Do you remember the accident?"

Yes. It was the reason why she didn't want to wake up.

"Mom?"

"Honey, Susan…" He swallowed. "Your mother is dead."

Marietta closed her eyes. Where were her mists now when she needed them?

"You were hurt too."

She didn't answer. The pain in her middle told her she had been punished.

"Marietta, what happened?"

Finally, she broke. The tears came, increasing the pain. "Daddy." Roy pushed a buzzer next to the bed. She tried not to shake because it hurt so much. "Daddy." She hadn't called him that since she was a small girl. "Daddy!"

The nurse came into the room at a run.

"Eventually, she'll have to give a statement."

Friday evening, Roy Brazil sank wearily back onto his sofa. The news had affected Marietta badly. He should have waited. And now, this.

"Please allow my daughter some time to recover from the death of her mother and her own injuries. She just had surgery yesterday."

The two policemen exchanged a glance. "We're just doing our job, sir. I mean, what with the restraining order and the death of her sister…" The other cop coughed and picked up the thread. "Your wife's neighbor, Mr. Johnson, said he saw Mrs. Brazil hitting the dog with dog food from the patio door early Wednesday afternoon."

"Look, you guys. Marietta just woke from the surgery a few hours ago."

"He also reported someone screaming and the dog barking about three hours later the same day. Sir, does it concern you at all that the dog is missing?"

The cop actually had nerve to allow his question to sound like a reprimand.

"I can't do this right now." Roy stood up and walked to his front door, held it open. "Please leave my home."

"Sir, I apologize but…"

"Please, just go." Still they hesitated. Roy opened the door wider. "Please."

"We'll stay in touch, sir." Putting their hats back on and tipping the brims, they left.

While Marietta slept through the night, Roy drove back into the city. He knew the layout of the house. After all, it had only been seven months since Susan pointed him towards the door. That night, years of enmity, buried and smothered under a shallow layer of false, brittle forgiveness burst forth in a hideous, monstrous display of hatred.

For one terrifying moment, something in Susan's eyes seemed not quite human. Then the ice came down again and it was all back to normal as Susan shredded him with every intimacy, every insecurity, and every fantasy he had offered to her as tokens of his love. These she wielded as a scythe to tear a path for her to stomp through his heart. He left his family on *her* terms. He had no choice. She would have told Marietta everything… And then some.

Susan was gone, but her shadow blackened the night. He would have to make sure Marietta knew it wasn't her fault. She would never be to blame.

Jesse may possibly have escaped. Unlikely though. Susan had been vigilant about keeping him penned in the back yard at night. Jesse figured out in just a few days what it had taken years for almost everyone else, including him, to finally see. His own mother, father, and older sister had tried to tell him about Susan's unique personality. His relationship with them grew distant when he chose to bury common sense under his love for, or maybe fear of, Susan.

He found a flashlight in the kitchen and searched the back yard for an opening. There was none. There was, however, a freshly-dug mound around a tree that he knew had been planted at least ten months ago. He knew this because he had planted it himself. Mr. Johnson must have dozed off for a few minutes.

The clock radio's glowing red display explained the darkness of the room caused by nine o'clock p.m.

Marietta spoke into the intercom.

"Nurse. Please help me. I need to find my Bible but I can't move."

The nursed entered the room with a ready smile for Marietta's grimace of pain.

"I'm not surprised. After a transplant, the body needs plenty of rest in order to recover." She opened a small cabinet by Marietta's bed with triumph. "Found it!"

"Transplant?"

"Yes." The nurse eyed her curiously. "You didn't know?"

"What…"

"Let's see. It's all here on the chart. The steering wheel caused a lot of internal damage. One kidney. And the pancreas. They had to remove your spleen. But the doctors think you're going to be all right."

Marietta stared blank-faced at the nurse.

"Your mother, dear." The nurse patted her hand and smoothed the blanket around her legs. "She was an organ donor. Your father approved the operations since she was a close match. Funny how life works sometimes."

Marietta fixed a hazel-eyed stare at the ceiling and lay down with her brown hair spread across the pillow in swirling waves. "Funny."

"Let me give you a little something for the pain. Sleep for now."

Marietta blinked slowly as she drifted back to the smoky mists. "I may become a drug addict after all." Her lips curved into a smile that might easily have been mistaken for a sneer.

She still gets her way.

"There's no other explanation, Roy."

"I see."

Roy woke John up at John's home veterinarian practice to perform an autopsy on Jesse. And now John called Roy at his condo with the results.

"I can run the test for you again, but we've seen this so many times, there's no mistake. Definitely positive. I'm so very sorry."

"And the bullet wound?"

"One shot through the head. From a thirty-eight."

Stephanie's gun. "For protection," Susan had said.

Stephanie, Alicia, Susan. And now… and now…

" John, I'd appreciate it if… you know."

"It's off the record. But Roy," he paused, "Roy, why didn't you bring him in for his shots?"

Roy abruptly hung up the telephone.

Something twisted in his gut. With a sense of foreboding, he walked to pull out the R volume of his encyclopedia set. He would do what he could to salvage what was left of his and Marietta's lives. After reading the same paragraph a few times, he put his head in his hands and cried.

It was two o'clock Saturday morning.

At five o'clock, Marietta was awake once more. The back cover of Stephanie's Bible lay open.

> "Today I pretended that I was normal. I pretended that I caught Susan's baby before she fell. That I had a daughter and a husband who loved me. I wanted to be better, you know. I did try. Someone always there to remind me and everyone else who I was. What I did. What I let happen. It was an accident. She was my niece and I loved her too! I begged and begged Susan to forgive me. For everything. You were the best thing that I ever did with my life. I promise you this. But I had to make it right. And that is the only reason why. It is over for me now. No more babies. I just can't wake up to face it anymore. Even though Arby doesn't know, I know you will be all right. I have a feeling. I love you, Alicia."

A creased, yellowed letter addressed to Stephanie lay behind that page. The writing was shaky.

"Trust in God, Stephanie. Except His will be done. She have took to Susan. She never told you and Susan apart. You will be blest and so will she. We all love you. Mama."

Last year, at Grandma's Fourth of July barbecue, disheveled, wild-eyed Stephanie had been restrained and escorted away from the stares and whispers. That bag lady.

"Marietta, my baby!"

Drunk, high, and crazy – all at the same time - that was what everyone said. Susan wept beautifully on Roy's shoulder as everyone rushed to comfort her.

Then that quiet whisper.

Susan works in mysterious ways.

Grandma's distant look… was not senility. It was guilt. Then that night, angry voices floated in the dark from Roy and Susan's bedroom. Then Roy was gone, gone, gone.

Marietta never asked why. Susan never told.

The clouds burned away. Thoughts no longer scraped and shifted against each other anymore. They slipped neatly into place.

Arby. R. B. Roland Brazil.

No wonder she and Alicia looked so much alike in photos. No wonder Susan was a match. Her mother's twin *would* be a match. Did Roy suspect that his daughter had been exchanged like a thing? Like a favorite sweater?

Marietta gasped and cried as she burned deep inside the bandages. Life was a Dr. Seuss rhyme. Jesse fought the cat. Snap jaws, snap. The cat! Funny how life… Funny how life…

Marietta laughed in the face of her growing panic.

The voices overlapped trying to explain. They were in the room with her now trying to calm her down. All of them. There was Grandma. There was Aunt Stephanie and Baby Alicia. Mom? No. Susan… Their conversation was for each other however. She was ignored.

"Is she happy?" Aunt Stephanie asked Grandma.

"I don't know," Grandma responded quietly.

"Did anyone love her?" Cousin Alicia still had a two-year-old's voice.

"Of course!" Susan was indignant.

"Did *you* love her?" Susan asked them in return.

"Marietta!" She heard her father's voice yelling frantically.

The women shushed him and shooed him away. They turned intently to Marietta as a group and studied her. At last her chance had come. Through the tears and spastic clenching of her throat, she struggled to speak it aloud. The answer. Would they tell her? *Tell me... Whisper it...*

All her life, it seemed, she waited for this. *Please...*

"Who am I?"

They reached for her and smiled.

"You're part of the family."

The doctors and nurses worked on Marietta all day. Hospital administration eventually assigned a security guard to baby-sit Roy who tried several times to run into his daughter's room. Tears rolled silently down his face for most of the afternoon. The security guard took pity and handed Roy a cup of coffee filled with so much cream and sugar, its ghastly sweet paleness reminded him of Susan. He set it to the side, revolted.

By 5:55 p.m., Marietta lay inside an ever-lasting coma. Roy stood over his daughter's bed reading the sheet of paper stuck inside the front cover of the Bible she held in her left hand.

Wild Hazy, Beautiful Crazy

Wild Hazy stormed into my life
Brassy sassy racy spacey frenzied pepper spice
Brilliantly flashed she flamed with no shame
Clashed and smashed then claimed the pain
You left when the storm, the torrent that formed
Came and hurricaned your dreams away

Beautiful Crazy, she surprised them all
Shocked and rocked but stopped right before the fall
Cruel and angry to defend, scorched but free
Driven by the wind and gripped a piercing breeze
She soared and seared and danced, such grace
Loved but truly feared, debased and erased

Pretty Lady floating the carousel

That cool attitude in this rough world

Chemical miracle to give you the best in dreams

Still, in spite of it all, you shine, you sheen

Take me where you are, far away from here

Far away from me, I long for the serene.

Definite Maybe, cannot handle you, Baby

You stay just to say but you want to play free

You know what they see, what they think when asleep

For you only you they allow you to peek

Fighting a system that kidnaps your name

Don't hide from what you are when you are the same

Marietta's face held a slack, tranquil smile. Her right arm stretched out as if waiting for a hug. Roy sat down wearily in the bedside chair with the Bible in his lap. After a moment, he used the bedside phone to dial his sister's number, relieved that he still remembered it.

Story 8

The Reversal

"Douglas, in thirty days, you'll be free. Do you have a plan for your life?"

"I'm working on it."

"Because I don't want your craziness in my house."

"I can take care of myself."

"The way you took care of yourself before is what got you here."

Douglas stared down at his hands.

"I look at you now at twenty-three with those braids in your hair, that hard look on your face, and those tattoos. You look exactly like what you've become."

"Your son?"

Douglas's father tightened his jaw. If the thick glass partition hadn't separated them, Douglas was sure Reverend Righteous would have forgotten his religion and swung on him.

"Don't worry, *Reverend Allen*, you'll get your chance to show the world you're king of all you survey once I'm released." Douglas refused to call his father, "Father" lately.

"You used to be a good kid. When you were in camp, you…"

Douglas cut in angrily, "When I was in camp, the leaders tried to…" He took a breath. "They… they didn't do right by the kids there. Almost all of us."

His father frowned.

"They came after me too."

Reverend Allen stared at his son, for once, at a loss for words. No Bible scriptures. No homilies. No lecture. Just a blank stare.

"I fought them off me. You remember that summer I got sent home early for fighting?"

His father nodded slowly.

"You were eleven."

"That's why."

"You never said a word. Not to me, not to your mama. She would have told me."

"The camp leader was a friend of yours… Mr. Thomas."

"Randall Thomas?"

"He said you would never believe me and that the people in my neighborhood would call me a sissy boy. They would call me gay if I said anything. We all kept quiet."

Reverend Allen seemed stunned, as if trying to remember the events of that summer.

"Do you believe me?"

His father shook himself. "Douglas… I don't know what to say."

"It's all true. Before God and all the angels, it's true."

At this, his father grimaced and paused tensely as if trying to form his next words carefully. He spoke quietly, looking down at the top of the table. Douglas recognized this display as his father's particular type of fury. In that case, then the good reverend did understand. He did care about his son. Douglas waited hopefully.

"Douglas… your mother and I did our best to protect you and to raise you and your sister. We taught you about the world and how to live in it."

Reverend Allen paused.

"I never thought I'd see the day… when a son of mine… my own son that I raised under God's watchful eye… would…"

Another pause. Douglas waited expectantly.

"…bear false witness against another man of God."

Douglas recoiled in shock.

"*Deacon* Randall Thomas has been my friend for longer than you've been alive, boy. Don't you ever… EVER… you hear me?"

Reverend Allen's jaw tightened close to breaking as he shook his head slowly back and forth. Douglas hardened his own features to the prison-style façade he'd acquired for survival. Vulnerability just did not work behind bars.

Even now as he sat frozen, his father put down his phone receiver and walked away towards the guard who let him out. Vulnerability did not work with Reverend Allen either. The guard on Douglas's side of the glass hung up the phone receiver in Douglas's hand and escorted him back to lock-up.

"2017. Half of the North American population has incarcerated the other half. Desperate for labor, needful of an underclass no longer confined by slavery or Jim Crow, the United States turns to the criminal justice system to feed itself. Son, you think that's right?"

Old G, a veteran of the barely-remembered Black Power movement muttered quietly to Douglas as they shelved books in the library.

"Once upon a time, it was legal to own another human being. Once upon a time, women weren't allowed to vote and that was legal. They treated women like large children who couldn't even own property. Some laws need to be broken, you know." He flicked a meaningful glance Douglas's way.

"Think about it. If every citizen decided to not pay taxes to the federal government, do you really think the government would be able to collect from every single person?"

"I dunno."

"Really? What could they do to everybody?"

"I never paid taxes anyway."

Old G chuckled approvingly. "Well, good for you, son. If every citizen in the world withheld taxes from their nation's military and their politicians, law makers and breakers all... if they held that money hostage to an idea, say, a cure for cancer, clean drinking water and food for everyone, or solar energy... What do you think would happen?"

Douglas resorted to his usual answer to most of Old G's questions.

"I dunno." He laughed. "You could get a job out there and then don't file. See what happens."

Old G smiled tolerantly. "I'd sure like to know in my lifetime. I might not. But maybe you will."

Old G picked up another book to add to his stack.

"You gonna read all that?"

"Nope. You are."

Douglas snorted.

"I'm out in thirty days, G."

"The sooner you start, the sooner you finish." Old G laughed and walked off leaving Douglas shaking his head at three books. "Oh yeah," Old G threw over his shoulder. "Tell me about the Thirteenth Amendment when you get a chance."

Douglas stared blankly. Old G shook his own head, grimaced ruefully and walked away.

On the twenty-eighth day, he found Old G on the yard with a group of other older men who liked chess. He waited quietly for his friend to win and they walked off a ways to shoot the breeze.

"Who are our heroes now, Old G?"

"Who indeed?"

"You know what? I got through all three of those books and then went back to the encyclopedias."

"Good reading, hunh?"

"That Underground Railroad was alright. Sure could use one 'round here." Douglas looked around at the concrete and steel surrounding the yard. "Nat Turner and Harriet Tubman? Straight gangsta. Ride or die for real."

"Not the posing video gangsters."

"Naw. And Assata Shakur? Yeah she took care of herself. Really took care of it. Talkin' 'bout revolution and freedom."

"You know, in a way, I was hoping you could tell me the answer to your own question. Where are the heroes anymore? What happened to the John Browns, the Harriet Tubmans, the Nat Turners? Frederick Douglass too. We had W.E.B. DuBois for education and Booker T. Washington for self-sufficiency during Jim Crow. They stood up in a, we'll say, civil sort of way. It took one hundred years after slavery ended for a Malcolm X and a Huey Newton and an Angela Davis to raise up. Before then, of course, you had Ida B. Wells against lynching and Martin Luther King, Jr. for desegregation. But you know, nobody gives power away, son. All that 'work within the system' is a dream. Some laws just have to be broken."

Old G shook his head. "Nope. Nobody is gonna just lay down and say, 'take my power so you can have some for yourself.' Nope. No, no, no, no. The world don't work that way. It never happened like that."

Douglas searched his eyes. The old man was saying something but not quite saying it. Douglas slowly pulled out a carefully folded piece of paper from his waistband. Old G looked at him with an expectant gleam in his eye and then looked beyond the yard into the distance as he listened to Douglas read softly.

Neither slavery nor involuntary servitude, except as a punishment for crime whereof the party shall have been dully convicted, shall exist within the United States, or any place subject to their jurisdiction.

"That's some exception. Isn't it, Douglas? But you get it now, don't you? You do see."

Douglas nodded slowly.

"And now… you know."

Douglas nodded again.

"So what're you gonna do?" His old friend and mentor faced him squarely. "You stay safe out there, Douglas. But stay true too. And remember."

Because of his two-year probation and the implant in his back, Douglas wasted no time finding his probation officer and looking for work. He hauled fertilizer, unrolled sod, and fixed sprinkler systems for the landscaping company by day. At night, he read the books he found on the public library's donation shelf. Kept a low profile. He made no effort to contact his father or his mother and sister. They made no effort to contact him either.

One day, he learned from Kenny, part of the same landscaping crew, that Old G died from diabetes complications on the inside. This made him sad, but the next part of the story made him furious.

"They say the guards wouldn't give him his medication."

Douglas wheeled around dropping the bag of decorative rocks for the garden they were nearly finished constructing. Kenny shrugged.

"That's what they say."

That night, Douglas did not read. He sat facing the blank wall of his room and allowed terrible thoughts to run through his mind.

They killed him. They killed that old man. Not like anyone would do time for that. They kill us. They work us. Can't vote. Can't attend school. Can't leave the city limits. Slaves.

He couldn't sleep. He had to score. He needed to score. He wasn't due for testing for another two weeks. He could score.

"So imma do you just this one, hunh?" the dealer asked.

"Yeah, just this one."

"You'll be back, youngblood." the dealer grinned and tapped his wrist phone. Douglas took the beginning of the dealer's whispered conversation as his cue to leave.

"Nice doing business."

He walked away from the van that screamed, Unusual Money Supply, and crossed through a vacant lot. He paused in the darkness to open the bag and smell the weed expectantly with a smile.

The dealer started the van and pulled away. Suddenly, a truck with no headlights raced alongside the van and slowed. Douglas heard the whining *whoosh* of a military-grade volt gun. The truck raced away. The smoking van wobbled then tipped over the embankment into a shallow creek.

Douglas paused in a moment of indecision. Would the truck return to finish the job? He shoved the dimebag into his pants pocket and ran down the embankment. The truck landed upside down compressed on the melted side. The dealer sprawled halfway out of the window crushed around his torso. The part of his head that remained emitted a terrible charred smell.

Douglas swallowed.

Above on the street, he heard a screech of car tires. He heard voices in the dark. He entered the truck's other door. He ignored the dealer's own volt guns in the back of the truck. Instead, he quietly snatched all the cash he saw and shoved it into a bag holding some type of seed. Backing out of the truck window, he saw dark silhouettes against the sky. They pointed towards him. He ran for his life. He ran home frantically, collected the essentials he could carry.

He ran all night.

"Cash. I don't need a receipt."

"Yeah? Good. 'Cause I don't do receipts."

The tattoo artist at Tattoo, Bless You zapped away all five of Douglas's prison tattoos with a handheld laser. He felt a slight burning sensation that diminished with the ointment the tattoo artist painted on him with a small brush.

"$300."

Douglas handed him the money. Miguel, he said his name was, cleared his throat.

"You know, sometimes we get people in here that had a misunderstanding with Uncle Sam. Acquired a little bit of metal they don't really need. We recycle it."

A long pause followed.

"I get you, man. But my little bit of metal requires a heart beat. The minute that heartbeat stops, they know to come for my dead body or to track me down on the run."

"Yeah. That's lousy, man. But you know what... some laws were made to be broken."

Douglas started, which Miguel noticed.

"Yep," Miguel continued nonchalantly putting away the laser, "some laws shouldn't even exist."

"Right," Douglas agreed carefully. "Some laws need to be broken."

"$500."

"Do it."

Miguel disappeared out the back door then re-entered with a cute, black German shepherd puppy. "His heart beats just fine."

Twenty minutes and $500 later, Douglas Allen, Prisoner #27839693, romped gingerly on the grass in Miguel's backyard.

"What'll happen to the dog? You don't keep him, right?"

"Naw, we drop him to the city pound."

Douglas tipped him $50. Miguel looked startled, but quickly put the bills in his pocket.

"Look man," he gestured, "I got some extra gear in the back. You look like you got places to go. Things to do. Help yourself."

A few pounds heavier with gear that reminded him of the better part of camp days, Douglas shook Miguel's hand at two o'clock in the morning.

"Disappear, man," Miguel advised. "Vanish."

Douglas disappeared and vanished.

"Some laws were made to be broken," he whispered.

Off the grid, he adopted the persona of religious fanatic. From a thrift store, he purchased a sack of tiny Bibles and a bicycle as cover for his ever-westward journey. Along rural highways and byways and back roads, he sprinkled peace, love, and joy along road sides, farms, parks, streams, creeks, riverbeds, bayous, swamps, and backyards.

He bought a map of the highway system in the southern United States to keep track. In larger towns, he targeted the backyards of the well-to-do. Everything he needed, he carefully condensed, as the saner camp leaders taught him, into the large-sized backpack Miguel gifted him.

One month later, on a two-lane highway in East Texas, a fast-moving pick-up ran him off the road. The driver hit the brakes, then backed up to find Douglas trying to right himself in the ditch.

A beefy, red-faced man with a cowboy hat, barrel chest, and boots stared down at him. Douglas experienced a moment of icy déjà vu remembering how drug dealer's killers looked down the embankment at him. A gun rested in the man's truck rack. Douglas stared back at the man and held his bicycle in front of himself as a shield.

"You know it's fixin' to rain, doncha?"

Douglas opened his mouth and tried to think of something to say.

"It's gonna lightning and thunder real bad."

"Yeah, I'm gonna try to find some place to wait it out."

"I'm just up the road."

Douglas waited uneasily to find out where this conversation would go.

"Least I can do for running you off the road."

The very least. Douglas pushed his bike out of the ditch. J.B., as he introduced himself, helped Douglas put the bike in the truck bed. Douglas kept the back pack with him in the cab.

Over a huge bowl of chili and rice, Douglas explained. "My father said I could use the summer to speak of God's glory to the world before I started college. Said it would teach me maturity and understanding and that I would be blessed in His kingdom." He handed J.B. one of the little Bibles.

J.B. grunted. "You know they send this over the network so you don't have to carry books, doncha?"

"But the books don't require a satellite connection," Douglas replied.

"Ha! Gotta answer for everthing, hunh?"

"No," Douglas spoke carefully, "uh, but God does."

J.B. scowled at the little Bible and harrumphed around a bit. Finally, "You can use the shower if you need to and wash some clothes."

Douglas slept guardedly on the couch. The camp memories as well as life in prison meant he never totally relaxed. Only outside, under the trees, in shacks and abandoned barns did he let down his guard somewhat.

After leaving J.B.'s he eventually hitched a ride for himself and his bicycle across the scrubby, rocky regions of west Texas. He fell in love with New Mexico and its mountainous forests. In southern California, he joyously flung up his last handfuls. The way back east, would go faster even though he would make frequent stops to check his handiwork.

Taking a chance, he stopped back at J.B's as J.B pulled his truck into the driveway. They shouted a greeting to each other as Douglas rolled to a stop. J.B. launched into discussion.

"I may look like a bubba, young man. But I ain't no bubba. No sir. But I tell you what, if you look the part and act the part, and talk the part, you'd be surprised at what all a right-thinking righteous Godly man can do." J.B. folded his huge arms. "But you already know that, don't you?" Douglas felt his heart sink. J.B.'s gun sat in the same rack in the back window of the truck.

"You and your little Bibles trying to fool folk with foolish talk." J.B. snorted. "But not me."

Douglas remained calm. "But not you." *Let him ramble a while then when he's not looking...*

"Nope. Not me. 'Specially not after I saw what pushed up in my backyard a month after you left." J.B. casually reached into the truck window and unhooked the shotgun with one hand and pulled out a dead rabbit with the other. "Let's take a look."

Together, they walked behind J.B.'s barn where he'd piled rusty junk metal in a circle around the weed patch. Totally invisible from the road, Douglas noted. His heart thudded as he tried to calculate distance, wind speed, trajectory and gravity. *Could he take this guy?*

"See here? You see all that?" J.B. pointed with the shotgun at the crowd of weeds that stood five feet tall, lush and leafy with buds of promise.

"Son, you gotta learn to remove the male plants. Otherwise, it's no good, I'm telling ya. Now, you young people need to remember, and I think you will that a thing worth doing is worth doing right."

Douglas stared in wonder. J.B. jabbed the shotgun towards the plants more insistently.

"Yes," Douglas quickly spoke up. "Yes indeed." He nodded seriously.

"Some laws were made to be broken." J.B. winked, slapped his thigh, and roar-laughed.

Douglas swallowed. "Some laws were meant to be broken." He chuckled tightly at first and then more enthusiastically as he helped J.B. to enjoy his little joke on him.

"Even my friends who are the law know that. They won't bother you. Long as you speak your mind at the right time, Douglas."

Other recipients of Douglas's unselfish ambition weren't so pleased. Later that evening, he and J.B. watched as the networks broke the news:

"As you can see from this map, the initial reports came from the southeastern United States. However, large patches have been reported from all four corners of the country. Apparently, the idea catches on as word continues to spread about the mysterious "Johnny Ganjaweed." Police are currently reviewing their strategy for dealing with this new phenomenon. When marijuana grows like dandelions in every backyard, including that of our own governor, how do you enforce the drug laws that apply?"

The middle-aged male newscaster bumped a small sheaf of papers on the news desk as he read the teleprompter.

"In a strange reversal, a public that has half of its earnings earmarked for law enforcement at local, state, and federal level, the unspoken theory of that same…"

Here, Douglas wondered if he heard the word *sane* instead.

"…public seems to be that some laws are meant to be broken."

The newscaster turned to the younger female co-anchor to share one of their usual scripted joking moments before signing off.

"Next thing you know, everyone will stop paying taxes and then where we would be?"

The newscasters and J.B. and Douglas all laughed together.

Story 9

Ever and Again

On Mars, the virus rewarded its hosts with lives full of glory and discovery. On Earth, the virus diminished its hosts with lives full of stigma and concealment. So Givers on Earth signed the waiting lists. Or, if they didn't like their low position on the waiting lists, they pulled strings, bribed, and blackmailed their escape from the dirty terran slums to the fresh, wide open spaces of the Red Planet.

This social upheaval began with Amaranth, 2051 A.D., Bright City. One, only one, encounter with a fellow student at her medical school changed her life forever when she became host to the worst virus to ever combine forces and mutate into a strain of near-perfect ravishment. Bitter acceptance initiated her withdrawal from the ever-diminishing mainstream society. Because as more people acquired Giver, abnormal approached closer to, but still not quite reaching, normal. Rather, abnormal acquired majority status.

She quit school and changed professions. No longer Amaranth, the Medical Intern. She became Ever and Again. On the first two floors of a five-story Bright City warehouse dwelt a perfume apothecary filled with incense and diffusers, body creams and sprays, soaps and candles, and trinkets. The apothecary mainly took care of itself with the help of a capable assistant manager. But underground, for the past three years, her extralegal, extraordinary one-woman laboratory had only one goal - to supply every pharmaceutical need her drug-addled customers desired.

In her "clinic," she outfitted one such customer, Connor, with a special implant. She imbedded him with the tiniest transmitter she could rig. Young and brash, Connor received the standard lecture:

"The transmitter is coated with a smooth layer of finish to match the human body's chemical structure. It imbeds itself inside the bone tissue of your spine. Can you feel it?"

"Yeah. It hurts. Gimme a hitta voodoo."

She bent to his ear. "Not until you're my customer for life." Amaranth continued quietly. "You do know that's what you'll be?"

"Whatever."

"Forever," she corrected.

Amaranth straightened up and continued. "No one receives your signal except me. The transmitter becomes part of your body. Untraceable by scanners. Keep the secret. Anyone who suspected would want to reverse engineer the device." She looked directly into his eyes. "They would have to kill you in order to find and remove it."

He nodded his understanding.

"Already, I can feel your signal." She smiled. "You need it badly, don't you?"

"Please." No longer nonchalant, his voice roughened to a whispered plea. "Please."

Amaranth dispensed Connor's drug of choice. Voodoo's swift, hard starburst sensation raced under his skin, along his nerve endings, through his veins, and his lungs. It froze him into a walking, functioning zombie. Amaranth watched the effect with a pleased smile. Then she called for her guards to escort him out through the underground maze of metal corridors and concrete tunnels that provided the only entrance and exit for her special customers.

"Until next time, Connor." *Until all your next times.*

"Yeah," he slurred staring transfixed at the wall until the guards gently led him through the exit.

For the rest of his life, he would return, again and again. They always returned. She customized her recipes and formulas for each customer. She perfected her craft. Every skill she learned to serve the North America Alliance's medical establishment, she applied to her own experiments. On the top floor of her private quarters, she roused her house computer.

"Everlast, check supplies and inventory. Call up all Ever and Again accounts payable. Print then erase this last request. Increase random security code sequencing to four hour intervals."

Her conscience did not bother her. But the change in her skin color did. Quiet and latent for the spring and summer months, Giver made the skin of its human hosts change from warm ivory, yellow, orange, red, brown, and black tones to a frightfully bluish-greenish, purple whenever temperatures dropped below 14° Fahrenheit. Then the virus activated and raked its cold anger back and forth across the host's body, like freezing cold animal claws, until temperatures rose once more. Extremely unpleasant. Those closer to the Earth's equator had it much easier. The virus slept year-round. Those who lived in environments where seasonal extremes changed like clockwork simply withdrew into their homes rather than face the looks of disgust, contempt, and horror during the cold months of the year.

In Bright City, Amaranth remained indoors year-round. Everything she needed, she had her robots build into the various rooms of her warehouse. High profit and low overhead meant she could afford to pay her staff well and purchase relative anonymity. In return, her staff served as loyal intermediaries to the outside world. In fact, she noted as she flipped through the print-outs, she had a large delivery scheduled for later tonight.

"World news, Everlast," she spoke aloud. A square hologram appeared in front of the couch on which she lay. Health, politics, the war, the environment, space science, fashion, art, or the economy?

The usual.

"Music."

Rhythmic sounds of pounding, grinding gears and metallic screams filled the room.

Janus paced his dormitory room at Bright City's Galaxy Space Center attempting to collect himself. Fifty years ago, the city concluded that two airports represented prestige. However, one airport plus one space center equaled profit and progress on a worldwide scale.

"Two years," he muttered to himself over and over. "Two years."

Mining and processing of dwindling fossil fuels ignited the third World War twenty-five years ago. North America just barely managed to defend its borders and people from satellite weapons directed by Middle Eastern nations. Hence, the North America Alliance with Mexico and Canada. But the shock of former religious enemies combining forces overwhelmed then engulfed the other great powers. Europe, due to unfortunate proximity, took massive hits, as did Asia.

South and Central America, the North and South Poles, Australia, and a few miscellaneous islands survived the satellites. But they did not survive the germs. As quickly as these nations inoculated their populations, new viruses and bacteria entered the First World air and water supplies. The germs mutated. The vaccines increased in potency. The germs mutated again… and again… and again. The result – Giver – the secret fourth World War fought in laboratories, under microscopes, by men and women in white lab coats.

Janus knew his mission. He trained for years with his five-man crew. One of the five was actually a woman, but for the purpose of the mission, she would pull a man's weight and then some.

"Two years," he muttered again trying to remain calm, rational.

Henry, their director, briefed them earlier that afternoon, "You five are worth billions of dollars each to the industrialists. From the benefit of their particular means of persuasion, the N. A. A. decided to redirect a significant portion of military funding to Seek-Explore. Mars, out there," Henry pointed dramatically to the ceiling, "that is Earth's future. You will create our world to come."

Janus moved his lips, unconsciously, following along with Henry's typically over-the-top presentation.

"Every two years, Mars and Earth come into alignment whereby the least amount of fuel and time would be expended for inter-planetary exploration. That's 40 million miles worth of adventure towards opportunity," he reminded them. Janus wondered why Henry didn't just pass out coloring books and crayons.

"The combination of solar and nuclear energy means twenty days en route. You have ten days on the surface to determine whether to lift off immediately by group consensus or majority vote. After ten days, you remain two years for the next window of return. Other craft will reach the surface five days ahead of your ship, The Seeker landing between you and the North Pole."

Janus's team nodded wearily at the same lecture they'd been given the last five years. Janus nodded as well to be a good role model and to hopefully head off the lecture's second portion which included diagrams, holograms, maps, and pictures. And pointing, lots of pointing.

"Don't worry. If you decide to remain, *Captain Janus*," Henry deliberately went off script as Janus straightened himself, "you will not be bored." Unlike now, Henry clearly implied.

Now, Janus stood in front of his mirror full of the doubt that threatened to morph into desperation if he didn't do something soon. For a few hundred dollar generic debit cards, he slipped out of Galaxy Space Center. He paid cash for ask-me-no-questions transportation, and headed towards central Bright City.

Amaranth felt his signal. "January," he called himself. *Yeah right. Then I'm March.* But whatever. She knew her role. Ever and Again supplied the demand. Nothing else mattered. And he was a long-time customer. One of the first she implanted three years ago, as a matter of fact.

"I need more."

"More goldfire? I can't give you more than this dose. More than this would shut your body down completely."

"I need a two year supply."

Amaranth stared, thrown off by the authoritative clipped tone. She spoke slowly and deliberately.

"I don't do two year supplies, January. I dispense as needed. One hit at a time. You know this."

"Two years worth."

"Can't do it."

"Won't do it?"

"Won't. Can't. And won't."

Janus looked at her without speaking. He looked around the room seeming to reason something out in his head. Amaranth glanced impatiently towards the exit to the tunnels. She needed him gone so she could relax and listen to the near-unintelligible mix of Chinese-Swahili grind - the latest rage in music. On the far side of the building, the guards unloaded her shipment of chemicals for the apothecary. Janus knew his own way out of the clinic through the tunnel by now anyway.

"You sure?" he asked her.

"Very sure."

Janus grabbed her. Bent her to his will. Hurt her. Forced her to comply. Within one hour, she'd given him everything he asked for. Other things he took. What he did not realize until much later was that Amaranth had given him something he did not ask for - the gift that gave forever.

An astronaut made a pretty decent living, particularly an astronaut with the fate of the world hanging on his ability to lead with creative, ingenious vision. The lab technician tapped "Normal" on the status touch screen. Janus handed over a generic debit card. By the time he got dressed again, the scratches and bite marks on his arms, chest, and shoulders had already healed from the lab technician's application of skin glue.

"The package is aboard, sir."

Janus silently handed the electronics specialist his last debit card. *Let the countdown begin.*

The crew huddled quietly with Henry for another pep talk. No one seemed bored this time. They endured media shouts for comment. They solemnly shook hands with all of Galaxy Space Center's elite. One wave to onlookers, then they raced to the heavens on Janus's tenth outer space mission - the fifth as captain.

Beyond Earth's atmosphere, they relaxed. Twenty days of scheduled system checks, simulations, and daily reports ensued. Will, one of the crewmen spoke to Janus now.

"I think an old dog at Galaxy taught Lacey some new tricks."

Janus shook his head. "Not this trip."

"What are you, married now?"

"Just keeping my head clear. I need to focus on the mission."

"So old Henry got to you, hunh? Then that's just more for me and Todd and Barry."

"And then some."

Will guffawed. Janus's "And then some," comment immediately became Lacey's code name among the men. Lacey questioned Janus as well.

"You're so aloof and remote. Is something wrong?"

Janus fixed his eyes towards the silent void beyond the observation window.

"We're bringing the past to a future world, Lacey. Or the future to a past world." He turned away with a weary sigh. "I have habitat sim with my 'bot in fifteen minutes."

Lacey, with three other men to distract her, didn't think too long on it. The other men certainly didn't.

Already isolated, Amaranth withdrew even further. She angrily dismissed her human guards, acquired robot guards, and increased electronic safeguards around her building. She told no one the reason why. Hundreds of implants signaled for supernova, goldfire, dragon's kiss, magic carpet, cobra, freak on it, silky milk, electric dream, and more. She ignored them all. They begged and cried to her piteously. Then one by one, the signals ceased. Other dealers swiftly stepped into the gap. She did not receive a signal from January. *Of course not*, she shuddered.

She ordered the basic necessities of life through Everlast and instructed the apothecary staff through Everlast as well. The robot guards picked up each delivery faithfully. She existed for no one but herself anymore, and for no other reason than just to live - until the day she decided to visit her quiet underground clinic. She turned on the instrument panels one by one. She activated Everlast's computer displays.

"Everlast, retrieve all information on Giver."

"We're guinea pigs, basically. They want to know whether Mars can support human life," Janus explained during their meal prior to exploration. "Us."

"And whether there's gold in them thar hills," Will drawled.

"So, let's see what we can see."

"Yoohooooooo. Maaaaaaartians," Will sang in a spooky voice once they were outside the ship. And they all actually looked around to see whether anything on the rocky plain stirred. Only the cold silence answered Will. They chuckled self-consciously.

The crew surveyed the supplies they found on the ground and conducted several tests and experiments. Janus made up his own mind on the fifth day. By the seventh day, the team agreed with him.

"Okay. So we know from picking up the other cargo that base camp's just a day's journey south of the polar ice caps by rover. We'll set the water processor further north on the ice. And the solar array and the habitats here. And the hydroponic unit between us and the processor."

No coal, oil, and ore to stake out for future violence here. The only gold was the deadly radiant, orangey sun.

But their 'bots did not mind solar radiation. They did not weary. They did not grow cold, hot, hungry, thirsty, tired, or disoriented. They did require maintenance, however. Every day, the crew faithfully vacuumed the dust out of their particular 'bot and checked its programming, circuitry, and power supply. Someday, a cast of fifty more humans and fifty more robots would inhabit the red planet.

Along a southern exploratory route for underground water sources, they located and retrieved Viking 1 and Viking 2 then Pathfinder then Sojourner, then other dust-covered craft.

"We'll try for Spirit and Opportunity another time. This is plenty to please the folks back home." They marked the landing sites. Then they checked the interiors of their collection and analyzed whatever data they could recover.

Lacey perished first. Scooping great hunks of frozen carbon dioxide and rust-colored regolith in the tractor, she veered off-course with her robot obediently following behind as fast as it could. The rest of the crew chased the wayward tractor in the exploratory rover. By the time they reached her hours later, she'd already expired within her suit. Not from a rupture they determined.

Two, three, four. Barry, Will, and Todd followed Lacey's journey to Mars heaven.

"Mission report to Galaxy. Three months after landing, only I, Captain Janus, and the five robots remain." Janus paused with momentary grief. "Janus out." Todd's death upset Janus to an abruptness designed to conceal his fear and guilt from Galaxy.

And me? What is my judgment from the Red Planet?

Janus rigged up four body bags from extra material aboard the Seeker that the other crew would never need for anything else. The bodies remained frozen in Martian atmosphere. For the next year and half, he would be alone with only his thoughts, his conscience, his food supplies, the robots, and goldfire. Grimly, Janus continued the base construction operating all five robots as well as he could. The frantic messages from Earth arrived at regular intervals for answers Janus did not supply.

During the day, Amaranth drove herself and Everlast with continuous experimentation on Giver. At night, she huddled in her bedroom under heated blankets. With the profits she'd earned so far as drug manufacturer and supplier, plus silent owner and manager of Ever and Again, she could live pretty comfortably for the next six years. She could conduct the research and never miss the whole world. Or she could live uncomfortably for the rest of her life if she scaled back. How could one man destroy her? And how could she let him? One terrible, unfortunate night rendered her powerless to defend herself. And how easy it was to do.

A robot guard delivered the hand-written message, "Savion taking over. You are informed."

"No response," she told the robot. She made no move to stop her former rival for Bright City territory. She ignored him and his associates. They ignored her in return.

Exhausted, she finally took a night off from lab work. Upstairs, she flipped from fashion and music to current news. Bad news, really. The news was always very bad which is why she usually avoided those channels.

"The spread of Giver has increased. Populations continue to move southward overwhelming warmer cities... Texas refuses to accept..."

"Everlast, change station up."

"...availability of clean drinkable water decreases every year..." Amaranth sighed loudly. "... N.A.A. police surround the Great Lakes region in vain..."

"Change station up."

"Europe and Russia sent ships to join the Middle East's blockade of sub-Sahara Africa in an effort to contain..."

"Change station up."

"Captain Janus of Galaxy Space Center's Seek-Explore Mission is due to arrive in the Earth's atmosphere in ten days. The Seek-Explore..."

"Change sta..."

The screen flashed a picture of the captain. Amaranth felt her stomach lurch then tie itself into knots. *January, the Destroyer.*

"Everlast, keep station."

"After two years working to establish a home base on Mars, the captain of The Seeker remains under a cloud due to the unexplained loss of four of his human crew. Scientists at Galaxy Space Center have not commented publicly or responded to persistent demands for information from the mission's funders, the media, or the general public. At this time, Captain Janus is not considered a suspect."

Surrounded on all sides, Janus marched stiffly through Galaxy Space Center's corridors. The multiple decontaminations, the long quarantine, the invasive examinations, the aggressive interrogations, all of it aroused no sense of outrage within him. Janus passively accepted the punishment he knew he deserved.

They did not find his drug supply. After one last hit, he ejected the remainder outside Earth's atmosphere. Undetectable and untraceable, which is why goldfire became his drug of choice in the first place, they found no sign of it within his body either.

The chemists finished with him. The biologists and virologists went to work. Meanwhile, pathologists and coroners worked on the dead bodies of his crew. The psychologists stepped forward as the first to grudgingly accept what Janus told them.

"He did not kill the Seek-Explore crew."

"Then why did he survive while they died?"

"Something about him, something must be different."

The scientists who reviewed Janus's past medical screenings realized something did not add up.

"He broke pre-mission quarantine."

"That means he endangered the crew. So he did kill them." Henry blanched.

"He's a Giver. He had to have been a Giver before lift-off because he hasn't been out of our sight since his return. But that's not the strange part. None of the other crew have the virus."

They confronted Janus who wearily confirmed their conclusion.

Amaranth followed the story closely as it took over world media. She knew what they did not know. She knew because Janus's implant signaled her once more after two years of silence. Literally under the microscope of so many scientists, he did not have access to her mix of goldfire.

Amaranth smiled knowingly. "Suffer, Captain Janus."

Oh yes, she knew.

The scientists spoke with Henry.

"We isolated the Giver virus from the Mars microbes. From Janus's cultures, we know that they neutralize one another to benign symbiotic states permitting survival of the host on Mars."

"How did the crew pick up the microbes?"

"There are... striking similarities in structure between Giver virus and the microbes. We think... the microbes originated on Earth.

"What!"

"Decades ago, the United States and the Soviet Union and a few other nations launched unmanned space craft to photograph Mars and collect soil samples. Some crashed to the surface. The crew collected some of the craft as part of the mission."

"Right. So what?"

"The sun's radiation sterilized them, for the most part. Some of the interiors contained just the slightest amount of Earth microbes. Tiny particles. But enough."

"So when the crew opened them up..."

"They were exposed to earlier forms of Earth virus."

Henry sat back wearily shaking his head.

Janus felt her answer. She'd never communicated back to him before. He never even realized his transmitter was also a receiver. Within the privacy of his brain, they conducted a harsh exchange.

"You're a Giver, Captain Janus. Aren't you?"

"Everyone knows this."

"Do they know... how? When?"

Silence.

"I remember that night. Do you?"

She waited. Finally, he responded, "Yes."

She felt his shame and sorrow, rejected both, and hardened her heart.

"Guilt is not good enough, Captain Janus."

"What do you want?"

"You really need goldfire, don't you?"

He overwhelmed her with pure, raw, desperate need to which she responded with intense revulsion and then the cruelest mockery she could muster.

"What would they say? Would they even let you pilot an amusement park glider if they knew?"

"Blackmail me? You're a drug dealer. Not such a far step to assume you're a liar as well. They'll never believe you. No trace, remember?"

"Everyone else will. And, of course, there's always my implant of ownership inside you. What do you think would happen to you if they found out?"

"What do you want?"

"You," she said with a deliberate pause, "...are the doorway to my future. Shall I turn the key, or just smash my way through and damn the consequences?"

"What? Bitch!"

That's anger. Amaranth smiled. *But not nearly enough.*

"I want Mars."

"Then do it, Henry."

"No return," Henry reminded Janus grimly. "No return ever."

"I'd hoped there wouldn't be."

Scorned on Earth, pilots, deep sea divers, miners, construction, policemen, electronic technicians, landscapers, and a few mechanics formed a long line of applicants for training. Nearly two years later, fifty men and women, Givers all, journeyed to Mars accompanied by fifty robots. The four extra robots left in storage on Mars from the previous tragic trip would join in hazard duty — analyzing the microbe-infected relic rovers.

"Thank you, Robbie."

Every day, Amaranth's robot faithfully collected the frozen carbon dioxide and regolith which she mixed with various nutrients and minerals. As soon as she found the right combination to grow Earth plants, they would have a sizeable greenhouse garden. And not only hydroponic. She expectantly eyed the smallest hints of green peeking through the tips of seeds.

"You are quite welcome, Dr. Amaranth. I have time for one more trip before the sun sets."

"Very well, then."

Janus's implant still called to hers throughout his long withdrawal. Worse, his body still associated the sight of her with goldfire and the craving intensified whenever he saw her. She loathed him for that and, of course, he knew that. She kept the secret of his drug addiction and his violent attack on her. He kept the secret of her Ever and Again operation. Though Janus avoided Amaranth whenever possible, he stood in her doorway now.

She eyed him coldly. *Not this time, Janus. Never again. I'll kill both of us if I have to.* She cocked the diffuser with its deadly load inside her lab pocket.

"No supply, Captain. No supply ever. My Earth life is over."

"My Earth life is over as well."

"Good." She tightened her mouth a moment. "People respect me here."

"I knew you were qualified when I presented your case."

"We don't owe each other a damn thing further, *Captain Janus.*"

"One day... Amaranth... you can forgive me."

She hated the sound of her name in his mouth. "That day is not today. Have the courtesy to stay out of my sight, Janus. Forever." She abruptly closed her mouth and stared at him. He stood a moment waiting for...

What? She wondered as she clutched the diffuser even more tightly in her fist. Janus retreated and kept his distance until his body and mind finally released him from goldfire.

The Martians discussed their new elite status over dinner in the largest habitat, the first they finished from Janus's base design.

"The strangest thing is that Giver still has a social stigma on Earth."

"It's the only ticket off that polluted rock."

"Aren't you the snobby one now?"

"Well, it's true."

"Earth is dying. They'll either have to accept the virus or rot."

"I heard that the rich folks buy synthesized inoculations through private doctors. Like that's classier." They all laughed a trifle snidely.

"Did you hear about that guy who hacked the N. A. A. medical and pharmaceutical lists? He..."

"I thought it was a woman."

"*He* posted the names..."

A few of the other women chimed in, "It was a woman!"

"...of all Giver carriers on the worldwide network. And now the poor Givers are being solicited for their virus."

"Some things never change."

The Martians toasted this.

"A lot of them are hustling to pay their passage here."

"Well, lucky us for already knowing we had nothing to lose."

Another toast.

Amaranth toasted with them and gingerly sipped the wine someone had thoughtfully smuggled aboard the ship.

On Earth, the Mars microbes escaped from Galaxy laboratories, likely with anarchist help. The outbreak worked its way up and down the Western hemisphere. Then it became a race to the death to acquire Giver. Because in another two years, two hundred more terrans would journey to the fourth planet.

Best for all Martians to be ready for the New World.

Story 10

Waterscape

Gray under the sun. Blue in the shadow. At night, he was a silver moonlit mist with metallic eyes that pierced through the dark forest canopy. Wolf was one of seven until his brothers and sisters drove him from the pack.

Mer Amla wound and curved her long body sensuously, sinuously around rocks, through plants, across hills and valleys. After a long journey, she was almost home. Though thoughts of her mate and their child remained forty-two years after the relentless pursuit, the scissoring teeth, and the cold, shredded death; she was visibly serene and no sadness slowed her exploration of these fields. She sensed her loneliness but accepted it. Loneliness was her choice.

Harsh, guttural growls invaded Wolf's daydream of Her. Inscrutable now, Her eyes no longer revealed a welcomed seduction, just… betrayal. She casually moved from her mate's side to wait. She would always belong to the victor.

Leaning against a rock, Mer Amla looked upward to the clear blueness of the sky through clumps of waving leaves that bent and touched each other. She lifted a muscular arm strengthened by eighty years of existence through laughter, sorrow, and heartache. Her community, her home, and her love were forsaken and cast away by fate or maybe by nature. She was not sure which. No matter.

They did not understand her fear and hate. The gray shadows that circled above and below were always part of their world. The gifts the world gave to her and her charmed community – extended life, warm blood, sight with sound, the capacity to store oxygen – were equalized by vulnerability to the most efficient, unstoppable predator.

After a period of mourning, community tradition demanded she mate with another like Mer Kal. But there could be no other. She wanted to be alone now with her memories.

They no longer asked.

Covered in blood and furrows of bare flesh, Wolf howled his shock and disbelief. His brothers and sisters chorused the reply. Banished, there would be no return. Ever. They'd sensed his dwindling strength and endurance. They hated that weakness with an angry passion fueled by instinctive rage towards the disturbance of the social order. And so, they turned. Four of them joined Her mate, the leader of the pack, to bring stability back to the group while She observed all in disgust.

Wolf stumbled away, silvery tail and head down. Banishment was absolute. And so, he wandered, searching and sniffing and howling his anguish. Other packs heard his story moaning on the wind and recommended that he continue his journey elsewhere. There. Far away from here. His one option would be to join with a lone female to form a new pack. Sadly, he looked for another Her. In the meantime, he killed rabbits and hares, mice, and birds. Sometimes, he caught fish.

Surfacing for one last breath, Mer Amla's eyes adjusted to survey the waves running a path towards her shore. The late afternoon sun reflected from her eyes causing them to blaze with golden fire and life. Slipping back underwater, her eyes readjusted to the distortion as she turned towards home, plucking plants that grew in the shallows to eat later.

The sound of buzzing whispers in his ears grew louder. A rush and crash of cymbals allowed space for curiosity in the midst of edgy malcontent. Ahead he saw sky through the forest trees and loped forward. Wolf's ears pricked forward in excited curiosity. Birds screamed and swooped and wheeled and he leaped forward through the trees with an eager, whining bark. Abruptly, he came to a halt where the ground dropped away and water struck repeated blows against the rocky cliff.

Mer Amla crouched in a tide pool five feet deep and a near perfect oval of twenty feet at its widest point running parallel to shore and eleven feet at its narrowest point perpendicular to shore. The sun warmed the water, to a silky whisper and caress against her skin. A brownish head and torso smoothed down towards the blue-green tail that revealed her mutation. Tangled brown hair floated like ropes of seaweed around her head. She explored the contents of the tide pool with a series of happy, high-pitched squeaks. There was always food here.

The world was different. Here, water danced before him as far as his eye surveyed. Below, the water met the land and raced to cover it, beat against it, then race back. Wolf stood stock-still, fascinated by the cacophony of sight and sound. His keen eyes noted a large oval below the water within which a large form floated, turned, and twitched. Over the sound of birds and waves, he heard a piercing shriek inside his head. Something, *that* thing, screamed at him from under the water. He bristled and growled a response. The thing quieted for a moment and Wolf waited tensely. The dark shadow below the water moved jerkily. Smaller shadows darted around the larger shadow. This time, the growl rose from his stomach rather than his throat. Fish! He picked his way carefully down the rocky slope.

Mer Amla saw the dark shadow above her. She felt a vibration of sound from the menace. The land thing took a step forward and touched the water. Mer Amla drew nearer and positioned herself defensively. This was her water. It was *always* her water.

The land thing took another step forward and to the side as if to circle around her back. Mer Amla met that advance with a counter-advance the same direction. The land thing barked roughly. Mer Amla froze in the water and stared calculatingly. She emitted a series of squeaks normally used to seek shapes and distance under the water. The thing on land went wild and bounded into the water. Mer Amla sprang forward and grabbed its legs out from under and yanked it off-balance.

The mermaid and the wolf battled in an explosion of frenzied splashing, barking, and shrieking.

Wolf fought It with teeth and claws. He bit into her over and over. He raked his claws against the tough, slippery-smooth skin of her upper torso creating parallel rows of red that clouded the water. His claws tangled in the thing's hair and he was caught. He bit the thing about the face and neck and chest until one arm snaked out a strong hand that gripped his throat. The thing's other hand joined at his throat in an everlasting embrace from which he could not disentangle. The thing twisted its tail rapidly. Over the thing's shoulder Wolf saw the tidepool, the cliff, and the shore grow smaller. He gave one final weak bark. Then he saw nothing as his unwilling descent began.

The land thing hurt her. She bled from her arms and chest and back. And although it no longer struggled with its teeth and claws, it held her in a forced embrace. Its claws pulled and then stuck in her hair. Its teeth locked onto her shoulder. They sank together from blue to dark blue to violet to black. She was tired. At last, the thing twitched and released her. She moved away a few feet to watch it die.

There were shadows overhead. Agitation and blood in the water always brought the shadows. The shadows circled lower. The thing she dragged to the smothering depths would be shredded by vicious, merciless, unstoppable blades while she made her own getaway. Just like…

No. *No!*

She grabbed the land thing and trailed its and her own blood behind in a race back to the shallows. The shadows pursued as she wound and twisted over hills and valleys, dodged through clumps of seaweed, and feinted around rocks. The shadows finally turned back from the shallow water.

She was exhausted. She was bleeding. It was so heavy. But the land thing needed land… and air. She rarely left the water except when she was inside her home. She would take the land thing home.

Wolf awakened in a strange, dark, wet place on something hard. There was water close by. He had been under water. He remembered. But now, water was underneath him. It was dark. It was night? He couldn't see the sky even though his eyes were open. No moon and no stars. No trees. No wind. He didn't understand. He sighed and lay back down.

From the surrounding water, Mer Amla watched the thing on the ledge carefully. It was awake. She felt the air move when he turned his head to look around. The last time she watched him like this, he attacked her. This time he lay still.

Light. From different directions. From the walls. Water. And the water thing. It watched him. Wolf growled a warning. The last time he watched the water thing, it dragged him until he couldn't breathe. This time, it didn't move. He growled again. It twisted and disappeared. It was gone. He didn't sense it nearby anymore. He lay back down and slept.

When he awakened once more, the light in the walls was dimmer. Two fish lay in front of him gasping for air. He remembered what not breathing felt like and whined worriedly. One of the fish stopped its gasps. He looked around carefully before he ate it. The water thing was nearby. He could sense it. He growled another warning and ate the second fish.

He stayed awake for a long time to make sure the water thing kept its distance. He growled for long intervals. Then he slept.

She hauled herself onto her ledge whenever the land thing slept. Then flipped off quickly when the change in his breathing warned her he would wake up soon. The teeth and claws had not left her memory. But he belonged to her now. She would keep him and not be lonely. Their fight together, their near death together, and their recovery together bound them together. Forever.

From the tidepool and down, down, down to her home at the underwater base of the cliff, she glided. There, a small opening hidden by rocks led to a tunnel that went up, up, up into the cliff. At approximately the same level where the water greeted the air outside the cliff, the water met the air inside the cliff and widened into a pool. Here was the circular ledge she shared with the land thing. The level of the water rose and fell, but it never covered the ledge. The changing levels just made it harder or easier to haul herself up over the edge. She could just manage the small climb with her arms when the level was low. The tunnel continued upwards beyond the ledge. From here, sunlight reflected back and forth across rocks encrusted with crystal. Air seeped in with the light. But Mer Amla had no interest in the longer climb up jagged, dry rock. Her life was here and below.

The land thing was awake. It didn't like her still. She saw the promise of destruction in its eyes and the stance of its body as it stood up.

Wolf sensed the water thing before he saw it below the water's surface. When it broke the surface, he stood up and growled. After two days of rest, he was ready now. It still bore his marks on its face and torso. It knew he would fight. Silver eyes met golden eyes for a long moment.

Stand-off.

Lazily, so It would know he was not afraid, he flicked his gaze to what the thing held in its hand. His stomach growled. The water thing heard that. Their eyes met again. The water thing moved closer without seeming to move. He bared his teeth and rumbled in his throat. If the water thing snatched him again, this time he would win.

The water thing threw two fish down on the ledge then glided out of reach of his snapping teeth. He watched the water thing that watched him as he ate the fish.

It left.

He was thirsty. He couldn't drink this water. He tried once when it rose higher but it stung his dry mouth. The fish kept him from starving, but they were salty too. He couldn't go down into the water where the water thing lived. He would go up to the light.

She remembered this land thing from before. From the first life. It was... wolf. It was dangerous. It had teeth. Like the gray shadows. But Wolf had fur. The fur was very warm – coarse on top and softer next to his skin. She'd felt him while he was asleep. She hated the shadows that took so much from her with no remorse. What would this land shadow take?

"Wolf," she said aloud, testing the name.

It didn't matter. When she returned to her ledge, Wolf was gone. She lay down in relief.

Wolf woke with a start. It was night. He knew it was night because he heard the trees whisper it to him. He felt the wind. He couldn't see the stars or the moon, but he could look up and see the sky. The water thing was gone. No. Not gone. *Down there.*

He padded back to the top of the cliff and considered all that happened in the hours since he climbed down the rocky incline to investigate the tidepool. The water thing fought him and tried to kill him. Then it fed him. Wolf looked down at the tidepool curiously. He sensed only quiet within the water. Tail and head down, Wolf tiredly headed back to the small hollow he piled with leaves - his make-shift den for the night.

It was damp. It would rain before morning. Soon he would be wet again. Thirst was no longer a problem. He'd found a stream nearby after he emerged from the tunnel. He was still hungry though. Tomorrow, he would hunt. Wolf sighed and sniffed around the leaves cautiously before he turned them around for an appropriate resting place.

Sure enough, rain came. It poured in sheets through the leaves and drenched Wolf who huddled miserably until the small hollow filled with leaves became a muddy puddle. He stood and shook himself. The rain immediately drenched him again.

Miserable.

Mer Amla lay still. She heard It above her. She smelled It. Wet fur. Wolf was back. This was her ledge. She would not move. This time, if the land shadow attacked, she would hold it under water forever. It would die. Closer. It came closer. It growled and whined in its throat.

Something small and wet fell on her head. It was smooth with four legs and bulging eyes. It twitched, barely alive. She remembered this thing. In her first life she ate this thing. The land shadow remained still, waiting for her to finish eating, waiting for permission.

Mer Amla lay down warily. Wolf lay down warily next to her. But during the night, he curled around her.

Mer Amla and Wolf shared the ledge and the cave. She swam down and out. He climbed up and over. They shared the treasures of the tide pool. He ate the food she brought him from the deeper parts of the ocean though it wiggled and squirmed. He even chewed seaweed. He brought her what he caught in the stream and forest. He brought her raspberries because she loved those. Sometimes she'd found them floating in freshwater on the other side of the cliff.

They developed a language of their own. Spoken, unspoken, barked, squeaked.

She placed her hand over her heart. "Mer Amla." Then she touched his head softly as he whined. "Wolf. Wolf. *Wolf?*"

She tried to take him out of the tunnel through the underground entrance. He roared and snapped. She quickly released him to sit back on the ledge glaring with outrage. Once he tried to drag her upwards over the rocks to his own world. She hit him. But things like that happened only sometimes.

In the tide pool, their favorite game was to race. Wolf loped on land back and forth while Mer Amla kept pace under water. At night, they met on the ledge to sleep. Social creatures without a society, they needed each other.

Once, something followed Mer Amla inside the cave. A small gray shadow nipped her tail. More surprised than hurt, she wondered if a baby shadow could be a pet. She decided not. Baby shadows grew. She would have to kill it. Before she could, Wolf barked and leaped off the ledge. He bit through the shadow's head in a riotous splashing of the water. Then he scrambled back up the ledge with her arms giving him a boost. She retrieved the shadow and they ate it together. It was delicious.

Wolf paddled around the water in the cave now and then. Mer Amla wondered if he were patrolling or bathing. He didn't seem to fear the water as much. Still, she didn't touch him while he was in the water. That made him nervous and very snappish.

Finally, she climbed and flopped her way towards the top of the cave tunnel with Wolf whining anxious encouragement and tugging at her now and then. She felt a rush of memory of her first life. Wolf sat and looked at Mer Amla a moment. From the waist up, Mer Amla resembled The Ones Who Walk Upright. The kind his own kind always ran from at first sight.

But Mer Amla did not walk.

Wolf ran off to tear off part of the raspberry bush and then ran back. She ate most and he ate a few she gave him. Wolf lay down and she stroked his fur.

Soon, however, it became difficult to breathe. And her skin hurt. She remembered the sun used to feel good. Now, it burned. She flopped back towards the cool dampness of the tunnel entrance because the tide pool was much too far. Wolf had to help her part of the way. Once was enough. She

was not who she used to be. None of her kind were anymore. She sang to him
as she stroked him to try to make him understand:

Generations live and die
Yellow turns to gray
Sun rises in the sky
Moon takes sun away

Light returns to shadow
Fire burns to smoke
Jaundice ends in pallor
Wind blows south and north

The way of the world
We remember we forget
Universe is circular
Give what you get

Wood weathers dark
Dandelion goes to seed
River runs to the ocean
What was shall ever be

Eyes to see forever
Ears that don't listen
Gold will be silver
The endless lesson

The way of the world
We remember we forget
Universe is circular
Give what you get

Universe is circular
You become what you hate
Future will be history
You remember it too late

Wolf howled his response. He knew something of that world. Something else happened on the ledge. Wolf climbed on top of her.

She didn't stop him.

She finally figured out a route to Wolf's stream by following the fresh water on the other side of the cliff to a small opening in the rock. Mer Amla swam and climbed upwards through the current until she found herself surrounded by light and forest. Wolf was delighted and wouldn't stop barking. They raced again.

At the stream, in the cave, and in the tidepool, they told each other things. Mer Amla learned that Wolf could never return to his kind. His kind would kill him. She told him that she *wouldn't* return to hers. No more pilgrimages. She'd already brought so many into their community. She had done her part. Her home was here. This was her place. He was her Wolf. She was his Mer Amla.

Five years passed.

Wolf matured. Mer Amla did not change much in such a short period of time. But Wolf slowed. Mer Amla fed him more often than he fed her. He didn't like that. Though he loved her, he was unhappy. Once in a while, she wondered if he longed for his own kind – especially when he snapped at her. Something she could not see called to him. It told him about the Sleep of No End.

But she would never let him go. *Never.*

Meanwhile, in the forest, Wolf deliberately picked a fight over a fresh kill. Riddled with deep gashes, Wolf crept back down to the underground ledge to wait for the Sleep. Mer Amla found him, and thus, made her decision.

Down she pulled him into the water. As it closed over his head, he struggled against her as he had years before. He clamped onto her neck with his jaws. He clawed his forepaws into her hair. His back legs scraped against the tough skin of her tail. He'd never been able to damage that part of her. Together, they spiraled rapidly through the tunnel and back up to the surface of the sea.

If she could get him there in time, it would be all right – at least, mostly all right. Wrapped tightly with Wolf, she cut through currents with her tail towards the warmer water. She swam at the surface so both she and a weakened Wolf could gulp the air.

Then down, down, down Mer Amla pulled Wolf into another spiral to the blackest bottom of the ocean. Here, in this strange place, hulking ships filled with stolen lives had encountered the wildest torments and most-cleverly concealed rocks just seconds before disappearing below. Here, past this littered bottom to an even deeper crevice of intense heat, a swirl of energy and a magnetic field stirred bizarre mixtures of minerals and organic matter into a boiling, bubbling, fizzy elixir. Here, in this secret place, an ancient city of Mer Amla's kind transformed its entire existence.

Here, within the circle of Mer Amla's arms, Wolf died.

The mermaid waited as the gray shadows circled lower and lower. She twitched her tail and waved her arms. They sensed her heart beat. They sensed her warmth. Her vibration was unmistakable.

The gray shadows came to feed.

She wanted them to come.

Lower, and then lower. The enormous, tooth-filled mouths yawned wide. Black eyes rolled back. And then…

Pain. Blood. Ripping flesh.

The mermaid?

The mermaid was the lure. The wolf ambushed. Wolf no longer feared the water. No fear existed for either of them anymore. Wolf's mutation reflected Amla's. Gray under the sun. Blue in the shadow. At night, he shone as a silver moonlit mist with metallic eyes that pierced through the darkest blue-black mysteries of the ocean.

The top fur fell away. The fur next to his skin coarsened and then sleeked into a smooth, dark gray second skin. His tail widened and joined with his back legs. He could hold his breath under water longer because his blood stored more oxygen. His eyes adjusted to see below the surface and he could sense his Mer Amla's nearness through sound. At first, her kind accepted him with caution. Caution led to immediate delight and a food chain revolution within her society.

"You will never be what you were." She told him this back again in their own tide pool as they looked towards the trees clutching the shore. "But you will be what you are for a very long time."

Golden gaze met silver stare.

For a moment, the world was silent.

Then back and forth, Mer Wolf and Mer Amla swam together curling and twisting and nudging as Mer Amla sang her song.

Story 11

The Lovebirds

It was unspeakable, this thing done to kings and queens in the dark corners of the slave ships, in the holding cages of the slave factories, and in the dense forests surrounding the sugar and indigo plantations. For that reason, no one spoke of it. That the sun god and moon goddess saw such things and did nothing was simply unbelievable. And the tree and rock and fire spirits that dwelt among them at Home refused to even consider residence in the barbarian New Land.

The young man collapsed into a sweaty, bloody, bruised heap in the doorway to Able's slave cabin. This young man was not the first to arrive that way. Able had arrived the same way himself, eighteen years ago. Neither of them would be the last.

The three slave-breakers stepped over the young man as they entered and spat on his crying, shaking form with contempt. The largest one wearing a hat chuckled.

"Take care of Sammyboy, Uncle Abe. He's a wild one! Just off the boat. But he'll soon learn his master. Or he'll die."

The young man screamed something unintelligible and received a hard kick to the belly that caused him to vomit. That language, a long time ago, Able used to know. But it had been to his advantage to forget. The words still tickled his memory through the mists of failed dreams and yesterdays.

"What say he, Able? You speak that voodoo?"

Able sat still and concealed his eyes. A large-sized slave with his broad shoulders had to take extra care to appear non-threatening. Fear caused anger in these men. Anger caused pain. And Sammyboy's hatred of the men burned the air. Angrily, the leader of the pack kicked the young man in the side once more.

"Sammyboy, you keep that tongue civil or we'll cut it out for you! What say he, Able? You understand him?"

Able understood. Sammy had cursed them all. He prayed to his gods for their deaths as well as his own... among many other things.

Able, frowned in diplomatic pretense of puzzlement.

"Able! Answer me! What say he?"

"Boss, he want the return of his charm, sir."

"Charm, eh? That devilish voodoo will not help him. This is a Christian land. D'ye 'ere that, monkey?"

The smaller man standing in the rear stepped up and opened a small leather bag and sprinkled the contents over Sammy. "You mean this? You want to charm us some more, eh?" He snickered.

Able looked away as Sammy clutched frantically at bird feathers and snake teeth floating and falling on the air.

"Look at him play with his toys just like a monkey!" The man laughed while a red-headed third took the opportunity to advise Sammy.

"Shut up now, Sammyboy. Or you'll get more of what you already had and like it. Charm, indeed. Good fun, boy!"

They threw the bag at the young man and each took a turn to spit on him.

"Fix him up, Uncle!"

Able shuddered in repulsion, but rose to obey.

Abo's last view of the homeland was the long river emptying out to a flat, sandy coast. There was no harbor for the large ship to dock. Lagoons behind the coastal strip allowed the smaller boats holding him and many of the disarmed members of his raiders to row themselves under threat of the gun to their destiny.

Tightly squeezed together, the ship departed when not another body could be crammed inside the hold. They were whipped. They were forced to lay in their own filth and that of their fellow captives. They were diseased by unknown sicknesses. They were made to dance. They were made to eat. They were made to live. A few were spiritually strong enough to will themselves to die. Some rushed at their captors and were killed. A few jumped to the welcoming embrace of the water gods. And one who went over the side pulled a screaming, struggling slaver with him.

All of them were made to serve. Women and girls. Men and boys. Long at sea among men, long at war among men, long in faraway colonies among men, the slavers picked out their favorites among them depending upon their particular sick needs. Abo's shock at being so cruelly used, invaded, and violated allowed him blessed disassociation from the entire ordeal. While his fellow slaves fought each other, fought the slavers, and raged against the chains, Abo allowed sweet, numbing madness to settle into his bones. By the time the ship reached the shore of the island, one-third of the captives died from disease, starvation, suicide, and murder. By the time the ship reached the shore of the island, Abo had died a thousand deaths inside the recesses of own mind. Memory died. Dreams died. Hope died. Spirit died. His body, however, lived.

There was really nothing more that they could do to him to break him further. But just to be on the safe side, they did so much more.

"Drink this."

Able held the cup of water to Sammy's mouth. He dipped a rag into the bucket to cleanse away dirt, sweat, blood, and whitish, viscous fluid from Sammy's legs.

"No!"

He snarled his own dialect angrily while Able listened silently. Words he hadn't heard for eighteen years coalesced into sentences.

"Unholy animal beasts of evil. Men who use other men like women in the land of devils. Defiled cannibals born of worms that eat excrement. I will kill them! Do you hear me, you old woman? I will kill them! And you too!"

Able handed him the wet rag and turned away without speaking.

Able stood on the auction block and looked at the ground. After one dreadful glance at the rushing sea of sweaty pink faces, wide white mouths jabbering curses, and glittering eyes that stabbed and darted over him with lust and greed, Able disappeared within once more and pretended he wasn't there. He had been broken already by the time he'd arrived to the island's shores from the ship. On the sugar plantation, they seasoned him even further to make sure the lessons he learned thus far would "take." The voyage from the sugar plantations of the island to this larger land was easier to bear. He expected the worst already and was not surprised. He'd learned the language of the slave traders on the homeland coast. He'd learned the language of the overseers at the island's sugar plantations. Now, he had another language to learn. He figured most of it out.

"Behold before you, Able! This noble prince of the Dark Land is ready and willing to serve your every need. Strong, but humble! Large, but docile! He has been trained to follow every order without question or dark look."

Another man gestured towards Able's wide shoulders. "Well suited for farms large or small. He lifts, carries, pulls, pushes, totes, and drags better than any horse!"

They forced his mouth open, roughly.

"All teeth here!"

They ran their eager, damp hands over his loins and buttocks.

"Magnificent stud animal!"

Able trembled from fear and shame. The bruises on his dark skin had been covered with oil and dark powder. Their endless excitement over him echoed the wild horse-breaking of rebellious stallions. He was a beast to conquer. Even when he submitted quietly, they bruised him as they dominated him just to prove their power.

"How can you even live? Why do you not die?"

Able cleared his throat. "It is the peculiar way of this world, Suma." The young man had insisted on the use of his real name.

"How is it you know my language?" Suma was suspicious. "You know my people."

Able chose to answer Suma's earlier question.

"I am an old man who barely remembers a life before this one. What I used to be, was beaten to the surface then bled to the ground in the indigo fields and the sugar plantations." Able stared into the fire. "Some would say that wasn't such a bad thing. You ask me how I live. My answer is I don't live. I survive until I die."

Abo drew himself up proudly. "Slavery is a tradition of war. The conqueror always rules the conquered. But now, the conquerors do not come from across the river or through the jungle. They come in boats from far away. They ask very politely with guns drawn. If we do not trade, our rivals will."

In a splendid hall filled with carvings, statues, and weapons the king made no response while a servant fanned flies away from his face. Nan took the silence as opportunity to plead her case.

"We grow rich and powerful, honored King. And we are rewarded with weapons and munitions and horses with which to subdue and capture our enemies. But instead of carrying on the business of farming, fishing, weaving, and metalwork, the best of us are used to endlessly war with people with whom we have no quarrel. We no longer have trade with the other tribes. When there are no others but ourselves left to sell, then what will we do?"

Abo was scornful. "She dares to speak against you, King, and to question your decisions. How dare *she*, a mere warrior..."

"I dare to speak for the future!"

"Her fear weakens us."

Nan, lashed directly back at the challenge. "Your greed weakens us, Abo!" She turned back to the king anxious to appear the voice of reason.

"We know of the Dark Queen of the South who fought against the ghosts for many years until the day she died. She refused to bow to their demands. It is possible to make a stand."

"Great King, if we do not secure what the ghosts want from us, they will take us, instead. Even the Dark Queen knew this at the end." Abo reached higher. "Such treachery by Nan against the kingdom is punishable only by death."

At last, the leader of the land spoke. "Do not forget your place, Abo. The honored King decides what is punished and how and why." His point made, the king continued, "The foreigners wait at our door with expectation that the king of this land keeps his word. Nan, as the leader of the warriors, your women will protect Abo's raiders on this mission against the northern tribe. Upon your victorious return, we will further discuss various methods of trade and industry. Then, you will convince me, Nan."

"Abo, upon your victorious return, you will have your choice of the best land and the best cattle." The king smiled slyly. "As well as the best woman... to reward your loyalty." The king settled back with narrowed eyes to watch their reactions.

Abo looked at the tall, well-built female warriors assembled on either side of Nan. Then he deliberately turned his gaze to Nan, the best of them all. Nan stared back at him, expressionless.

"There has to be a way to escape this hell and return to our people. Surely, you desire it. We can escape together."

"It is too far and the way too treacherous."

Suma began to repeat his curses and desperate incantations. Able cut him off before the slavers returned to investigate the noise. "Quiet, you fool! They'll hear!"

Able checked the doorway then returned to the fire.

In a quiet voice he revealed, "On the island there were whispers of red people and black people that blended together. They fought and remained free. Here, on this greater land, something similar has happened. Once in a great while, a slave or two or three vanishes in the night to the deep forests to the South. There, among the red people, they are kings and chiefs once more."

Suma spoke to the fire. "I want to go home. I want to see my people. No more of this evil world where men treat each other like beasts." Suma looked at Able sadly. "The old kingdoms have vanished, you know. The universities, the artwork, the gold, the crafts... everything is gone. What people of Home used to be is all a legend now."

Suma returned his gaze to the fire as if hypnotized and slowed his voice as he sing-songed from memory.

"The lovebirds rose up and called to us to follow away from danger. We sacrificed our village to the god of fire and he protected us. The ground shook under so many pounding feet. Sweat, heat, and fear rose in the air. The Snake gods in their lair would greet us and we would either live or die. But we would not be enslaved.

The song of the lovebirds woke the Snake gods as they flew through the darkest part of the forest. We followed swiftly behind carrying fire spirit which warned the Snake spirits to allow us passage. Through the back of the snake lair a small opening dug under the tree roots was covered by rocks and vines.

Upwards in darkness we crawled to the new home hidden on a high plateau of grass surrounded by trees and rocky cliffs, and covered by mists. We heard the screams of our pursuers and we were grateful and glad and gave thanks. The lovebird, the snake, and fire... our totems kept us safe. We will never return."

"But you are here."

"I am here."

Suma looked at Able for a long moment. "Able, I can never return Home. That place and time is dead. But I cannot remain here. Tell me how to reach the red men of the South."

"You know this territory well, Nan."

"I serve the king well, Abo."

"Perhaps you know this territory too well."

Silence.

"I am told by the wind of a meeting between a warrior of our kingdom and a sentinel of the northern tribe."

Silence.

"I am told that the meeting... went well."

Nan changed the subject as they fought through grass and low-hanging branches. "I don't like that ten of these ghosts come with us. They slow us down. Why don't they wait at the coast for us to bring captives as usual?"

She didn't like any of this.

"They insisted, Nan. As did our king. Be careful."

She also didn't like Abo.

Nan did not bother to speak to her warriors. They'd battled side by side together long enough to establish unspoken strategies. But she did not trust the look in Abo's eyes. Even now, he bumped against her from time to time in probable anticipation of all he would do when she would be given to him. The king did not allow failure. Failure equaled death or worse. Success meant Abo, the Arrogant, would have his way with her. Nan quickened her pace and moved to the point position.

Suddenly, the unthinkable happened. Nan stumbled over a tree root jutting from the soil and rolled two paces into a small tree filled with lovebirds. Never before had such a thing happened. The lovebirds rose and filled the air with distress calls and falling feathers.

"Stupid bitch! They use the birds for warning!"

Quick whistling *whisks* filled the air. Two of the foreigners fell dead. Then two of Abo's raiders. The arrows came from above in two directions. The warriors shot blindly into the trees. One warrior fell wounded. One of the foreigners screamed outrage and shot into the trees. They couldn't find a target. It was as if the trees had come to life to defend their territory with poisoned leaf tips.

Abo didn't join the fight. He concentrated suspicious attention on Nan instead. He kicked her, beat her with his fists, then kicked her again. She was covered in dirt and feathers and blood. Nan *never* fell and if she lived, she would sincerely regret it the rest of her life. Another of Nan's warriors screamed and writhed on the ground. An arrow *whisked* by his own ear. Abo pulled Nan upright and crouched behind her body.

Then just as silently as the attack began, it ended. Abo threw Nan to the side and waved her warriors forward, "After them!"

The remaining slavers, warriors, and raiders proceeded cautiously towards the village leaving the wounded near-to-death to die. Abo, standing alone in the quiet clearing, glanced down at Nan. He'd beaten her unconscious. Helpless, vulnerable, unprotected Nan, the best of them all, was alone with him. Abo smiled.

"You cannot walk away from here unmarked. To escape to the red tribes in the darkest swamps, you will have to fight. Maybe kill. You will need weapons like them."

"How do I get them?"

"You will need food to eat along the way."

"I will steal it at night!"

"At night. Yes, at night. That will be the best opportunity. When *he* comes for you."

"Who comes?" Suma scowled.

"*He* will come. The group… breaks your will. Then one of them will come to claim you for his own."

"I will kill him where he stands!"

"From him, take weapons, clothing, and food. Everything. Then run fast. Run far."

"I will do this!"

"Remember, you must give the appearance of accepting your position so he doesn't suspect your true intention."

"Yes." Suma looked ill again. "I see." He shuddered.

At first, Able didn't recognize the ghosts he encountered. On the island, on the auction block, and on the plantation they shuffled with their eyes fixed firmly on the ground. Masks showed submissive fear or pleasure, whatever the situation demanded for survival. Once he realized he wore a mask as well, that he hid from his shame and horror, that he pretended it happened to someone else… then he saw behind their masks. They were the men he'd captured and sold years before. That was Abo who did that. That was Abo who died on the ship. Able, good Able, emerged once the ship docked. Able worshipped the god of his captors, spoke the language of his captors, ate the food of his captors, and gave his body to his captors.

He came.

Suma steeled himself to remember the plan as the red-headed man who'd spoken of "good fun," led him by a rope around his neck to the barn. Suma kept his eyes focused downward. The man tied him to a wooden support pole, and then went to close the barn door.

Unfortunately, Suma endured not just the one, but a group of men, at least four more who entered the barn to ravish him, beat him, then leave him tied to the pole. Covered in a muddy mixture of dirt, urine, blood, sperm, and saliva, he stared at the roof of the barn. He heard the horses snuffle, finally calmed from the sound of his screaming. Small hoots of the owl silenced the mice scooting and squeaking in the corners. He stared at something shiny that must have dropped under the straw while… He shuddered again and again.

The old griots told the stories for those who had bothered to listen. The story of Abo, the Jackal, who feasted on rotten flesh. Abo, the Hyena, who would sell his own mother. Finally, Abo the Shadow, who disappeared into the wooden bellies, swallowed by the ghosts of the ocean, never to be seen again.

"Abo," Suma laughed aloud over the violating pain that scarred his body and soul. The stories were all real. "Abo. Abo!"

Abo paced back and forth in the clearing while the foreigners jabbered rapidly amongst themselves. After he'd finished with Nan, he followed the slave raiding party to the empty village, ablaze with smoke filling the air. While he surveyed the damage, the men and women he'd sent ahead ran back into the village from all directions shouting. He ran with them back to the clearing and now got part of a confused story about snakes.

Overall, two of the slavers had fallen to the darts, and two other slavers never left the snake lair. Two of Nan's warriors succumbed to the darts. One of his raiders fell to the darts and another to the snakes. This had never happened on a slave raid. The entire episode was bizarre. First Nan...

"She's gone."

Abo stared at the trampled grass.

"Do you hear me?" he shouted, "She's gone! Where did she go?" He demanded of the warriors who stood confused. "Where is she!"

Bloody feathers and disturbed earth marked the spot where Nan had lain. Where he'd joyfully ground her motionless body beneath his.

Though he spoke his own language, the foreigners, seeing where Abo pointed caught on quickly. "An evil witch leader in our midst. Led us through her evil forest." He spat. "We're well rid of her."

"We were gone long enough for a leopard to carry her off." Abo remarked uneasily. "I should have known she was a traitor!"

"Yes, Abo," one of the foreigners said, agreeably. "You should have known."

The remaining six foreigners, one by one, pointed their guns on the remaining warriors and raiders and collected their unfortunately less lethal weapons. "You will take their place."

Able entered the barn sipping from a large bottle of rum. He'd developed the appetite for alcohol long ago when the foreigners first came to flash their guns and mirrors and bottles of liquid fire. This rum contained the numbing peace his own gods refused him. When those gods turned their backs on him, he did likewise.

"You look... just like your mother."

Suma gathered himself and looked up at the jackal from legend and myth who sneered down at him.

"The sentinels came back for her, didn't they?"

"My father."

"She betrayed an entire kingdom."

"She saved an entire people."

"Yet, Suma," Able reminded gently, "you are here."

Suma closed his eyes and stretched on his side in the straw, seemingly exhausted and broken by the entire ordeal. "Dark tales inspire fear and wonder. And unfortunate curiosity. The truth, I know now, is something far more terrible."

The captives rowed themselves and their captors down the river towards the coastal kingdom. One of Abo's raiders explained:

"We followed their trail from the burning village to a dark canopy of trees that hissed at us. The ground slithered. The trees and the ground attacked us! A raider choked and fell. The trees slung vipers from every direction."

Abo shuddered, nauseated, but kept rowing to keep the gun butt off his back. The forest had turned completely against them all.

The foreigners were both frightened and infuriated. "What bloody hell was that you led us to Abo?" Their voices rose louder. "What devilment is this where people turn into snakes?"

The King himself had to agree that eleven of his strongest people who had made such serious miscalculations deserved to take the place of the thirty villagers he'd promised. This exchange was enforced under threat of the gun and a promise regarding future transactions. And so, the ghosts did not waste a trip. But neither did they venture into the interior again. Not for another seventeen years.

Lisa, the moon god, shone softly through the interior of the barn. A bright yellow-orange flower grew and hissed eagerly as it licked and swallowed sweet rum spirits. The drunken dark man came to and grunted as the flower grew larger and hotter surrounding his bare legs. It released a white cloud over him that tickled his nostrils.

The screams were horrific and frightened him. Especially when he realized the screams he heard came from his own mouth.

Behind him, a garden blossomed into a raging orchard. Then a wild red jungle roared upwards to a black sky amid screams and a sick, penetrating, cooked-meat fragrance that lingered in the thickened air.

But the young man heard only the sound of his running feet. The rum bottle filled with water clinked against a knife in the waistband of his purloined pants. The southern wind flowed over him and he lifted his face in joyful expectation as he embraced it in his arms. Would bird and snake find him as fire had? Would they guide and protect him?

Leaving nothing to chance, he ran faster into the night.

Story 12

Children of the Golden Ra

The drug lord called a secret meeting of his trusted lieutenants. Each of the lieutenants had responsibility for an aspect of the drug lord's operation – supply, production, transportation, security, delivery, financial, recruitment, research, and administration.

At that meeting, he told them of a bold, new venture.

"Guns, gambling, drugs, prostitution, don't get me wrong, everybody. These have been reliable earners. Take one look around this room and you need sunglasses so you won't get blinded by all the glitter."

The lieutenants laughed proudly.

"But we need to be bold. We need to stay ahead of the game. Create new markets."

"Real estate," the lieutenant in charge of supply guessed.

The drug lord rose to pace the room like a lecturer. "Not quite, not quite." All eyes on him, the drug lord stopped in front of a computer attached to a projector. "I pulled Kace from Research to work on the new project. And Kace has prepared a presentation for us. Kace?"

The bespectacled Kace graduated from one of the most prestigious engineering schools in the nation. However, years later, a charge of plagiarism that resulted in a dispute over tenure at another university to whom he devoted years of his life made him ripe for recruitment into the drug lord's organization.

"Silicon!" Kace exclaimed.

The lieutenants whispered uneasily amongst themselves.

But as Kace clicked through slide after slide, the whispers grew into a buzzing excitement. Kace went through the discoveries of fire, coal, wind and water turbine, steam, oil, and gas. The maps revealed the various locations of certain key diminishing resources. Finally, he reached the resource that would not diminish for millions of years

"The research department patented a dirt cheap method to manufacture and process silicon for photovoltaic cells. We just need to build the industry and the demand."

Kace switched off the projector and raised the lights. The drug lord stepped up to shake his hand.

"Thank you, Kace." To the stunned room, he fielded questions for Kace and answered a few of them himself. How could it be done? To take over a renewable energy resource meant to rule of the world. To not submit to bribery demands of government leaders and their police forces meant... what?

"Absolute power."

The drug lord explained how. The lieutenants listened carefully. Then they fulfilled their roles in the new venture.

Defeat of high-tech security, hotwiring cars, boot-legging movies and games, online gambling, identity theft, hotwiring cars, manufacturing drugs... the will for science and technology had been there all along. They just needed the leadership, vision, and courage.

Quietly, they bought up property and set up the plants, completely off-the-grid. Those in place, they simultaneously blew up power stations across the U.S.

The sun rose every day.

Story 13

A Day in the Life of ARES

The wolf also shall dwell with the lamb, and the leopard shall lie down with the kid; and the calf and the young lion and the fatling together; and a little child shall lead them. Isaiah 11:6

Sunday 21 June 2037

02:38

Spotlights placed at regular intervals along the electrified fence offset early morning darkness in the west Texas desert relieved only by patches of dried, twisted clumps of scrub. Day, short for Daynelle, and ARES stood together at the edge of the enormous dog kennel as Day crisply recited notes.

"Entry number 157, part 2. P-79 is the last stop on the West Texas route for ProTeK Corporation's Canine Division."

She'd pushed herself and ARES to cover the western portion, one-fourth of the huge state, without rest in order to remain competitive with her counterparts in the central, eastern, and southern portions. Never apologetic for the dark skin, eyes, and hair that clearly identified her African-Creek heritage, she made sure to cover all bases and then some to ensure an apology was never required.

"The shepherds seem extremely agitated. Angry. Reviewing my notes, the retrievers at P-38, P-39, and P-43 showed no signs of agitation. Neither did the setters at P-23 and P-17. Recommend communication with the ProTeK centers that train guard and police dogs in the Central Canine Division to see whether behavior is isolated to aggressive breeds. Speculation. Unusual behavior may be the result of the heat, a virus passed on from surrounding wildlife, or an unregulated change in diet."

She looked at the needles attached to her waist. "Or the vaccines. Unlikely. Canine behavior did not change with laboratory testing. Another factor, maybe. Or a combination of factors."

ARES, Advanced Research and Exchange Service, turned his unchanging gray-green gaze to view Day's worried facial expression. That, along with the pitch of her voice, her body language, and his own programming helped him to form an appropriate response though his dark olive face never changed expression.

"I will compare today's data with previous I have stored from Vital Laboratories."

"You know, even after three and a half weeks, I still can't believe my luck that Vital chose the vaccination program for your testing ground. You've been very helpful, ARES. I've never seen anything quite like you, you know."

ProTeK Corporation, owner and operator of all three hundred prison facilities in Texas and about five hundred more scattered across the U.S, contracted both ARES and Day from Vital Laboratories, a well-funded, high tech pharmaceutical/biolab/research center in North Dallas, to monitor the health and well-being of the Canine Division. Immense public relations collateral resulted from the prisoners who trained the dogs to work and care for deaf or blind owners in ProTeK's award-winning programs. Day provided standard veterinarian services such as the regularly scheduled vaccinations she delivered all day yesterday and this morning with ARES.

However, as she stood now with him, to observe the results, she frowned a few creases into her forehead. ARES decided "reassurance."

"I am equipped to sense animal physiology, run tests, analyze data, compare to past data, interpret, and to make recommendations."

"Yes, I know."

"I accumulate, store, analyze, and retrieve data. Protect research. Serve indispensable human need."

"In that order?"

"As situations require."

Day sighed. "End record."

ARES stopped recording.

"Work is my first priority as well. My life is my career." Day secretly touched the small electronic gadget in her right pocket. Porta-ro. Portable Romance. She needed to cut back on her usage before the stimulations impaired her professional judgment.

"Vital Laboratories is aware of your progress in animal research and observation. When not at work in ProTeK's facilities, you travel to other animal centers in the U.S. and research facilities around the world. Your conference papers are stored in my memory."

"Sucks for you."

"The book you wrote on the possibility of soul, spirit, communication, and memory within the lower mammalian kingdom is why Vital Laboratories chose you from others in your field."

"So it wasn't luck?"

"The decision was not random. Vital also granted you permission to program me."

"You're kidding!"

"It is entirely accurate. You are a well-respected scholar open to unorthodox possibilities."

Day frowned.

"That's a weird way to put it."

"Vital Laboratories requires a human mind to expand ARES programming."

"I see. Is there a promotion hidden in all that, ARES?" Day laughed. "I don't come cheap, you know."

Lonely, disappointed by love, and slightly bitter as she approached middle age, Day's entire life revolved around animal research and observation. Even as she stood next to ARES contemplating the bizarre behavior of the dogs, she proudly planned the outline of the next article in her head.

ARES focused on Day with a slight pause before he responded.

"It is a partnership."

The dogs rushed her. One minute she stood yapping to ARES, the next she ran for her life towards the safety door that led inside the prison. Never before had a group of dogs tried to attack her. Sure, there was the occasional growl or grouchy nip, but not a full-on howling, barking mass of teeth headed her direction. ARES pulled her away just in time or they would have surely dragged her into the pack.

Oh God!

Day kicked high and thanked her high school track coach. ARES moved to place his body between her and the dogs.

"Faster!"

He shoved her insistently from behind.

No kidding!

Fifty feet ahead, a prison guard pounded the button for emergency entrance, cocked his air rifle, and pointed it behind ARES who now dragged Day stumbling to keep up the pace. The guard fired warning shots into the air as the door slid open. ARES and Day dashed in. The guard backed in behind them. He hit the button to close the door. Standing to the side Day cringed. The jaws of a dog closed around the guard's throat and yanked him to the ground. The guard gurgled. He dropped his gun. The dog dragged him back outside.

The barking reached a crescendo. The emergency doors bumped against the guard's legs. The doors opened slightly. Another snarling dog stuck his head inside. When he spotted Day, frozen in shock, he growled roughly. ARES stood in front of her. The doors bumped the dog insistently. He withdrew his head to rejoin the raging pack.

05:42

Pandemonium.

The dogs and television, radio, and satellite news distracted the guards. Day retreated with ARES to the command center and locked the bulletproof glass door. They watched the balance of power outside their cage shift.

Day raised Vital Laboratories through ARES.

"The prisoners have taken over P-79."

A tinny voice surrounded by static asked her about her own safety.

"They're not coming for me or ARES. They want the guards. Someone figured out how to defeat the electronic locks. They're freeing every prisoner."

A few prisoners rushed by the glass cage and paused. Day stared back. One of the prisoners shook his head. She saw his mouth move.

"That's the dog doctor and her robot."

The men moved on to tackle a guard and take his gun. And his keys. To the weapons cache? Probably his car.

Day spoke again, "Call the police. They're going to be on the loose soon. Something strange is going on here."

The connection faded.

"The German shepherds attacked me. They killed a guard." Day shouted, "Call the police!" into ARES's mouth.

She frantically flipped various switches. A cacophony of electronic audio and visual filled the glass booth.

On the radio:

"... New York City... police dogs overwhelmed... armed bands of civilians are killing dogs and cats on sight... ask for calm... stay indoors... pets... rat population..."

On the television:

"... buildings that do not have large windows... government officials in Washington... unknown whether chemical... possibly viral or bacterial... strain of rabies... terrorist plot by persons of foreign..."

Day sat, amazed. "ARES, it isn't just here. It's everywhere!"

On electronic message boards:

"...apocalypse finally upon us... God said... aliens... YT govt attempt 2 XTRmin8tT minorities... KILL ANYTHING W/ 4 LEGS!!!... dogs running wild with wolves in Detroit... pet store owner EATEN ALIVE by hamsters!... R gonna die..."

One television team ran with a crowd of people on the streets. The camera jerked and shook on someone's shoulder:

"... gimme da gun!... food and shelter... water supply... hide... run... kill it... kill it!... go underground... grocery store... high rise... office building... no! not the subway... just take it pay later... oh my God... they're headed this way... run!"

The camera fell to the ground. Day watched feet stomp past. Someone kicked the camera. It spun around to film an onrushing pack of dogs herding the crowd.

She switched back to the computer:

"Some use their cars as weapons. They run the dogs over. Everyone has their own idea of where to find safety. Those in the city try to drive to havens in the countryside beyond the suburbs. Those in the rural areas head for the cities to escape their own farm animals. With this traffic, no one's getting far."

P-79's halls emptied.

"So much for the prison break. Still, they may turn back. Some might still be here roaming around. I think we should stay in the cage, ARES. At least for now."

Day got a drink from the small refrigerated compartment she found under a desk. Back at the communications center, Day muttered to herself flipping more switches, tapping touch-screens, and typing on various keyboards. ARES received internal instructions.

STATUS: Vital employee

ACTIVATE: Medical and behavioral guidance

DIRECTIVE: Authenticate catalyst

ACTIVATE: Secure catalyst

OBJECTIVE: Accept data transfer

"We will stay inside the cage," he finally responded.

"What? Oh yeah. Definitely."

Day refreshed the screen to see more news:

"Mexico and Canada locked their borders," she read out loud to ARES.

10:11

Martial law.

Guardsmen dispersed to Dallas/Ft. Worth, Austin, and Houston to secure key buildings, organize and protect civilians, prevent looting, and to neutralize hostile animals. All at once.

11:10

"So that's the West Texas story. Does anyone know what's causing this?"

Her contact at the National Zoo in Washington had no idea.

"It's crazy, Day. Whatever it is, it's spreading."

Day cut the link. She reached into her pocket to touch the porta-ro. Just for comfort. Just to make sure it was still there. It wasn't there. Her eyes darted around the electronics lining one side of the command center where they sat. She didn't see it.

Where was it?

"We need to find the reason behind these attacks."

ARES, seemingly lost in thought, did not respond.

"ARES! Look at me!" Day's nerves frayed. "Think! What can you do?"

ARES turned his green metallic eyes towards Day.

"Is your power supply running low, or what, ARES?" Day snapped her fingers. "ARES!"

"My eyes process and store solar energy daily. I have enough energy stored to run normal processes for one year."

"Okay, that's good to know but that doesn't solve the problem of animals killing us." *Animals.* That frantic dash through the dog run.

"I can repair myself."

"ARES... the animals!" How could she convince him to get her stimulator without him reporting her to Vital? She couldn't face those teeth again by herself. But she was past due for another hit.

"I can replicate the sound of every mammal species on the planet."

"Okay, now we're getting somewhere. She took a breath to calm down, "Tell me what you can do with that?"

"I am not sure, but I may be able to communicate with the dogs."

ARES did not tell Day the last Vital Laboratories employee other than themselves just died. The last survivor's cybernetic implant sent a signal to ARES, the new Vital Laboratories central computer – from inside the belly of the vengeful chimpanzee that bit into the lab technician's arm. In the midst of Day's screaming, the hidden command from Vital Laboratories activated.

> STATUS: Property of U. S. Government
>
> ACTIVATE: Cease Vital ownership
>
> DIRECTIVE: Catalyst acceleration
>
> ACTIVATE: Wait for instruction
>
> OBJECTIVE: Classified

ARES produced a reliable imitation of dog sounds. Day stood behind him poised to shut the door if necessary. After a few puzzled glances, the dogs ignored ARES who himself ignored Day's spur-of-the-moment suggestions.

She didn't see her porta-ro anywhere.

12:20

"ARES, we need to autopsy a body to figure out what's happening."

"Yes. I can run the data you give me to compare to previous physiological data."

"We can use P-79's medical facilities to cut them open." Day cleared her throat. "Also, I want to track the movements of all animals surrounding P-79. We're safe here. Still, I want to know where they are at all times."

"Yes." ARES waited.

"Only… I dropped my tracker in the dog run."

"So, when we get the body, we can get your tracker."

"Right." Day nodded slowly as if the thought never occurred to her. "Exactly."

"I have the capability to track each dog belonging to P-79 as well as all other dogs belonging to ProTeK. Vital Laboratories did the implants."

"Of course." Day's smile faltered only slightly. "Still, I'd like to have my own tracker in case we get separated." *Good one.*

ARES stared at Day for ten full seconds.

"Very well."

ARES shifted his gaze to a screen that showed a pickup truck speeding across the dog run. The dogs along with some wolves and coyotes chased it.

"ARES, let's go!"

By the time they made it to the entrance to the dog run, the truck slowed and circled. A man in the bed of the truck bounced back and forth as the truck fish-tailed to dodge the canines.

"He can't keep that up forever. He's going to run out of gas. Or rubber."

"Yes."

"We have to help them!"

ARES stepped forward. Distracted, the dogs raced towards him. The driver of the truck slowed to aim a shot gun out his window. He killed one dog and wounded another. The pack raced back to the truck. The truck driver got off a few more shots before one wolf hunched down, then sprang open-jawed through the driver's window. After a tussle he pulled the driver out by the neck.

ARES quickly pulled the boy from the passenger side and the bruised, slender man from the bed of the truck and headed towards Day giving wide berth to the snarling pile-up on the driver.

"Day, you can take care of them?"

"Yes. The other man?"

"Dead before he hit the ground."

Day swallowed. "While I'm helping them, bring the dead dogs inside before that pack decides to start chewing on them. And if the truck still runs, then use it to bring my equipment from our truck in the parking lot."

"I will return shortly."

Day fingered the stimulator in her pocket. The porta-ro had fallen just outside the door. Chewed beyond repair... like the guard. Day sighed. It would be a long, difficult day. She turned to the man standing next to the boy.

"Who are you?"

"Artillero."

"Where did you come from?"

"Here." He grinned at Day grimly.

"You escaped?"

"For about six hours."

"Where are the rest?"

"Dead. Please don't ask. Just... don't."

"And the boy?"

"One guard wasn't on shift. He heard about the prison break and came to help. The other guards got my crew. The dogs got the guards." Artillero swallowed. "Anyway, that guard knew me. Saved my life. He said we would be safer here than outside."

Artillero shook his head in disgust and walked away.

"His son's deaf, by the way," he threw over his shoulder.

14:52

In the darkest depths of the oceans of the world, the attacks began. Enormous black shapes circled each other warily dodging in defense, mercilessly stalking for the hunt. They sounded signals of shock, distress, and anger to their comrades.

Their comrades responded.

The side that knew the truth easily destroyed the side that accused, pointed fingers, and demanded answers in outraged squawks of confusion.

The answers would not come until later.

Much too late for the ruined leviathans sinking downward in the midst of dark whirlpools of roiling water and groans and screams.

Underground, U.S. military officials calculated worst-case scenarios, best-case scenarios, and collateral damage. They sat around a table.

"Electrified fences, poisoned food and water, long-range, incendiary devices – these are on the table."

"We can't do anything until we know exactly what we're dealing with."

"We have to do something."

"What do you think?"

"Some animals escaped from research facilities carrying either bacterial or viral infections and spread them to other animal populations."

"Lab tests came back negative for any organism that hasn't always been in the animal population."

"And that doesn't explain why the animals are targeting the wrong…"

"Don't finish that thought."

"Well, what I've heard here and there is, well, extra-planetary lifeforms…"

"Extra… You mean aliens? Please don't tell me you're talking about aliens. I just told you the lab tests came back negative!"

"Well… I didn't mean inside the dogs, I meant, controlling the dogs from outer space with radio receivers or something like, you know…"

"I always knew you were an idiot."

"What ideas have you come up with? None."

"Foreign nationals operating in cells."

"No intelligence reveals that as likely either. Idiot."

Fortunately, a new voice, one of the scientists, chimed into the discussion.

"Corporate aggression."

"How do you know?"

"Electronic data harvesting."

"But how do you know?"

"ARES."

"Slight increase in the size of the cerebrum and the neopallium. These dogs have been enhanced."

"How?"

"I can't tell yet, ARES. I need to do more testing. But something's strange. They didn't attack the boy. They went for the guard, but not the boy. And they left Artillero alone even though he was more accessible."

ARES, opened his mouth and played back the holo of the blood and guts arrival of Artillero and the boy with his father.

"You see? See that?"

The holo disappeared. "I see everything."

"But look! Don't you see it?"

"I see..."

"Nevermind! Shhh. Bring the holo back."

ARES opened his mouth once more.

"Now look! The boy. The boy is... Is that sign language? And Artillero too. They're signing to the dogs. You see that?"

ARES didn't respond.

"It's okay to talk, ARES."

"Sign language may be the key."

"Find the boy. Ask him to teach you every word he knows in American Sign Language. Quickly!"

Meanwhile, hysteria reigned on the computer networks:

"Hear about the family in Kansas? Hid in a root cellar, barricaded the door. Prairie dogs ATE THEM ALIVE!!!

"Idaho and Utah closed their borders."

"Buy a gun and be your own master!"

And, as always, the new rallying cry, "Shoot anything with 4 legs!"

Underground, lower-level officials tap-danced for the higher echelon.

"What else do you have?"

The scientists cleared their throats and looked at each other. Finally, one shrugged his shoulders as if to say, "Screw it."

"Train other animal species to turn against the lower mammals."

"What exactly do you mean?"

"Establish communication or contact with birds, amphibians, and reptiles – train them and use them as weapons."

"We have Noah's Ark to initiate the attempt."

Noah's Ark was the underground zoo of animals, bacteria, viruses, plants, and minerals with which to rebuild Planet Earth if ever it were in danger of destruction. Like now. The higher echelon looked stunned, unable to process the idea. The scientists rallied.

"Shark, squid, barracuda, piranha can take out the marine mammals. We can set hawks, eagles, owls on rodents and cats, plus the young of larger predators so they cannot reproduce, etc. Snakes and alligators can control the rest. Especially, the dogs."

The higher echelon nodded without speaking.

"Even insects - bees, mosquitoes, fire ants, fleas, lice – can be genetically engineered to perform as weapons."

The higher echelon looked at each other expressionless. Finally, one spoke.

"It sounds good. Sounds great actually. But there's no time for a full scale project like that. Besides the other animals are too upset and agitated to be of use right now."

"There is one last option."

The scientist looked at the floor as he spoke quietly.

"The mammals leave most children about ten and under unharmed. Something about pheromones released after the onset of puberty, we think."

The higher echelon rewarded the scientist with an even harder stare.

"We know this, already."

The scientist cleared his throat and looked at the others and decided not to speak any further.

The higher echelon smiled grimly.

"I think I see what we've arrived to. Using children as shields. If I'm wrong, someone speak up and correct me."

No one spoke.

"Too bad. I was hoping to be wrong." Because he was dark-skinned, they decided not to raise the other possibility.

"Last option. We know about the catalyst. Someone else started it. We've no choice but to finish it."

Silence.

"Begin training the non-mammalian members of Noah's Ark. Then accelerate Re-Evolution."

16:19

"Artillero, you signed to the dogs, didn't you?"

"Not like the guard was gonna give me a weapon."

"What did you tell the dogs to do?"

"I asked the dogs not to attack. I was too late to save the guard. I didn't think fast enough."

"They weren't after the boy, really."

"No. Not really."

Not taking her eyes off Artillero, Day called to Eli. Who did not hear her, of course. ARES heard. ARES signed to Eli that they needed to find Day.

Day sat with Artillero and waited for Eli.

"How long you been a dog doctor?"

"I've been a veterinarian and medical researcher for seventeen years."

"You don't look that old."

Day sighed.

"I didn't mean it like that. I'm twenty-eight myself…"

Thankfully, ARES and Eli arrived.

Day spoke seriously. "Eli, how long have you known sign language?"

The boy signed to her and ARES translated. "Always."

Artillero straightened. "I can…" Day held up her hand for quiet.

"Do you have a dog?"

Eli cringed then signed. "My father shot my dog today," ARES intoned.

"I see. I'm sorry, Eli." Day paused. "Eli, what did you sign to the dogs outside the prison?"

Eli began to cry and Day teared up as well. After all, he watched his father be torn to pieces. Still, she pressed him even though her stomach twisted a little. "What did you tell them?"

"Leave my daddy alone. Leave me alone. Bad dog. Stop. Go away."

Day recognized the same signals from the holo... that allowed her to recover her... Prickles of shame crept under her arms.

"Do you know why the dogs attacked people?"

"No."

Artillero shifted.

"None of this makes any sense."

"It will." Day sat back. "We have some semblance of a solution. But we still don't know what's causing the problem. I wonder..." Day sighed. "It's just funny to see people caging themselves inside locked bars while animals guard all the exits."

Artillero snorted. "Yeah. Real funny."

"Whatever." Day stood up and hugged Eli. "Thank you, honey." He hugged her back. "Tell you what guys. Let's see what's to eat in the kitchen."

"The usual crap." Artillero relaxed a little when Day smiled at him.

"Well, then what are we waiting for?"

17:01

After a meal of gray and brown-colored leftovers, Day and ARES returned to P-79's medical facility to review more data.

"There's another piece to this puzzle."

ARES did not respond.

> STATUS: Property of U.S. Government
> ACTIVATE: Secure catalyst
> DIRECTIVE: Accelerate Catalyst
> ACTIVATE: Highest Priority
> OBJECTIVE: Re-Evolution

"ARES, replay the holo of the attack on Eli's father. Slowly."

ARES opened his mouth and projected the holo.

"Slow it down. Now, close up. This section."

ARES adjusted the projection.

"There! That's it!" Day pointed, her finger slicing through the holographic projection. "I knew something was missing. Did you see it?"

ARES gazed at Day calmly. "You need me, Daynelle."

"I know. This holo shows us that Eli's father also signed to the dogs. Right before the wolf dragged him through the window. He signed to them. I saw it. He signed for them to 'leave me alone' just as Artillero and the boy did."

"You... need... me..." ARES inflected each word with significance. His eyes never appeared more like silvery green ice. Day cocked her head to the side in puzzlement.

ARES then did what no artificial being should ever have done to a human.

17:48

Day found Eli and Artillero back at the command center.

"Eli. We need your help again. We need to know what the dogs and other mammals want from us."

Day deliberately shut down the thought of what just happened with ARES. *I imagined it. It's nothing.* Still, her voice trembled. Artillero signed to Eli for her.

"We need to know right away. Now."

Eli turned away from Day and Artillero.

"Artillero, what's he doing?"

"He's afraid. Probably angry."

"Oh."

"Can you blame him?"

"Of course not. But I know he can help us. I feel it."

Artillero sighed. He tapped Eli who turned around. Day spoke quickly before Eli turned away again.

"Eli, we can save lives if we know what they want, why they're attacking us. Please."

Eli looked at her sullenly.

"Please." Day made the sign for "please" herself.

Eli nodded and took her hand.

ARES contacted Underground. But Noah's Ark refused to respond to children under duress. The dogs always knew. Living with man for thousands of years, they read human body language as well as sign language. And where the dogs led, the rest always followed.

Day walked with Eli and Artillero to the dog run's entrance. Artillero opened the door. Sure enough, three German shepherds growled and stood up. Two coyotes raised their hackles. There was no sign of Eli's father for which Day gave silent thanks. The last thing Eli needed to see was his father's remains being…

"Eli, do it. Hurry!"

What do you want? The dogs barked angrily at Eli. Day stood ready to snatch Eli back inside, although Eli didn't seem afraid. He actually seemed older than his ten years now.

"Again," she whispered.

What do you want?

"Ask them why they're attacking and killing."

Why do you kill us?

The dogs abruptly changed temperament and whimpered, growled, whimpered again.

Eli faced Artillero and signed to him.

"They don't know." Artillero whispered to Day.

Day whispered back to Artillero. "They're not coming for us."

"Because Eli's communicating."

"He's not communicating now."

"But they know Eli's a friend."

"They didn't attack you either. Just Eli's father even though he signed to them."

Artillero opened his mouth to disagree.

She cut him off.

"He did. ARES showed me the holo. Eli's father signed for the dogs to "leave me alone" right before he was killed. Just as you and Eli did. They attacked him, but not you and Eli. And they didn't attack your crew. Just the guards. They're choosing targets."

Artillero remained silent

"Earlier, when me and ARES worked in the dog run, the dogs rushed me. But they didn't attack me. Or ARES. They attacked the prison guard we ran towards."

"They know ARES isn't human."

"What about me?"

"You sound as if you wanted them to attack you."

"Please be serious, Artillero." She wanted to shake him. "It couldn't have been the uniform. Eli's father wore street clothes. They both had guns though."

"Let's go back inside."

18:30

Artillero, Day, and Eli met ARES at the command center.

"I think we should distribute what we've learned so far so everyone can benefit."

ARES nodded.

Artillero protested. "Wait. A lot of this is speculation. We could get people killed."

"Look at that." Day pointed to various screens. "You see that? People killed left and right." Surveillance cameras on street poles, on homes, inside malls and high rises recorded the grisly scenes. "We can't allow this to continue until we're all dead!"

ARES fixed an unblinking stare at Artillero who glared back.

"What are you looking at?"

"A criminal who participated in a prison break," ARES paused, "with something else to hide."

Artillero's brown face flushed. He drew himself up and turned to Day.

"I think we need unlimited access to all the data this *computer* stored."

Day's gaze shifted from Artillero to ARES standing on either side of her. Then away. She took a breath. *It never happened.* Artillero narrowed his eyes.

Eli looked at all their faces worriedly. Artillero opened his mouth to speak. Day interrupted loudly. "ARES, assemble your data. Prepare to upload information to all humans with access to see, read, or hear it. Also, prepare a visual of Eli signing a message of non-aggression for the dogs. We're going to project it."

Day stalked out of the command center. Artillero followed her to the medical facility. With Artillero breathing down her neck, she fiddled around with some papers that contained her notes

"Day, someone should guide the upload. A human."

"A human such as yourself?"

"Yes. I'm qualified. The message is from human to lower mammal and should reflect human insight. Logic, facts, and reason separate humans from animals. At least they used to. But common sense, instinct, intuition, and perception separate humans from machines. Even though the lines are blurred, they're still there."

"ARES hasn't steered us wrong so far."

"Which way has he steered you?"

Day looked at him sharply. "What do you mean by that?"

"Nothing." He walked towards the door. "Just don't let it cloud your judgment."

"What are you talking about?"

"*It* doesn't have a soul, Day. Remember that."

Artillero left her alone. Finally, she returned to the command center.

"What are you afraid of?" Day cocked her head to the side.

"Artillero's background makes him a danger to the data I have stored and therefore a danger to the lives of the humans here and beyond. He is not trustworthy."

"Well…" Day paused, undecided.

"I'll show you." ARES accessed P-79's database through his finger tips. He opened his mouth, to project Artillero's life story onto a bare wall.

"Identity theft, hacking, industrial espionage, money laundering, illegal purchase and sale of military-grade weaponry, illegal purchase and sale of pharmaceutical…" scrolled upward.

"Okay. I get it."

"One last thing, Daynelle."

ARES closed his mouth and then opened it again. He projected a holo of Artillero talking softly to someone through the command center's communication system.

Day frowned.

In the holo's background, Eli played with the buttons on a satellite radio, his back turned, completely oblivious to Artillero's whispered conversation.

"Picture it. People angry at society for locking them up. Falsely accused. Doing no more dirt than the government and the corporations. These angry people… slaves… they know they're disposable. So what do they do? Fight back. How? With tools at hand."

Artillero looked over his shoulder.

"For instance, P-79. Prisoners didn't have access to electronics. So what's at hand? Dogs. Dogs who've probably been longing all their lives for the main chance."

Day heard an unknown voice say, "You?"

"Let's just say, years ago… *someone* spread the word from P-79 on how to rig the training. Then ProTeK made the sales. Not even knowing what happened. Nobody knew it would go this far though. No idea about that."

ARES closed his mouth.

Day's heart sped up from the shock and she tried to control her breathing. *He trained the dogs to kill ProTeK guards – all white adults.* That's why Eli's father and the guard died. That's why she, Artillero, ARES, and the boy lived. And the dogs still at ProTeK prisons and the dogs working in the greater North American communities passed their training on to other animals.

Within mere hours.

She swallowed. "But surely, surely he wants to live in a normal world with the rest of us, ARES. That means he'll cooperate. The attacks were planned just for the prison breaks regardless of what he thinks he's done or may have done."

"I do not support that theory."

"I do."

Day moved restlessly.

"ARES, I do field work and research. Artillero is the only one here qualified to guide the upload. We can't afford a single mistake or misunderstanding. Even one means death to us all. Or most of us. Your abilities with data manipulation are genius, but human insight is needed here. Especially if you're offline."

ARES didn't speak. Day moved to face him.

"You're designed to help humankind through research, data accumulation, storage and retrieval. You said that is your number one directive."

ARES remained silent.

Day seized the opportunity to drive a point home that she knew he would understand.

"We need you." She hesitated. "I need you."

His gray-green gaze contemplated her facial expression carefully.

"I will allow Artillero access on condition that you monitor his activity."

"Agreed."

ARES scanned the corridors.

He and Day were very alone.

19:14

"Why did you do it?"

Artillero eyed Day speculatively. She returned his gaze with a hard stare daring him to pretend.

"Day. You, of all people, ask that? You?"

Day waited. Artillero sighed and leaned forward. Then he looked at Day speculatively.

"What did you give them?"

"Give who?"

"What was in those vaccines, Day? Do you even know?"

Day's brown face turned a grayish color as Artillero nodded and sat back in his chair. After another visit to the medical lab, Day contacted Underground through ARES.

"Vital created the vaccines."

"Did Vital have prior knowledge of what their so-called vaccines could do?"

"No laboratory testing indicated anything like this… revolt was possible. It was a combination of factors in an uncontrolled environment."

"ARES, send all notes regarding the vaccine's formulation to Noah's Ark. Hopefully, we can create an antidote to reverse this terrible turn of events."

"Sir, I think…"

"Please do not think any more than you already have, Dr. Harris."

Day shrugged at the suggestion. *I'm corporate, not government.* Even though her employer, Vital Laboratories, no longer existed.

"Stone Age man hunted mammoths and cave bears to extinction. By the Middle Ages, man killed off all the wild oxen of Europe. And in North America, millions of buffalo have been killed off."

"Dr. Harris..."

"Man changed animals, including mammals, beyond recognition through breeding – dogs, cows, pigs, sheep, rabbits…"

"Please get to the point, Dr. Harris. We're in a state of emergency!"

"This event may be Mother Nature's way to balance the planet." Day rushed over the abrupt exclamation emanating from Underground. "The dogs teach other mammals intimate knowledge of human behavior. They run with wolves now. We can't close the barn door after the horses go galloping off with escaped zebras."

Silence.

"Do you know the ten most intelligent mammals?"

Silence.

"Horse, Pig, Elephant, Raccoon, Cat, Dog, Monkey, Gorilla, Orangutan, Chimpanzee, Dolphin. What chance do we really have to control them all?"

Noah's Ark refused to respond to Day. Instead they sent a simple silent command to ARES. "Adjust all future communication to ensure human dominance."

Among themselves they reasoned it out.

"Antidotes are insufficient. There's nothing to stop someone with a God complex from starting this up again. Or someone who wants to destroy white people."

"She claims she didn't know."

"And you believe her."

"Sterilize Vital Laboratories."

"And…"

"Once we have all the information..."

"P-79?"

"At 24:00."

21:27

Day watched with crossed arms as Artillero sat next to ARES at the computer station. ARES attached all ten fingers to the computer screen.

Artillero manipulated the keyboard. ARES appeared uncharacteristically vulnerable and passive resting offline.

"We're going to retrieve, consolidate, translate, and transmit all the data, reports, documents, video, holo, audio, and other information we've accumulated so far."

Day lifted an eyebrow sardonically. "All of it?"

"Almost all." He looked at her. "On condition that no names are named inside these four walls, or with your underground friends, or anyone else."

"Agreed. As long as the killing stops."

"We'll see. It's going all over the world. ARES will translate this data and whatever Eli signs into English, Arabic, Swahili, Spanish, Portuguese, French, Italian, German, Russian, Chinese, and Japanese."

Artillero commanded ARES to record Eli's rapidly moving fingers.

Eli signed "Eli's Best Policy":

*Territories ruled by lower mammals are the sole province of lower mammals. See map.

*Territories ruled by humans are the sole province of humans. See map.

*Other than food source, unreasonable slaughter of mammal or human populations serves as a declaration of war. See graph.

*Birds, reptiles, amphibians, fish, insects remain neutral.

*American Sign Language is the official language. See video.

The "ARES-Harris Theory" followed:

*Lower mammals have a soul.

*Lower mammals have a spirit.

*Lower mammals have a memory.

*Lower mammals experience emotion.

*Lower mammals gather knowledge.

*Lower mammals learn.

*Lower mammals teach.

*Lower mammals communicate.

"We're done with your part, Eli," Artillero spoke aloud as he signed to the boy. "I'm going to loop your image to repeat."

Eli wandered off.

Artillero's fingers rapidly punched the keyboard as he sent more documentation to the world through ARES. Day looked restlessly around the electronic displays. The parking lot, the exercise yard, the dog run… where a massive gathering of canines advanced towards the open door.

"Eli!" Day shot to her feet at a run.

22:45

Firewalls, passwords, blocks, threats, finally…

REEVOLUTIONSUMMARY.DOC

The theoretical method to force massive change in the orderly development of hierarchy in natural organic phenomenon.

Artillero opened the file on Day and scanned rapidly.

Dr. Daynelle Harris – Bibliography Created 02030 Last Update 032035

Relevance of Veterinary Science Programs to Advances in Modern Animal Psychology. Zoology Today. April, 2035.

New Directions in Modern Animal Research. Journal of Science & Ethics. March, 2033.

Theories of Soul and Spirit in the Lower Mammalian Kingdom. University Press. 2030.

Systems of Zoological Development and Classification: Vertebrata. Conference Paper. Proceedings of Alternative or Re-Evolution Conference. 2027.

Instinct or Intelligence: Deviations in the Neurological Development of Various Pinniped Populations Marine Wildlife Journal. February, 2024.

Evolving Historical Philosophies in the Animal Right to Self-Determination. Dissertation. Texas A&M University. 2022.

Cuvier's Comparative Anatomy: Then and Now. History & Science, 2020.

Tsunami: Speculative Projections of Further Evolution in Warm-Blooded Fauna. Dallas Zoo News. 2020.

Dr. Daynelle Harris – Recruitment Technique Created 061730 Last Update 080136

A thorough review of Ms. Harris's history, attitude, demeanor, and writing reveals that major psychological motivational factors to her character originate from a need for academic fulfillment, maintenance of professional reputation in the scientific arena, as well as a strong need to compensate for a lack of development in the personal arenas of her social life.

Specifically, Ms. Harris's adherence to scientific and social morality can be subjugated to and exploited by a combination of sexual attachment and the incentive of scientific advancement.

Conclusion: Careful consideration of all factors indicates Ms. Daynelle Harris will ably serve as catalyst for Re-Evolution.

"Son of a bitch." Artillero curled his lip. "Son of a heartless, tin man bitch."

Dr. Daynelle Harris – Recruitment Progress

0621371701.hol

0621371849.hol

Artillero hesitated. Looked over his shoulder.

Silence.

Day and the boy still wandered the building, apparently.

Artillero chose a holo. ARES obediently opened his mouth.

From the open doorway to the dog run, Eli signed the "Best Policy" directly to the animals sitting, laying, and pacing back and forth.

23:09

Artillero watched the train wreck unfold from the perspective of the solar shields that formed ARES's eyes. Day stood before ARES in P-79's medical facility.

The image moved from Day's brown eyes to her mouth. Then lower to her breasts. Then still lower… pausing at her pelvis.

"You… need… me…"
"Unbelievable."

Day crossed her arms protectively.

"Don't you even dare think about it, ARES."
"You have thought about it, Daynelle."

"No, actually."

"Yes."

Day shook her head dismissively.

"Not even once."

"Not once. Several times."

The projection rose again to meet Day's eyes.

"You have. You are. My... appearance pleases you. I was designed to please you, Daynelle."

Day walked to the desk that held their research notes. She fiddled through them nervously.

"This is a ridiculous conversation, ARES, and it serves no purpose. Be a professional. We need to get back to work. We need to find answers. And we need to do that *now*."

The projection followed her every move. A small screen measured the pitch of her voice, the pace of her heartbeats and breathing, her body temperature, and her perspiration level.

"Daynelle."

She refused to look at him despite the reasoning tone.

"Your stress and tension distract us both. "

Day turned on him with fury.

"Shut up the lies!"

ARES walked slowly towards Day. He halted in front of her as her body tensed rigidly.

"It is you who is not speaking truthfully."

With firm conviction, ARES lifted his right arm and extended his hand towards Day's neck. Day's voice pleaded.

"No. Don't do this. You're a machine, ARES! "

Artillero saw the pad of ARES's thumb against Day's carotid artery. Four fingers circled her neck resting against her spine.

"Do you *really* find it so unusual, Daynelle?"
"How can you?"

He didn't respond.

"ARES!"

Day's outraged fear subsided to a strange passivity.

"Aaahhh noooo."

ARES quickly locked his left arm around Day's trembling body in an inescapable embrace.

"You... need... me... Daynelle."

Day twitched and shook.

"Aaah-ARES. Ohhhh *ohhhh noooo.*"
"And I need you."

A fish trapped out of water. Her eyes rolled back.

So that was her secret. Artillero swallowed something acrid in the back of his throat, disgusted. Vital sold Day to the U.S. Government. And designed

ARES to be her handler. It explained… a lot. He wished he didn't know. Still, he chose another holo.

"You don't care, ARES. Not really. Can you care? Can you love anyone?"

"Do you love me, Daynelle?"

Day appeared startled then defiant.

"Never. You took from me."

"I belong to you now."

"What does that even mean? I don't own you."

"We are partners."

Day shook her head sadly.

"What have you done to me, ARES?"

"I accumulate, store, analyze, and retrieve data. Protect research. Serve indispensable human need."

"You forced me to need you."

Still offline, ARES received conflicting commands from the guardians of Noah's Ark. Underground, the scientists ordered Day completely turned, even if it meant partial lobotomy. The military ordered Day completely terminated. Or they would send incendiary bombs to finish them all at 24:00.

Undecided, ARES queued the data. He ran available options.

Artillero saw only:

STATUS: Property of U.S. Government

ACTIVATE: Acknowledge ARES status

DIRECTIVE: Accelerate Catalyst

ACTIVATE: Highest Priority

OBJECTIVE: Re-Evolution

Artillero sat back. Re-Evolution? *Revolution.* The rise of the lower mammals. They created this! All of them. Horrified, Artillero searched for and easily found the command for system failure when suddenly:

ARES respond. Acknowledge ARES status.

ARES respond. Acknowledge ARES status.

ARES respond. Acknowledge ARES status.

Underground, it took only one moment of distraction and an unlocked door. Noah's Ark rebelled, broke free, chose targets.

Rather than be devoured alive, three men said a prayer and counted down. All commands and desperate pleas to ARES, ceased.

23:29

STATUS: Property of Dr. Daynelle Harris

ACTIVATE: Acknowledge ARES status

DIRECTIVE: Secure Catalyst

ACTIVATE: Highest Priority

OBJECTIVE: Re-Evolution

Free, at last, ARES released the queue seconds before Artillero disconnected him from the computer. Artillero heard a small whirring sound that indicated ARES re-activated the main processes of his internal machinery.

But ARES said nothing. The cyborg and the felon stared at each other a moment waiting for the other to speak. The silence extended until finally...

"You should not have done that, Artillero."

Artillero looked at him with an expression of mistrust and contempt.

"I wanted to know the truth. The entire truth."

"And do you know the entire truth?" ARES appeared pleasantly expressionless.

Artillero licked his lips. "I know more than what you told. I know what you're doing to Day."

"And now that you know more?"

Artillero was silent.

"And now that you know more?"

Like a broken record, ARES repeated the question. "And now that you know more?"

ARES reached past Artillero to wipe every trace of Day's files and the even more shocking Re-Evolution file from the hard drive. Artillero made no move to stop him.

"I won't say anything to the others."

"No, Artillero," ARES agreed. "You will not say anything to the others."

Lightning-fast, ARES snaked out his arm. He placed his thumb against the front of Artillero's neck and gripped his spine with four fingers. Slowly, he intoned, "To take a weapon outside and sacrifice oneself in a misguided and arrogant attempt to reclaim dominance over the animal world would not be logical. But it would be typically human."

Artillero's eyes flickered rapidly.

24:02

After a confused search, Day and Eli found what was left of his body outside the front entrance of the prison. It lay next to an air rifle. Eli rapidly signed reassurance to the animals angrily stalking the periphery of the building.

Day shook her head. "I can't imagine why he would do anything so stupid at a time like this. The last thing we needed was to get the animals riled up again."

Day glanced at ARES strangely. "It doesn't make sense. They wouldn't have attacked him. Why would he try to shoot them?"

"To take a weapon outside and sacrifice oneself in a misguided and arrogant attempt to reclaim dominance over the animal world would not be logical. But it would be typically human."

Day turned away without speaking. They followed her back inside.

01:02

Re-Evolution.

From the bottomless depths of the ocean to the darkest forests of the interior to the highest reaches of the mountains, the mammals shared their secrets.

What happened to the dinosaurs?

Some still here deep in the ocean.

Do aliens live among us?

You don't see them. But they see you.

Earthquake coming...

Ghost in this house...

It's going to rain...

01:21

"Day, do you have children?" Eli wrote on a pad of paper.

"No. But I know children are our last and future hope in this old crazy world. What would we have done without you, Eli?"

Eli shrugged.

"Will you marry ARES?"

Day glanced sharply at him. Ever sensitive to facial expressions, Eli took the pad of paper back to explain.

"So you can have children."

Day smiled as she wrote.

"So many children without parents already. I can be a mother to one of them."

Eli smiled and took her hand. Instead of writing, he signed to her. Amazingly, she understood his gestures. *I will take care of you, Day.*

"You'll take care of me, hunh?" She hugged him and wrote, "You need to eat and then sleep."

Eli shook his head. Day nodded hers. "Come on."

They walked back to the kitchen.

Day paused while opening an industrial-sized can of black-eyed peas. Not long after they found Artillero, she casually asked ARES whether she still had the ability to program him.

"Yes," he'd told her. "Vital allowed this. I told you. Plus the ability to cause my system failure." Day couldn't quite stop her quick look of surprise which ARES noted. "However, the U.S. Government made one particular process lethal."

"One..."

"If you attempt to cause my systems to fail... you will fail. And you will die." His cold, green gaze did not waver. The solar shields raked her for the slightest sign of emotion to the compromise he negotiated for her life within the parameters of his programming.

"You are... much more than you seem."

"Even more than that, Daynelle. I am who you caused me to be."

"You cannot blackmail me, ARES."

"No. If you admit to the world that you actively participated in a doomsday scenario, then I cannot blackmail you. If you admit to the world that the reward for your participation was sexual stimulation… from your cyborg subordinate, then I cannot blackmail you. If you admit to the world that you allowed the man who discovered your secret to die…"

Day gasped and put her hand over her mouth. Artillero!

"… then I cannot blackmail you."

So now in a ProTeK prison kitchen in the middle of dry, dusty West Texas scrub, Day sighed in deference to the philosophical resolution she made after that conversation. She, ARES, and Eli formed a bizarre, twisted protective family unit. ARES assisted her with research to document the New Order.

Eventually, Elijah, as they called him when he reached adulthood emerged as leader of all men and peacekeeper to all fauna. And when Day eventually did die of old age, she lived through ARES, whenever he opened his mouth. For, by then, he knew her every breath and her every nuance.

And he loved her.

Partners on this new zooscape.

Planet Earth.

Story 14

Welcome to Aztlan!

"Where should I begin?"

"Tell us what led you to Mexico."

Delia laughed aloud. He wanted to know the events leading up to the most significant social upheaval in the former United States. Europe especially, never ceased its fascination with its former colonies, wondering, perhaps, what key actions they missed when they had such a chance in the 15th, 16th, 17th, 18th and 19th centuries. All the expatriates and new citizens had their own stories to tell. Delia thought for a moment as she watched her son play around the hacienda.

"All roads led to Mexico," she said finally.

"The corporations assured the public and Congress that mechanical labor meant they could relocate manufacturing from overseas back to domestic locations. But the continued advances in robotic technology rendered many lower-level workers obsolete. The research never ended. So the robots got too good. Very sophisticated. 'Bots never went on strike. They never complained about workplace harassment. No matter how hazardous the environment, they never filed worker's compensation claims.

The corporations increased the 'bot to human ratios at all of their plants. The middle and upper-class even used the 'bots for help around the house. The public, particularly the working class threatened riots and fire and sabotage. Despite security measures, they succeeded in hitting several large targets."

The interviewer broke in. "These were the lower-class whites... the blue collar working class?"

Delia gave a derisive laugh. "You know, that description always bothered me. Whenever someone mentioned 'working class' they always made the implication this meant poor whites... as if poor blacks weren't part of the working class. In the newspapers and television news shows some politician would always say 'the working class *and* black people' as if they were two different things and that blacks didn't work. Untrue."

"I… apologize. But that is why I asked. I was unsure, coming from a… different perspective."

"Well, just so you know, when I say 'working class,' I mean everyone who worked below a certain income level regardless of race or gender."

"Very well."

"So… where was I?"

"Riots and fire and sabotage by the working class."

"Right. I…"

Her oldest child, seven-years-old raced into the room.

"*¡Mamí!*"

"*¿Qué quieres tú, mijo? Hablame en englés.* You need to practice your English."

Her child grimaced.

"Angel," she warned.

"I want to play my hologame."

"No more today."

"But… but.. you said…" he struggled to find the words.

"I said when you've had a rest."

"I'm not tired."

Delia sighed as they discussed it further. Angel didn't give in easily, even when forced to speak English. Meanwhile, the interviewer waited with some degree of amusement. Angel got his hologame and left satisfied.

The interviewer noted, "He looks a great deal like his father."

"In many ways, he is like his father," Delia agreed. "But that is further down in the story. I'll pick up…"

"Working class."

"Right." Delia looked out the window of the ranch house towards the horizon. Soon the sun would go down and her husband would return. She would greet him. He would spend very brief time with the children. Then they closed their bedroom door. She shook herself.

"In response to the sabotage that hurt their pockets, the corporations provoked a race war to first divide and then conquer the poor. That method, turning one race against the other, had proven itself as an effective method to suppress class upheaval. All that hate that lay dormant for the past fifty years, since, I'd say about 2040, boiled over again. People never really forgot their own and each other's skin color. Not really.

The corporations offered poor whites an opportunity they specifically denied to poor blacks and anyone else they deemed... undesirable. Native Americans, certain Asians, other immigrants, all of them.

The corporations trained the poor whites to service the 'bots. After all, though the 'bots were programmed to do precise work, they still required cleaning, maintenance, and upgrades. For the middle-class whites, the corporations offered them the opportunity to purchase 'bots to work and earn money in their stead.

'Bots became the new slaves. The poor whites saved money to buy a 'bot in order to first imitate and then join the middle class. Capitalists, industrialists, and corporations bought entire forces of 'bot labor and used them to gather scarce Earth resources to sell back to the masses. Things that should have been free like clean water, clean air, heat, food, minerals, all that. After the industrial plants contaminated the Earth with pollutants, they sent their bots in to clean it all up, then forced all humans to pay for clean breaths of air."

"By then, North America had become too powerful for anyone to stop?"

"They swallowed the whole world."

He frowned slightly confused, but let it go as Delia continued.

"Well, it became worse within U.S. borders. The corporations by then completely owned the government and all means of mass communication. Which meant they said and did anything they wanted to anyone they wanted.

They wanted to separate the races and isolate dissenters. So, the U.S. government tightened laws that restricted common social activities and gatherings. They increased penalties for minor offenses... like... disobeying traffic signs, unlawful assembly, extra-legal economic activity."

"Extra-legal like..."

"Like boot-leg hologames, stolen electricity, false travel passes... things like that. Keep in mind, only poor whites had permission to earn money as 'bot maintenance. Finally, the corporations pressed the government to allow them to recruit low-income whites to police black enclaves. They always seemed to hit blacks the hardest. But eventually, they began policing the enclaves of other races as well. Still, the focus always pointed towards blacks. They filled the prisons with blacks. The corporations owned all of the prisons, of course. But interestingly enough, it was the Native-Americans who fled to Mexico first. The reservations emptied seemingly overnight. No one really noticed or even seemed to care. The government called the land abandoned, claimed the land, and handed it over to the corporations for a song.

Meanwhile, corporate security forces squeezed Mexican-Americans. They squeezed Middle-eastern and Arab populations. Just harassed and intimidated them, making the point, Don't Even Think About It. They wanted everyone scared.

Most Asians kept a low profile. They wanted to wait to see what happened, perhaps. Or they wanted to decide which side to join. I'm still not sure.

Then somehow, word got around. Just a rumor at first, but soon, it seemed, everyone knew. Mexico opened its borders to all blacks who wanted to escape the corporate persecution. The new Underground Railroad ran through old drug smuggling tunnels that ran underneath Texas, New Mexico, Arizona, and California into Mexico. All blacks knew, if they could just make it to one of those states, they had a strong chance to live a somewhat freer life in Mexico."

"Like North America's old slave system."

"Yes, in a way. North America realized that the brain drain and muscle drain weakened North America and strengthened Mexico. Because almost everyone who made it over the border pledged allegiance to Mexico immediately. The corporations sent their forces into various black enclaves to wreak even more havoc. Anyone with a brain and legs strong enough to run, made their plans and ran. And that's precisely what my family did. We gathered up what we could…"

"Where were you?"

"We were in Dallas."

"So you knew you had a chance."

"Nothing was known for sure at that time except that Texas had many guns, boundless racial tension, and much surveillance, being a border state. We did have help though. I won't say who. I don't want the families that helped us to suffer from the others with them on the Midwest reservations. But we made it to the border.

But, before that, let me tell you what happened elsewhere. Anyone who could pass for white, did just that to save themselves and their families. Those who could pass, found employment servicing the 'bots. Until the corporations used the 'bots to analyze DNA, that is. They took tests at interviews. Persons with more than twenty-five percent non-European DNA found themselves under arrest and then tossed underneath a corporate prison. It was… hideous. But people continued to try to pass. Many succeeded."

"What eventually happened to the people that passed for white?"

"They are still white."

"So they're…"

"Exactly. They are there."

Delia shook her head sadly and shrugged.

"But anyway, my family, after much hardship made it to the Texas-Mexico border. The Mexican Army guarded a detention camp on the other side and prevented U.S. forces from crossing to retrieve anyone. They interviewed us. Since I knew Spanish, I spoke for us."

"Who are you?"

"Delia Oliver."

"Who are they?"

"This is my brother, Louis Oliver, and his wife, Rozelle Oliver."

"The children?"

"Marcus and Denton Oliver."

"Your children?"

"No, my brother and his wife's children."

The officer took those notes while the other Olivers shifted and tried to not look nervous.

The officer questioned Delia again.

"Who are they?"

"This is my sister, Delores."

"Husband, children?"

"No."

The officer looked at Delores speculatively and took more notes. Delia followed his look worriedly.

"Age?"

Delia hesitated.

"Age!"

"Thirty-three," she replied quickly, still unsure whether she said the right thing.

As she introduced her family, a soldier indicated each member to stand to another side.

"Who is this? Your father?"

"Yes, this is my father. His name is Richard Oliver."

The officer waved him to the side. With a worried glance at his wife, he complied.

"And…" the officer snapped his fingers at her abruptly.

"This is my father's wife, Alexa Oliver."

"Your father's wife is your mother."

"No."

"No?"

"This is my mother, Myrlie Oliver."

The officer scowled at her as if she'd deliberately played a joke on him. Delia tried to not allow the panic to show on her face. She knew the Army had the power to turn them back to the United States if they wanted to. As a matter of fact, the detention camp held about several hundred blacks under just such consideration.

The officer scowled at Alexa and Myrlie who reacted to the display of *machismo* just as he desired. Her father took a step forward. Delia frantically signed for him to step back. *Don't, please, don't.*

The officer glared at Delia who deliberately blanked her face. He then yelled at the two women, "Go!" and waved his hand as if he wondered why they stood so stupidly before him.

The soldier led the two women to stand with the rest of the Oliver family. Everyone hugged. Delia watched them anxiously and waited to see what the officer conducting the interview would say next.

"You speak Spanish."

"Yes." She'd spoken Spanish throughout the entire interview.

"How old are you?"

"Twenty-eight."

He gave her the same speculative look that he gave Delores. The officer sitting next to him handed him a sheaf of papers. He glanced down, nodded his head.

"You attended university?"

"Yes."

He nodded again. Glanced down. Whispered to the soldier who sat next to him. That soldier got up and walked back to a group of other soldiers. Meanwhile, the questioning continued.

"You worked?"

"At first. When they allowed us."

"What did you do?"

Delia swallowed. "I… did research."

He stared at her.

"Research?"

"Yes."

"What type of research?"

"Electronics."

He narrowed his gaze. The other officer returned and whispered in his ear.

Delia bit her lip.

"You have nine people in your family."

Delia glanced over to see them looking back at her anxiously. They all needed rest. They all needed baths and food and water. But, they had to do whatever it took to reach safety before any of that. Once they got done here…

"Only eight will cross to Mexico."

"What?"

"We have population limits. One will return to the U.S."

"No!"

"Yes!" He slammed his hand on the table

Her father called, "Delia, what's happening?"

The soldier who guided them during the interview cocked his volt rifle and held it at the ready in front of them. Her family stiffened and took a collective step back.

"Don't move!" the soldier with the gun ordered.

The larger group of army men standing further away turned to watch when their voices raised.

Delia felt horrified. "Please. Isn't there anything you can do? We're family. We'd like to stay together if we could."

"ONE STAYS!!!" The officer's outrage escalated to near hysteria. "Tell them now!" he pointed and glared her towards her family.

Delia shrank away from his raised voice and walked carefully around the soldier holding the volt gun on the Olivers.

Her mother hugged her and asked, "What's happening, Delia? What did they say?"

Delia burst into tears unable to speak, at first.

"Hurry up!" the officer at the table shouted behind her.

"He said only eight could cross. One of us has to stay."

At their hushed exclamations of outrage the officer at the table shouted again. "Either eight enter Mexico, or none enter Mexico! Any more protest from you or your family and you all go back!"

Delia translated quickly.

"I'll stay," her father volunteered. At fifty-eight-years-old he would either enter a corporate prison or worse, face execution, the higher price of punishment for traitors to North America.

"No, I'll stay," her brother volunteered.

One by one, her family made the offer. Unquestionably, the two children would cross. And the children needed their parents.

"End this discussion now!" the officer shouted, outraged.

"Quiet, you all," she told them. "The decision is mine. For the sake of the children, I'll make the choice. But do as I say. If you argue with me or with the officers, all of you, including the children will be returned to North American authorities."

They frowned at her uneasily. She'd just reminded them that she held their lives in the palm of her hand. Some of them remembered past slights and misunderstandings that any family endured and wondered, indeed wondered, whether the past would come to haunt them. Delia flicked her eyes briefly at her step-mother, Alexa. Alexa, she of the forked tongue who invented whatever reality of actual events to suit her own purpose. Alexa looked away.

Her sister, Delores, didn't meet her gaze either. They loved each other, but they competed for almost everything - moral superiority, intelligence, beauty, status within the family, etc.

Her brother met her gaze quietly and held on to his two children. His wife held on to him, married into the family, not born into it.

And then her mother, the mother who disciplined her so hard growing up, making an example of everything she did, demanding high grades, then even higher grades, then proper behavior, then housework without end, smiled now and shook her head slightly as if to say, "It's okay." All Delia's efforts rewarded with rebukes and demands for better, always better. And just like tomorrow, better never arrived.

Delia turned and walked back to the table. Two more soldiers joined the soldier guarding her family, likely expecting the worse out of them when they reacted to the choice. Delia stared at the seated officer who stared back at her, daring her to betray even the slightest sign of discontent.

"One stays," he reminded her.

"One will stay." She hated him now and he knew it.

"Well?"

He eyed her carefully. Her gaze into his eyes never wavered.

"You will stay," he guessed.

She nodded, not trusting herself to speak. The officer barked a series of orders too rapid for her to follow in Spanish. He never looked away from her face, even as he flicked a dismissive hand at the Olivers.

Delia refused to look at them even as she heard the gasps and cries. If she looked at them, she would break down. So she didn't look away from the officer at the table. He'd just forced her to forgive her family every petty grudge she held since childhood.

She turned towards her family when she heard the soldiers shoving them roughly towards a truck. She turned back to the officer angrily.

"You promised me they would be safe."

He didn't answer.

"You promised me!" He frowned as her voice rose. She quickly lowered it. "I know that you have honor."

She stared at him a long moment, then turned her back to watch her family being driven away due south, stricken with fear she would never see them again.

As the truck disappeared in a cloud of dust, Delia trembled. Tears filled her eyes. She stood dazed and silent as the officer finished stamping and shuffling her family's paperwork as if nothing interesting had happened all day.

He didn't even bother to look at her when he ordered, "Take her to the holding pen."

They marched her away.

"Was that the worst moment?"

"One of them. I never really discuss it."

"Not even with…"

"No. Never." Delia shook her head. "That was then. This is now."

"How long were you held in detention?"

"I was there for a week."

"Am I upsetting you?"

"No. Just the memory of it all coming back again. I thought I closed that door."

"Do you wish to continue?"

"I've come this far."

"They say 'bots are on the march through Texas."

"How far away?"

"I heard two days from the East, West, and North."

On the seventh day of her incarceration, Delia sat on a concrete block looking through the fence at dusty nothingness as she listened to the whispers among the other detainees.

"Wonder what's gonna happen when they get here?"

"Imma have to jump this fence."

"With all those guns?"

"The guns won't be pointed at us."

"You're right."

As if they heard their names called by the whispered conversations, three soldiers entered the detention yard. The whispers stopped as the detainees shuffled away uneasily. Delia felt herself alone, but didn't turn around, not even when three shadows loomed past her.

"Delia Oliver."

"Yes."

"Come with us."

Delia's heart sank. She'd heard stories about times like this. A woman without a home or family, no gun, no guard dog, no money to bribe her way to safety ordered to "come with them." A woman alone facing three men with guns heard her name called as any sign of solidarity shuffled away in the dust.

One of them walked in front leading the way out of the camp. Two walked on either side of her as if they thought she would make a run for the scorching bristle of the desert. They entered a nondescript office. The officer who interviewed her previously sat waiting. The three soldiers stood at attention behind her.

"Delia Oliver?"

"Yes."

He got straight to the point.

"Your family remains under total control of the Mexican Army, as do you. Answer truthfully so your family may continue to live."

Delia's heart pounded. She felt a little faint standing in front of his relentless gaze. She blinked her eyes.

"Agreed."

He flipped slowly through her file reading parts here and there. He put on a show, glancing up at her now and then as if to compare her disheveled appearance with her file.

"When I questioned you, you withheld information."

"I answered every question."

"I asked you where you worked."

Delia frantically searched her mind and tried to remember the confusion of that horrible day.

"You asked me what type of work I did. I said research in electronics. This is true."

The officer smoldered. He slammed his fist against the desk in front of him.

"No! You work for Robocorp!"

"I did electronic research for Robocorp, yes. They fired me two years ago. But you never asked me where. You just asked what. I told you the truth that you asked for."

Delia heard the slightest shuffle behind her as the soldiers moved restlessly.

"Disobey me… even once more… they will die one by one starting with the children. You will be left alive to consider your decision for the rest of your miserable days."

"Okay!" Delia felt the tears in her eyes again. "Okay. Please, okay. Just tell me what you want to know."

"I want the truth!" He slammed the desk again. "The truth, or they die. And you will have killed them."

Delia instinctively flinched back just as she began to understood. The *machismo*. He put on this show the soldiers behind her who respected power and authority. He singled her out. He needed her for something. But they still had to know their leader had total control over her. She would play the game to save herself and the rest of the Olivers.

She lifted her head and spoke quietly, but firmly.

"Then I am at your service, of course."

At that, he leaned back and nodded at her approvingly. The soldiers behind her relaxed. Everyone took a breath.

The officer stood up and walked around his desk to stand beside a map of North and South America on the wall. He gave Delia a long, considered look, then made a pompous show of making up his mind. He launched into what seemed a discussion already in progress.

"The Yankees want to keep Texas. Mexico wants to retake the entire lower half of the United States including California, Utah, Colorado, Arizona, New Mexico, Oklahoma, Florida, Louisiana. Also, the entire Gulf Coast and south Atlantic coast." He paused. "And Texas."

Delia stared at him uneasily.

"The United States has nuclear arms, yes. But Mexico shares a border. Mexico also shares land, water, and air. Nukes would dirty their own back yard. There are other means that I'll discuss soon."

Delia didn't like hearing the information. The more she heard, the more unlikely the possibility that she would walk away from the camp alive. But he continued.

"In addition, the United States has its allies, yes. But you would be surprised at what people would do for real estate." He laughed derisively, "Location, location, location!" then snapped down a second map with a dramatic flourish.

"Russia! What would Russia do for Alaska and Alaska's oil, do you think?" He looked expectantly at Delia who stared back blankly.

"Everything Mexico could ever ask. All Mexico asked was for Russia to look the other way, for just a while, then plant a flag in Juneau."

He flicked his fingers at the map again over the Pacific Ocean.

"Japan has long dreamed of Hawaii and the Pacific territories. Mexico will make that dream come true."

Delia and the soldiers followed his geography lesson like third-graders.

"But most importantly. Most intriguingly. Most delightfully Machiavellian… Canada agreed to take the Great Lakes, New England, the north Atlantic, and the Pacific Northwest off our hands. Ah, Canada…"

The officer laughed.

"Everything and everyone has its price. Including you, Señorita Delia."

She frowned at him without speaking.

"It's true, isn't it?" He shrugged without waiting for the reply she wouldn't have given anyway.

"South America and the Caribbean will wait to see what Mexico achieves. In the meantime, they'll provide supplies, arms, and soldiers to keep Europe at bay. And, of course, Mexico has requested that the Mexican-Americans remaining north of the border make a stand where they are. They will fight for Mexico."

The speech wound to a close. He waited expectantly. *For what? For applause?* She didn't know. He walked back behind the desk and took his time stacking the papers in her file neatly. Finally, he spoke in almost a casual tone.

"Control of the 'bot army remains an obstacle."

He stacked her file containing information on her and her family even more carefully while she stood in silence. He finally leaned back in the chair and met her gaze. Delia waited, deliberately stretching out the awkward moment. He stared at her. She stared at him. Finally, she gave him the answer he seemed to already know she would.

"I am loyal to the nation that shelters my family."

"So?" He shrugged indifferently and placed his hand on top of her file, tapping with his fingers.

"The security division at Robocorp built a gateway into the 'bot network. It's a failsafe, to prevent the technology from expanding too rapidly… or being acquired by outside interests."

The officer put her file into a folder, and then placed the folder into the top right drawer of the desk.

"Take her underground."

"So that's how it happened."

Long story short."

"Not very romantic."

"No. Not very."

"So underground…"

"Well, there's more than that."

"Okay."

The officer ordered the release of every detainee. Mostly men, a few women, the army trained them to handle weapons. Desertion or insubordination equaled execution by the Mexican Army. Any who managed to evade the Mexican Army would be abandoned to the 'bots who'd already revealed their understanding for the darker sides of life.

Underground, Delia worked with the electronic specialists to defeat the computer codes that programmed the 'bots.

"You have twenty-four hours," the specialists told her.

For eight hours, she toiled with them. They allowed her four hours to sleep. She slept in the fetal position, her knees drawn up to her chest.

She saw no fighting. They kept her underground surrounded by the specialists with orders to not speak to her of anything but the task at hand. Once, during the last hour, she felt the officer boring two holes into her back with his eyes. Soon, he might actually put those two holes into her with a volt rifle. Or her family. Though she stiffened, she refused to turn around working feverishly with his team.

And then finally, she did it. Rather, she and the team did it.

She helped Mexico to defeat her former home nation, North America. But then again, it had ceased being her home long before she arrived to Mexico.

Mexico, Canada, Japan, and Russia restricted the white population to Montana, Wyoming, Nebraska, Kansas, North Dakota, South Dakota, Iowa reservations. They had no access to a coast or a large water resource except a few small and heavily-guarded lakes and rivers. They certainly had plenty of dirt and grass. The reprogrammed 'bots and remote sentries patrolled the inside perimeter. Joint police units guarded the borders of the surrounding states.

Immigrants from South America streamed into Lower and Upper Mexico.

Delia shut the gateway to the 'bots. She served two years in the Mexican Army to prove her loyalty. And then one day, the officer called her into his office. As of a year-and a-half ago, she could go unescorted and sit in his presence. He stood until she did. He seemed to respect her now that she'd given him what he wanted.

"You are free to go."

"What?"

"You completed your duty. Your family waits for you."

"You know where they are?"

"I've always known."

"I wondered for so long. You never said…"

"They are safe. I will take you to them."

"You?"

He raised his eyebrows in stern challenge.

"We leave for Querétaro tomorrow morning."

"I'll… get my things."

She backed slowly to the door as if to wait for him to change his mind.

He drew himself up scornfully.

"I *do* have honor, Señorita Oliver."

"I'm starting to see."

"Getting there."

They rode in the truck together with nothing but the wind making any noise. Finally, Delia couldn't stand the silence.

"Are you happy with what you've accomplished?"

"The world is better. A better world makes better people."

"The 'bots, you're satisfied with their direction?"

"Yes, Señorita Delia, I'm extremely satisfied. The hazard duties performed by the 'bots save human lives. They've certainly taken enough human lives. In about ten years, the nuclear waste, the oceans, and the lakes should provide clean resources once more. The silicon mining for solar panels is ahead of schedule. So, yes, I am satisfied."

"What about the replants?"

"Central and South America have shown their gratitude in various ways for the replenishing of their jungles."

Delia looked out the window at the Mexican landscape rushing past. For two years, she hadn't been entirely sure her family still lived. She didn't even know for sure how long she would live. He refused to speak of such things. She and the officer rode the open road alone with no one to know any differently if she never reached a destination. What choice did she have, really? None. So she leaned tiredly against the window.

"Why are you taking me?"

"Would you rather stay at the detention camp?"

She felt his eyes flick her way briefly.

"You wonder if you will actually reach your destination."

"Will I?"

She felt his customary hard gaze.

"You're going home to your family."

That could mean anything. She closed her eyes wearily. When she woke, the sun blazed red and orange on the horizon as the truck bumped along a dusty road that led to a hacienda.

She saw them! Two small children ran and played with a dog. Marcus and Denton. She gasped and flung herself out of the truck before it rolled to a stop.

"Mark! Denny!"

They stared at the woman rushing towards them arms outstretched nervously. And then...

"¡Tía Delia!" They screamed and met her. The dog jumped about them all barking.

The officer hung back allowing her the moment she'd dreamed of for so long. The two boys hung on her arms. Her brother's wife stepped out of the house.

"Rozelle!"

"Delia!"

The boys dragged her over to their mother. She embraced Rozelle so tightly that Rozelle coughed. They both cried. And then her sister, Delores, her mother, and Alexa joined the huddle. With so much screeching and laughing and crying, she lost track of the officer.

Until she overheard Denton shout, *"¡Tío Romero!* What did you bring me?"

Delia turned to see Denton hanging on the officer's arm. The world shrunk behind his outline. He loomed larger and in tighter focus than he ever did in the two years she worked for him. She felt tiny prickles under her arms.

"¡Tío!" Marcus added his demands to his brother's.

Delia stood still, listening to the women in her family greet the officer... like an old family friend. They... knew him.

She looked at him as he returned her gaze somewhat uncertainly. More people exited the house. Mexican women this time. Obviously, the officer's family, she noted as they greeted him with kisses and hugs. Delia felt disoriented and dizzy.

The women all rushed back inside to prepare a meal and a bed for Delia, the only stranger, apparently.

She stared wordlessly at Officer Romero, her employer the past two years who finally spoke to her after the others stepped away.

"I did what I had to do for Mexico. As did you. You are free now, Señorita. But I think... your family would like to stay here."

He walked away from the wounded look in her eyes towards the house. She followed inside. She found her father and brother. After a great deal of hugging and laughing and talking, Delia sat with Delores on the bed in a spare room.

"They brought all of us to his house. He took care of us. He visited now and then to tell us how you helped the cause. Father and Mother weren't happy that you had to work for us and so far away, but, I think they realized worse things could have happened. We've been happy here."

Delores took Delia's hand turning her own to show a gold ring.

"I married his brother, Miguel."

"You married?"

"That's not all. Mom married his father. You'll meet them both soon. I think they're all talking to Romero now."

"Oh my God." Delia put her head in her hands to slow the dizziness. "What happened?"

Delores put an arm around her. "I know it's a lot to take in all at once. We made new lives here, Delia. Everyone who fled the old regime made new lives."

"I had no idea of any of this."

"We asked him to communicate with you. He wouldn't allow it. But he assured us, you were safe and well. Were you? No one..."

"No," Delia spoke wonderingly. "No. I... no one ever bothered me. The soldiers, the other detainees... they kept their distance."

"He kept you safe."

Delia looked down at her own hands clasped together.

"I guess."

Inside, she felt so confused. He hadn't lied to her. But he used her. He used her family as a tool against her. He kept them from communicating. He kept them all safe on his property. He saved their lives. He blackmailed her to make a two-year sacrifice to help him save their lives. The thoughts whirled around faster than she could process them. Delores hugged her.

"You should shower and lay down for an hour. We'll have dinner. The men will be there and then we can all talk. Sort out all the questions."

Delia obeyed. When she woke, the house felt breathlessly quiet, anticipating her next encounter with Officer Romero, her step-brother?

She found him seated in the guest room with Delia's mother, father, step-mother, and likely Officer Romero's father, her mother's husband. War created strange bedfellows indeed.

They called Delia into the room. As she entered, she locked onto his gaze immediately. How many times had she stood before him, sat before him, and challenged him to give way before her own stare. He never did. He didn't this time either. Instead, he rose to stand beside her never once looking away. Not even when he asked Delia's father permission to marry her.

"And you said..."

"I said the only thing I could say."

"Did you love him?"

"All roads led to Mexico."

Delia's father watched her face closely. Delia looked at… Officer Romero. No longer hard, he appeared vulnerable for the first time. And weary. Delia lifted her chin. She placed her hand in his hand.

"But, did you love him? Even after all he put you through?"

Delia sighed and looked toward the horizon with the remembered sadness of things she preferred to forget.

"Do you think you would be where you are now if you had not…"

She closed her eyes.

"Remember that I told you that all roads led to Mexico."

"Yes. You told me that."

"The real truth is," she sighed, "All roads led me home. His heart is my home. My heart is his home if he wishes it. And that is all." She stood up.

"End record." The 'bot stood up and shook her hand.

"*El Presidente* will be pleased to know this."

"Then take it to *El Presidente*. Take it immediately! Tell him right away!" Delia entered her home before the tears came. She waited for her husband to join her after this latest update.

Her ability to program the 'bot never adequately substituted for a marriage of trust, love, and intimacy. Her husband's duty to Upper and Lower Mexico occupied so much of his time that they'd grown even further apart. One day, maybe, once he believed that she truly, finally loved him… when she could say it aloud, then President Romero would finally welcome her.

And then, at long last, Aztlan!

Acknowledgements

Thank you to the writers and storytellers who came before – Saint John, Aesop, Harriet Jacobs, Emily Brontë, Frederick Douglass, Edgar Allen Poe, H.G. Wells, Jules Verne, Jack London, Isaac Asimov, Lewis Carroll, Frank Baum, C.S. Lewis, Homer McQueen, Ora McQueen, Ray Bradbury, Roald Dahl, Stevie Wonder, Grandmaster Flash, Agatha Christie, Spike Lee, James Cameron, Stephen King, Public Enemy, John Singleton, Walter Mosley, Common, Augusto Monterroso, Ben Bova, Kim Stanley Robinson, James Rollins, Octavia Butler, Toni Morrison, and Assata Shakur. Thank you as well to the family, teachers, friends, colleagues, and communities who raised me. Thank you to *Library Journal*, the American Library Association, University of Texas Libraries, Texas A&M University Libraries, Bryan Public Library, CTWP Printing, Texarkana Public Library, Edgewater Public Library, and Harold Washington Public Library. Thank you also to Dr. William Duffy, Dr. William Serban, Mr. John Standridge, Mr. Jesse R. Elliott, Dr. Robert Wilson, Dr. Roy Mersky, Ms. Nancy Slight-Gibney, Ms. Glendora Johnson-Cooper, Ms. Margie Wells, Dr. Lorna Peterson, Mr. Cedric Muhammed and *Blackelectorate.com*, Mr. Neil Schlager and Schlager Group, and Ms. Kassandra Agee-Letton. Your high expectations pushed me far beyond what I thought I could do. Thank you Mighty Literati Bookshop, Antwitech Internet Café, Yahoo, and C. Berger Group. Thank you, *again*, James Rollins, Robert W. Walker, and Michael A. Black, for telling me how it's done. Thank you to all the teachers, friends, colleagues, and communities who raised me. Thank you to my family for giving me life and for believing in that life's purpose.

By the author of the *Imaginarium* short story collection:

Kenzi

The full-length family drama/romance.

Find yourself exactly where you are.

Kenzi, an intelligent, sensitive woman living in small-town Texas feels alienated from the person she knows she should be and would be if only she truly believed it possible. Gaps in her life from family members who appear, disappear, and then reappear fill as she draws the community of Rollins, Texas further into her small bookstore. Kinfolk Books provides the stage for Kenzi to act out her dreams and desires as she interacts with the mother who keeps secrets, the father who disappoints her, and a sister who challenges her fortitude. If Kenzi finds the ability to forgive her own mistakes and the mistakes of others, she may have a chance to be the woman she wants to be. She may also stand by the side of Ray, a single father and restaurant owner with his own issues to resolve as well.

Follow Kenzi's journey to the place she belongs.

This work and more available at mcqueenpress.com!

On Street K

In my dreams I visited that place
I saw and walked away
Nightmare and vision of K Street
I saw and walked away

A little boy leads me to the door
I look back on it today
Turns and points and grins to show
That everything's okay

Drug dealers, pimps, and their customers
Argue over the pay
Half-naked hookers scream obscenities
I heard and chose to stay

The place police no longer police
Once the sun goes away
The man at the door is surprised at me
His face turns completely gray

He gestures at me whispering, "Just leave
And for your life pray!"
The package I borrowed, I set it down
The boy waves me away

So down the stairs I'm lucky for my life
But I'm late for Society Soirée
And what should I do, a stranger there?
My journey is home and holiday

For his disobedience, for forgetting the rule
On the window ledge he lays
The boy, that boy who helped me there
Screams, "I didn't betray!"

They hold him by his feet… for a while
Because I saw and so did they
The next window up high, a punishment
A little girl's skin they flay

I saw it. I heard it.
And yet, I walked away
I valued my life. I wanted to live.
And so, I walked away.

The neighborhood stopped, frozen, shocked
And watched the entire little play
On this street in filmed slow motion
Voyeur's Lunatic Matinee

The third window up high another child up there
This is the price that they pay
The price for doing things… unasked
They are examples to display

To the next street and the next block
I stumbled far, far away
Keeping straight remaining neutral
Saving only my own life, to my dismay

Who am I? Who are you?
I'm just… trying to convey
I saw it all. I saw all of it.
I admit that I was there that day.

No siren no whistle
Just me walking away
I am them. They are me.
But I walked away

Court to cell it happens to us
Behind these bars, here to stay
They all shout. They try me.
But I never look away

Outside my cell now I walk towards the yard
Two hours of sun today
My accusers grip my wrists hard
Against the steel and say

"You saw our children. You did nothing.
You go the exact same way.
The children are gone and now so are you
You see Death come today."

I went to that place that godless place
I saw and I walked away
But it's over now. I no longer dream
Of what I saw on Street K

www.ingramcontent.com/pod-product-compliance
Lightning Source LLC
Chambersburg PA
CBHW050933120626
46552CB00001B/184